In Sita's Shadow

An Anita Ray Mystery

Susan Oleksiw

Hale Street Press ◊ Prides Crossing ◊ MA ◊ 01965

Hale Street Press
Prides Crossing, MA 01965

Cover design by wickedsmartdesigns.com

ISBN 978-0-9973520-6-1

Dedication

For Mark and David

Also by Susan Oleksiw

The Anita Ray series

Under the Eye of Kali
The Wrath of Shiva
For the Love of Parvati
When Krishna Calls

The Joe Silva/Mellingham Series

Murder in Mellingham
Double Take
Family Album
Friends and Enemies
A Murderous Innocence
Last Call for Justice
Come About for Murder

The Pioneer Valley Mystery Series

Below the Tree Line

Acknowledgments

Once again I am indebted to several individuals for helping me with this book. Usha Ramachandran explained several technical aspects of life in contemporary India. Dr. Charlene Allison caught my mistakes on life in traditional India, as well as many other missteps. Elenita Lodge offered valuable insights and suggestions on early drafts, as did Leslie Wheeler.

Sita

The wife and queen of Lord Rama, Sita represents the ideal of womanhood—faithful, pure and dutiful. While in exile with Rama and his younger brother, she is kidnapped by the demon Ravana, setting in motion a great war. After she is rescued by Rama, however, Sita endures suspicions about her purity from her time as a captive in Ravana's palace. Unwilling to live with the rumors about her character, she calls on her mother, the earth, to testify to her virtue. The earth does so.

In Sita's Shadow

One

The light cast from the tube bulb high above washed away Deepa Nayar's shadow when she stepped onto the veranda, but she didn't notice that. Her glance went to the night sky where a plane banked, turned and dipped toward the airport several miles north of the beach resort. She stepped onto the powdery sand and watched the descent of the plane. As it disappeared into the night beyond the highest palm trees she let it go.

Her glance drifted to the lane in front of her house, and she met the stony expression of Bhadar, the self-appointed guardian of this neighborhood. A frisson of fear ran through her followed by a flash of anger. How dare he stand there and watch her at this hour? She shook off the urge to shout at him, berating him for being there. He couldn't possibly know why she'd stepped outside on this night. He stared hard at her. She lifted her chin and flicked her fingers at him, not caring that he would be insulted, as she meant him to be. Then she turned and went back into the house. Of all nights for the tube light to be reliable. Why couldn't it flicker and fade tonight as it did on other nights?

Bhadar would tell her daughter and her daughter would want to know why she had risen so early, earlier than was her custom. And that would be only the beginning. The questions would multiply, and Bhadar would watch even more closely. And as soon as he got the chance he would dribble a comment into a casual conversation with her neighbors that he had seen her earlier than her usual time standing outside, dressed for the workday and looking up at the planes coming in from overseas. He would plant doubts and suspicions.

She strained to hear any sound telling her the self-appointed night watchman had passed on. But however hard she listened just behind the half-opened door, she could hear only the waves crashing on the rocks and crows planning an assault on a plate left forgotten on a terrace dining table. Soon the sounds would include the morning call to prayer from the Muslim mosque at the end of the peninsula, and music from the Hindu temple awakening the goddess Kali to receive her devotees. It was well past four o'clock in the morning.

The last twenty-four hours had been the most difficult of her life. And now, today was full moon day. The moon would be full very soon, at sixteen minutes past the hour of seven, an early hour, but moonrise would not occur until late evening. She tried to believe the timing was auspicious but sometimes she wondered if the heavens wiggled in their courses, just to disrupt life for those who turned to them for comfort. She headed back into her kitchen and the special work for the day.

Three hours later the hinges on the gate leading into her compound squealed. She'd been so lost in the familiar aromas that she hadn't heard the little scooter coming down the lane. Deepa pushed the door open wide and again stepped onto the veranda. She strained to see her daughter's expression below the helmet, but her little granddaughter, standing on the platform in front of her mother, stole her attention. Deepa smiled as the little girl waved. This too had to be an omen, a good one.

Two

Anita slid a plate onto the hotel registration counter and climbed onto a stool. Something had awakened her earlier than her normal hour, and she lay in bed thinking about how fortunate she was. She was in good health, her auntie Meena was in good health and, even better, had been in a good frame of mind for at least a week, and Anand, her former boyfriend, now in love with an art dealer, was still a friend. The world seemed a good place. When she threw off the single bed sheet, she felt buoyant. Even her dark brown curly hair seemed bouncier. She showered quickly, pulled on a yellow khurta and white churidar, and prepared to meet the new guests.

Running a hotel in a South Indian tourist resort seemed like the ideal place for a photographer, and Anita had gladly joined her aunt in her long-running venture, giving up her flat in Trivandrum and opening her gallery near Hotel Delite. Her mother was delighted to have her daughter living with family while she and her Irish American husband lived in the States.

"What do you think of these? Have you tried one?" Anita asked her aunt as she picked up the small pastry and took a bite. The request from the new tour group for the famous little pastries had seemed odd in the extreme, but never one to quibble with a paying guest, Anita agreed and set about placing the order. The restaurant that served them sent her to the baker Deepa Nayar, who brought some in for her to sample. Deepa was apparently the only baker in the area who knew how to make them as they were supposed to be made.

"I prefer vadai." Auntie Meena held up a small savory donut and took a bite.

Two young men came tumbling out of their room and waved to Anita and Meena on their way to the inside dining room. Located down the hall from the office and reception desk, this dining room was reserved for hotel guests only. The terrace and dining room on the lower level, open for lunch and dinner, welcomed all visitors, and filled with guests from other hotels. Anita could hear the upstairs dining room filling up. In another few minutes she would walk among the tables and visit with the guests, making sure they had what they needed for the day. Anita finished the pastry and licked her buttery fingers. This was going to be a busy week.

Hotel Delite had only nine rooms but they were always filled. This week was unusual in that six of the rooms were reserved as singles. Tours liked to put two in a room, as a cost-saving measure, but the tour members arriving this morning had insisted on booking singles. They had taken almost the entire second floor to themselves, including the large family room. The remaining three rooms, on the first floor, were occupied by pairs, two married couples and two young men traveling together who seemed to make enough cheerful noise for a small soccer team.

Auntie Meena nodded to an elderly couple on their way to the dining room. "So very nice," she said to Anita.

"You only like the wife because she is modest and never wears a bathing suit." Anita pushed her plate away. "You didn't tell me what you think about offering this."

Meena broke a small piece from the pastry. "We are very sophisticated now, isn't it? We are offering many cuisines to our guests." She chewed thoughtfully, her hotelier's mind running to taste, cost, and appeal to foreigners. "Will they like this?"

"Indian food is popular in Europe and in America and Chinese food is popular in India, and European food in Fusion cuisine is popular here. This is very popular at the French Bakery here." Anita leaned back to wait for her aunt's reaction.

"But costly."

"Here it's costly and time consuming."

"It is costly. But for occasions we are testing." Meena pushed the plate away. "You are not using this in your photograph series?"

Anita shook her head and laughed.

"Yes, it is too foreign even if we are showing ourselves to be modern and sophisticated." It was always important to Auntie Meena to keep up with the times. She prided herself on being modern and sophisticated.

"I've included a photograph of idlies and chutney." Anita had agreed to promote Hotel Delite with a photo essay to appear on a popular online travel site sponsored by a private tourism company. Excited by the assignment, she had begun taking and selecting the photographs. She settled on the traditional Indian breakfast because foreigners seemed to recognize the steamed rice patties, and they photographed well. She also liked them and the cook made excellent idlies and chutney.

"Tell me again why we are having this?"

"The organizer of this new tour asked especially for it," Anita explained. "And we are nothing if not accommodating."

"And the tour has arrived," Meena said, glancing at the block of key cubbies. "Sanjay is reporting only five are arriving on the tour." Auntie Meena looked worried as she counted on her fingers. "Not six?"

"That's right. Five, not six."

"Then it is the large family room that is vacant?" Meena cheered up. "Such rooms are not so common, isn't it? I shall pass the word and we are filling the room very quickly. This is much better, isn't it?"

"The other guests may not think so, Auntie. Children can be noisy."

"Nonsense," Meena said. "They are precious." With a changed expression on her face, she turned to Anita. "Perhaps . . . someday?"

Anita knew what she was thinking. If Anita were married, she would soon know the joys of motherhood. "No digressions, Auntie. We have a lot to do today."

With that, Anita pulled a lanyard from which dangled a number of keys from around her neck, found one, and headed into the office. She unlocked a drawer and pulled out a clutch of passports, and began flipping through them. “Perhaps now is a good time to do this.” She pulled out several sheets of paper and began transferring the passport details to the government forms. She had completed the task by the time the constable strolled down the stairs and up to the desk.

“I'm ready for you.” Anita handed over the passports and documents, and waited for him to complete his review.

“Full house, yes?”

Anita nodded.

“You are giving discount?” The constable was young and new to Kovalam, and not yet used to the large numbers of tourists who descended on the beaches, which to him seemed hot and sandy and messy. All in all, a terrible place to be stuck on a hot day.

Anita shook her head. “We have a tour of Americans traveling through Asia, and each one has taken a separate room. The entire upstairs is given over to them. Only one room remains empty.” She paused and glanced up at the ceiling, as though she could see through it to the goings-on above. “I think I made a mistake. I expected six but only five came.”

“Perhaps the one is arriving later.” The constable completed his inspection and went off to collect the same information at the next hotel, farther up the hill.

“Perhaps,” Anita said to his departing back. But the empty room wasn't what bothered her. She'd asked the tour leader about the missing tourist and he merely waved away her question, repeating that the group was only five. She couldn't really argue with him. But what bothered her was the obvious error she'd made.

Anita was certain that six had been booked on the tour in Athens but only five had arrived in Trivandrum. She was certain because after a fiasco a few years ago that nearly put Hotel Delite out of business, she had taken the precaution of double-checking on tours. A competitor had booked the hotel in the name of a Dutch tour group and canceled at the last minute, hoping the abrupt loss of business would cripple Hotel Delite. And it might have if not for Auntie Meena's good reputation among the other hoteliers, as well as Anita's penchant for helping others out of trouble. Including murder charges. Hotel Delite filled up overnight. But Anita learned to check on unknown tours, and the Maxinter Tour Group had arrived in Athens with six members.

No hotel manager would complain that the tour members were paying full value for each room, but the change in numbers left Anita uneasy. She liked foreigners to behave in predictable ways, and she had learned to appreciate their gift for becoming fast friends with anyone they met on their journeys. Thrown together with a stranger for a roommate, most Westerners established a rapport and set out to enjoy the trip. But Mr. Maxinter, the tour leader, had been most particular about the requirements for this group.

The members do not know each other well, and each wants privacy, he explained in an email. They are willing to pay extra, he added. There were always one or two in a tour who were willing to pay extra for a private room, but Anita couldn't think of any other tour in which everyone wanted a private room. Peculiar, thought Anita.

Just to be safe and to honor the booking, Anita decided to leave the last room empty for a day or so anyway, in case the missing tour member showed up. And, while she was waiting, she'd get in touch with the last hotel where the tour stayed, in Athens. Perhaps someone there knew what happened to the sixth tourist.

* * * * *

Anita locked up the passports and headed for the dining room. She made a point of greeting every guest who arrived for breakfast, to ensure they were satisfied with the hotel and had plans for the day. She would suggest and arrange activities if asked, but otherwise she limited herself to answering questions and left them to their own devices.

"Good morning!" Anita said. She smiled down at Mr. and Mrs. Allbret happily settled at their window table. They had reached the age when married couples look so much like each other that it is hard to tell who is the husband and who the wife. If anyone had asked her to describe them, she would have had to say tall and thin and gray. This couple had turned the table so they could sit side by side, facing out the window and enjoying a view of the small beach. Of course, this meant they had their backs to everyone else in the room. Anita smiled encouragingly.

"Namaskar!" Mr. Allbret said. "Ravi taught us that last night." Ravi was the young desk clerk who filled in as needed. He seemed to know just how to charm the guests, and after they left India they often wrote asking about him. He had lost his mother as a child, was still unmarried, and had that lost look about him.

Anita pressed her palms together in anjali and repeated the Indian greeting. "You'll make many friends with that courtesy." To her surprise, Mr. Allbret turned pale, well, paler.

"It's not an invitation for anyone to become familiar, is it?" He pulled back against the chair and tried to control his dismay. "We're not inviting intimacies, are we?"

"Not at all," Anita said. "It's a courtesy, a respectful greeting." And, she wanted to add, Indians are not as likely to become instant friends as are Americans.

"Ah, well, it's all right then." Mrs. Allbret rested her hand on her husband's forearm, and he smiled at her. Their obvious mutual warmth and affection won Anita over, and she wished them well in their plans for the day, whatever they were.

Auntie Meena ushered in the young couple in room three, which had never been designed to host guests, but younger visitors seemed to like it. They could enter and leave by a doorway opening into the back hall. They had a small terrace looking out onto the compound where laundry was washed and hung, a goat meandered, and people passed on the way to the beach. Anita left her aunt to cope with them and turned her attentions to the two young men. The shorter one, just her age, had invited her to join them for an evening of music in one of the hotels in Trivandrum but she had declined. They continued to offer enticements for the evening, in a good-natured manner, and Anita continued to make suggestions for their excursions throughout the city. Walking seemed to be their chief interest.

"From Kashmir to Kanya Kumari," the shorter one said. "He said it could be done in a matter of months."

"In bare feet," the other one said. "Have you ever tried it?"

"No." Anita shook her head. "But those who do are much admired and revered. There are plenty of holy sites to visit along the way." She wondered if the two meant to give the hike a try. "There's a highway now, and people drive. Do you want a map?"

The two shuttled words back and forth while they considered the offer.

"Yeah. Can you get us one?"

Anita was about to suggest where they might find one when someone behind her interrupted them.

"Is this the dining room for the hotel?"

Anita glanced over her shoulder, but the sight of the woman in the doorway blocked out whatever she was going to say to the two walkers. She knew from the passport photos that this was Angela Deetcher, in her midfifties according to the passport but looking as though she were in her seventies as she stood before them now. Anita hoped the guest didn't collapse before she reached the table. Angela walked across the room, careful to make each step identical, though it was clear to Anita the woman had a limp and wore a shoe with a heel to compensate for legs of uneven length.

Angela Deetcher preferred a private table instead of the large one in the center of the room. This was where tours usually gathered, but this tour was different, and Anita seated her along the inner wall at a table for two adjusted for one. Angela was clear about that, explaining she wasn't up to conversation at the moment.

Moonu appeared at Anita's elbow, hovering and eager. Not for the first time Anita felt enormous relief that neither she nor Auntie Meena had fired the waiter for his awkward movements and horrible singing voice, which he often chose to share with the guests. It was a wonder any of them returned for a second visit, but they did. Moonu had a way of overcoming his flaws. Now was a case in point.

"You are wanting idlies, Madam Deetcher. I am recommending them personally." Moonu pressed his palms together and leaned forward, elbowing out Anita, and proceeded to extol the virtues of the steamed round buns and certain other foods that he would have prepared for her at a moment's notice.

Cook was fond of him, he insisted. He could bring her anything she desired. Anita didn't know if it was Moonu's persuasive powers or Angela's exhaustion, but she opted for the idlies.

"You're overwhelming her, Moonu," Anita told him in the kitchen.

"She is needing idlies." Moonu let his eyes fall half shut as he pursed his lips. "I am knowing this."

Anita propped her hands on her hips and snorted. "You mustn't be too pushy, Moonu. Tourists don't like this."

"Not pushy, Anita Chechi. Kind and helpful." He gave her his mischievous look of innocence and backed away, talking to her as though she were his older sister. When he'd gone, she turned an uncertain face to Cook.

G. Prakash Pohty was a middle-aged Brahmin who had done something his caste members considered inappropriate and he in turn had considered their reaction to him unacceptable. The two sides had reached a stalemate, and he had left them and refused to speak to his family or other caste members thereafter. Though his family lived in the area still, he had not seen them, according to his occasional cryptic comments, in years. Anita knew the truth of his situation but only Auntie Meena knew the whole story, and she wasn't talking. As usual in the morning, he stood bare-chested over the counter, wearing an ochre-colored lungi knotted at the waist, the standard wrap-around garment for South Indian men, with a kitchen towel draped over his shoulder.

"He is wise. No harm done." Cook stirred, his eyes on his work.

* * * * *

Anita reached across the large mahogany table in the center of the parlor to gather up the newspapers and magazines. Guests were encouraged to borrow books from a large bookcase standing nearby. This morning, however, the only reader was Larry Forche, another member of the tour that arrived in the early hours, everyone coming straight from the airport.

He sprawled in a reupholstered chair near the window overlooking the terrace and waves crashing on the rocks below. As Anita tidied up, he gave her a distracted smile and went back to his newspaper. She turned her attention to the reticulated teak screen, which now stood along the wall; its correct location was behind the settee, blocking the view of the stairs to the second floor. She lifted the light wood and began to move it back into place when Larry objected.

"It helps with the air flow to have it over to the side," he said.

Anita left the screen as it was. "Are you having breakfast?"

"Hmm, probably. Not sure yet." His glance returned to the stairs.

"You are not tired from your flight? Some rise early on the first day, and others sleep until noon." She couldn't take her eyes away from that newspaper, which she could now see was upside down. The loose pages were drifting closer and closer to the terrazzo floor.

"I slept on the flight." He shook the paper, as though to remove creases but had to rescue the sheets from scattering across the room.

Anita knew from her review of the passports that Larry Forche was in his fifties, and born in New Jersey. He now lived outside Boston. His passport was new, and the only stamps were for those on this tour—London, Copenhagen, and Athens. He had bright red cheeks but a pale forehead beneath his wispy graying hair. He might have a double chin, but it was hard to tell beneath the tall collar of his white shirt. He had rolled up his shirtsleeves and the cuffs of his slacks. He seemed to have forgotten to pack clothing for a tropical vacation. She waited for him to ask for advice on shopping and tailors in the area but when he continued to stare at the staircase, Anita tried another tack.

"Have you special interests here? Certain things you want to see?"

"What?" Larry's face seemed to pale. "Oh, you mean tourist sites. Ah, well, I hear there's a nice temple in town."

Anita assumed he meant the magnificent Shree Padmanabhaswami Temple in Trivandrum. "We have several wonderful sites to visit. May I suggest the Attukal Bhagavati Temple? It's very interesting and open to foreigners."

He managed to pull his glance away from the stairs to mutter his thanks.

"Did you enjoy Athens? I've always wanted to travel there." Anita shuffled a stack of magazines and waited, hopefully. Perhaps he would offer some comment to explain the reduced number of tour members.

"Yeah, nice place." It was clear Larry was being polite. At the sound of a door closing upstairs, he folded up the newspaper and moved to the edge of his seat. Anita saw a pair of women's shoes descending the stairs. "Ah, Sandra! Good morning." Larry tossed the newspaper onto the table and took a few steps toward the stairs as a middle-aged woman came into view. Anita recognized Sandra Stover from her passport photo, but Larry was the more interesting one. He acted, in Anita's opinion, as though he'd been hanging about and just happened to notice Sandra.

"Oh, hello, Larry." Sandra nodded and turned to walk down the hall to the dining room. "Have you already had breakfast?"

"No, I've been waiting." Larry fell into step behind her.

"I thought I heard you go out some time ago," she said.

"No, no. I've been reading down here, that's all."

"I'm not very hungry but I think I should eat something." Sandra addressed the empty space in front of her.

Anita followed them as far as the registration desk and watched them enter the dining room.

"Ooh, she is very fashionable," Auntie Meena said. "You are noticing her very sleek style, isn't it?" The two women spoke in Malayalam whenever guests were in earshot. Meena raised a hand to her black hair, only now beginning to show signs of gray and all tied back in a neat bun. Well into her fifties, Auntie Meena longed for the dignity of a head of white hair.

Anita continued to stare at the dining room doorway long after the two guests had found a table out of sight. She hopped onto a stool behind the desk, still thoughtful. Sandra Stover was fashionable. Auntie Meena was right about that. She wore pink silk crops, and a white blouse with a flowered border. Her necklace of glass beads might be heavy but it was quite beautiful. The little that Anita could see of her blond hair beneath the pink and green print scarf was well cut and curled. But then, wigs always were.

"She's wearing a wig," Anita said.

"No!" Auntie Meena stepped into the hallway as if to see more clearly though the guests were out of sight. "I am not believing this." She marched down the hall and after a few minutes returned. "Yes. It is so. Perhaps she is worrying about the climate. I am hearing some women saying it is bad for their hair styles." Despite this opinion, Meena looked like she didn't quite believe it herself. "But so lovely, isn't it?"

"Yes, Auntie," Anita agreed. "She's very lovely."

"And her gentleman friend. So very devoted."

"Ah! Larry."

"No, no. Not Larry Forche. The other man. Mister. . . " She paused to look at the registration book. "Kenneth Maxinter." She stumbled over the last name.

"He's in there?" Anita wondered how she'd missed him.

"He is out walking and coming in through side doorway and going straight to dining room." Meena looked pleased at the idea of an early-rising guest. "And he is most solicitous of Madam Stover."

"So, he went out for a walk after just arriving."

"You are miffed that you missed that." Auntie Meena preened at the delightful sensation of for once knowing more about a guest than Anita did.

"I seem to be missing a lot this morning."

Anita slid off the stool and headed to the dining room, to get a look at Kenneth Maxinter. She had missed the tour group's arrival, feeling no need to welcome guests who were going straight to bed anyway. Sanjay handled this part well enough, and there were never any problems. She stood in the doorway and spotted a man hovering over Sandra Stover's table, his back turned to Larry Forche, sitting opposite Sandra.

Kenneth Maxinter was a tall, lean man with thick wavy white hair, the kind that made older men look more attractive and distinguished than they ever had in their earlier years. He managed to seem interested in Sandra to the exclusion of all else in the world, as though he were almost flirting with her. She seemed charmed by the attention, as a polite woman is charmed, but unmoved. His duty as tour guide performed, he stepped away from the table, gave a perfunctory nod to Larry, and looked around the rest of the room. He spotted Anita in the doorway, and came straight to her, looming over her with a perfect smile reaching all the way up to his green eyes.

Three

Anita walked down the hill from Hotel Delite and crossed the sand to the Promenade that stretched the length of the beach, linking hotels and shops and restaurants as well as the narrow lanes running deeper into the resort. She was still surprised at how long it had taken to find common ground between Larry, who was eager to please, and Sandra, who was listless and so uninterested in her surroundings that Anita wondered why she had come. Sandra agreed she wanted to see the sights but couldn't focus on any of them. In the end she and Larry settled on a basic tour of the city, including museums, and lunch at a nice hotel followed by a brief boat ride along a canal. Relieved, Anita waved them out the door.

Kenneth Maxinter knew exactly what he wanted to do, and described at length to Auntie Meena his plans to visit an Ayurvedic clinic, to which he had written months ago. Angela Deetcher assured Anita she knew what she wanted to do and marched out the door, to the extent that her frail form would march. She hailed an autorickshaw and disappeared into it.

No one expressed interest in the beach, which surprised Anita, since that was the chief attraction for most of the tourists who came to Kerala. Perhaps the last member of the tour, the only one who hadn't appeared yet, would break the pattern. Crocker Dawes had closed the door on Sanjay after finding his way to his room at five-thirty this morning and had not been heard from since. It wasn't unusual for a new arrival to sleep until midafternoon or later, but the other tour members had commented at various points during breakfast that Crocker Dawes was usually the first one up and out of the hotel.

"He wants to see everything," Larry said with a tinge of disapproval, as though the missing Crocker should be more selective in his interests.

He still hadn't appeared by the time Anita decided she had to get her photography gallery open if she was going to snag any customers that afternoon. She left Auntie Meena with the task of sending Crocker Dawes off into the hot afternoon, perhaps for a swim, or even a full Indian meal at one of the restaurants along the Promenade.

She smiled at two boys running into the waves, turned onto a lane bright with colorful cloths shifting in the light breeze, passed an open-air cafe, and came to her shuttered gallery.

"Ah! You have come!" A wiry old man with straight pins sticking out of one side of his mouth leaned out of his open shop and wiggled his eyebrows by way of greeting. Anita smiled and waved, then slipped a key into the lock on her storefront. She folded back the shiny new wooden doors, painted blue, and stepped up onto the cement floor. The interior was a cool, dark space, and quiet, very quiet, but now, without its wall of folding doors, all that would change. At the sound of someone calling out in the distance, she leaned out to see Chinnappa, the tailor next door, and nodded.

"And you alone must open the shop." The old man grumbled.

"He has ESP," Anita said to the tailor. "He knows I have just arrived." Chinnappa never missed an opportunity to disparage the character of the small boy who had attached himself to Anita, insisting she needed his assistance.

"Hah!" Chinnappa escaped into his shop and slid behind his sewing machine. He had a visceral dislike of Peeru, who came racing down the lane at that moment. Despite his often voiced feelings, however, he was not beyond calling on the boy for assistance when necessary. Chinnappa would never admit it, but little Peeru had potential.

"Am I not here?" Peeru, fourteen years old but still short and thin, as though he were eight or nine, flew up onto the platform and bolted for the closet in the back, which Anita had just unlocked.

"I always wonder how you know I'm here," Anita said.

"He has his spies!" Chinnappa's voice carried around the cement wall.

Peeru went at once to the business of setting up easels and arranging photographs. Anita hung a few select ones on the back wall, stepping away to evaluate the arrangement and make any necessary adjustments. When she was satisfied, she positioned a chair near the front, but instead of sitting down, she strolled over to the tailor's shop.

"Full house at Hotel Delite?" Chinnappa said.

"Full house." Anita watched him work on a blouse, stitching the hem before adding the embroidered trim. "One guest did not arrive, so one room is empty. All the other rooms are filled, eight of the nine."

"You are having a good season, isn't it?" Chinnappa had perfected the art of speaking around his mouthful of pins. "Not everyone is doing so well. Many problems that side." He nodded his head inland, and Anita guessed he was thinking of some of the more expensive hotels up on the hill.

"It's a good season but we've had a lot of special requests, which can eat into the profits." Anita's mind had wandered to the western-style foods that had been purchased for this group. If they hadn't been requested, and if Anita hadn't known whom to hire to make them, she would not have gone to the trouble—and expense—to purchase them.

"There is more," the tailor said. He leaned back from his machine and began removing the pins a few at a time from his mouth. He stuck them into his shirt lapel. "I am seeing this on your face. And you are not joking with Peeru about the spies."

Anita laughed. "I give too much away, don't I?" She glanced at the tourists walking down the lane, the damp of their bathing suits soaking through the thin, colorful lungis wrapped around their torsos. She turned to the tailor. "They don't seem like other tours. They're quiet, like strangers traveling together who aren't comfortable with each other. There's no joking and calling out to one another. There's a strain among them. I can't identify it, but they're not the usual tourists. Something's different."

* * * * *

A sense of uneasiness kept bubbling up in Anita throughout the afternoon, and she tried to push it away. Just when she thought she had finally shaken the miasma of worry she looked up to see Angela Deetcher walking down the lane, a small folded-paper bag dangling from her right hand. Wherever she had been, the shop used recycled materials—newspaper and coir rope.

Angela stopped at the edge of the gallery's raised cement floor and studied a framed photograph propped on an easel. Peeru inched toward her with such tiny steps that he seemed to be drifting on air.

"Is this all your work?" Angela asked, looking up. Anita allowed as it was, and Angela blinked at her as though never seeing her before. "So you do more than run the hotel." Angela didn't wait for an answer but turned again to the photograph. Intrigued, she climbed onto the platform and began moving from photo to photo. She flipped through the canvas bins, pausing now and then to study an image more closely.

Anita took the opportunity to read the name on the paper bag, Guru Vasant's Herbals. This was a new shop deeper in the resort, near the old paddy fields and poised on a cross lane connecting two paths running back from the Promenade. The owner, Guru Vasant, was a quiet, stout man who sat behind his tiers of herb and spice-filled jars with sleepy eyes and the occasional grunt of weariness. Guru, as everyone called him, hailed from Delhi via Mysore, where he took up the practice of herbal treatments. He confided to the craftsmen in the stone sculpture workshop next door that good sea air, clean of all pollutants, was a great assist for the treatments he recommended. Anita had once seen him standing outside his shop at six o'clock in the morning taking a deep breath, smiling, taking another, and so on for several minutes. His eyes closed, he looked like a beatific Buddha on his way to enjoy continued enlightenment beneath the Pipal Tree.

"I see you've been to the herbal shop." Anita wanted to get to know the tour members because they seemed so out of sync with the usual guest staying at Hotel Delite. Angela looked down at the paper bag dangling from her fingers and held it up.

"He seems quite knowledgeable," she said. "Do women really put those dots on their foreheads with colored powders?"

Anita didn't have to answer because just then a gaggle of young Indian women with arms linked and smiles like sunshine circled past, seemingly incapable of moving in a straight line. All three women wore bindus on their foreheads, in various shades of red.

"A mark of auspiciousness, isn't it?" Angela watched them pass by.

"And a sign of beauty." Anita decided that a young Indian woman in a sari with a bindu might be a good image to include in the photo essay she was working on.

"They are pretty, aren't they?"

Anita knew she meant the girls rather than the bindus. "Some people wear the ones you can buy and stick on. They come in all different colors and shapes, some like tear drops, and others in diamond shape. You can buy packages of them and stick on a new one every morning."

"That's quite funny, isn't it?"

Anita kept her smile in place.

"I mean, when we think people in other countries modernize, we think they give up Indian clothes for western outfits, eat western food and start using more technology. But they keep the clothes and instead of putting a paste of colored powders on their foreheads, they use plastic stickers. That's modernizing."

"Have you ever worn one?" Anita asked. "No? Perhaps someday." Anita changed the subject at the other woman's dour expression. "What are you hoping to do while you're here?"

"I thought I'd visit some of the sights, perhaps gardens. Are there good tour guides for botanical gardens?"

This was something Anita could deal with, and she gave the name of two tour offices that she relied on for organizing activities for Hotel Delite guests. Both were near the lane to the hotel, and charged reasonable prices. Angela thanked her and wandered off, the paper bag dangling at her side.

"I wonder what she bought," Anita said. At the sound of her voice, Peeru darted down the lane, away from the beach. She let him go and turned to make a sale to another tourist. A few minutes later, Peeru was back.

"She is purchasing Ashvagandha concoction from Guru Vasant," Peeru said, standing as though ready to salute.

Before Anita could reply, she heard the familiar voice from the tailor's shop next door. "Hah! Sleep aid." Chinnappa stepped into the lane and strode over to where Anita was sitting on the edge of the gallery. He was of average height for an elderly Indian man, thin and growing stooped. His fingers were shaped into a curve from working needle and thread since childhood, and his sun-lightening hair and mustache blended with his sun-darkened skin. Anita wasn't sure of his age, guessing he was somewhere between sixty and one hundred.

"It's a common concoction," Anita said.

"These foreigners. They come to rest and cannot sleep."

Once again Anita settled down to listen to Chinnappa's well-worn complaints against the world and traditional Karnataka music coming from his mobile phone.

* * * * *

The stream of tourists dwindled as the evening thickened. This was the time when visitors gathered in their rooms or hotel lobbies and settled on a restaurant for the evening meal. Unlike Indians, foreigners didn't eat a big meal in the middle of the day, and restaurants had adapted. In the evening guests strolled the Promenade inspecting the tables of fresh fish sitting in front of restaurants, with open-air tables and chairs four rows deep, touts doing their best to attract the strollers' attention without crossing the line between selling and harassment. Constables assigned to the beach watched and yawned, but sat up occasionally, looking alert. At such a moment Anita followed their line of sight, wondering which of the many men and women had caught their eye.

There were more families with children this year, which Anita took as a good sign. It meant a lot of things—the economy was improving, travel was more affordable, and parents felt the world a safer place. Still, parents never let children wander far, and several parents hired a nurse, or ayah, through their hotel.

Anita trailed after one gamboling child and her parents as she made her way back to Hotel Delite. When the family veered off to the right and a second-floor restaurant over a row of shops, she veered left and walked along the canal. She stopped at a shop selling toiletry goods and asked for a few sticks of incense. She'd run out and forgotten to put it on the shopping list.

"Business is good, isn't it?" asked the clerk, a ten-year-old boy named Rajan. He often managed his parents' shop while they worked elsewhere for the evening. The family owned the entire building, the shop on the first level and the two rooms above, reached by a narrow staircase along the side, which led also to the flat roof. Both rooms fronted on a narrow walkway that served as a balcony. In a good season they rented out both rooms and stayed with relatives in a village nearby.

Anita allowed that business seemed to be improving. "Have you a tenant yet?"

Rajan shook his head and screwed up his face in disgust. "One came to look and asked to inspect. Just today another one came. I closed the shop and got the key to show the room. But she didn't like the stairs—too steep."

Anita walked to the side and glanced at the steps. The shop sat on the edge of the canal walkway, and the first step, almost a foot high, was also on the edge. The staircase was narrow, and steep. "Did she like the room?"

He lifted his hands, turning over his palms, and shrugged. "She looked and looked. She took so long I began to worry but she said I should go open the shop and let her think about it."

"How long was she alone up there thinking?" Anita smiled at the image of the foreign woman calculating the cost of the room relative to its size, and whether or not she could get a better deal elsewhere.

"I pointed out the ocean view." He lay the incense on the counter. "And the restaurants are right there." He pointed to the curving canal and walkway. At present flow in the canal was reduced to a trickle among the pieces of trash, but later, if it rained, it might fill up and be more picturesque.

"An asset," Anita said, pulling out her change purse. "Did she ask for a reduction in price?"

He rolled his eyes and shook his head. “I offered to get more furniture. There is bed and chair. I could get a table. The closet is full sized—an alamirah built into the wall.”

Many rooms had armoires built into the walls, with wooden doors added at the end of construction. “You're a good salesman.”

“Very good.” Again he screwed up his face for emphasis. “But she is most particular. She asked about noise. She said the coconuts falling are very loud.”

“Well, that is true.” Anita's thoughts went at once to the many coconut trees on Hotel Delite property that had to be harvested, an ongoing challenge with the decline in climbers willing to do the dangerous if lucrative work.

“So she climbed to the roof to inspect the number of coconuts coming to the roof.” He would have said more but another customer stopped to buy cigarettes. He tried to pay in a large denomination of rupee note but the boy would have none of it. He'd rather not sell the cigarettes than have to run around looking for change. The tourist relented and came up with smaller bills. Rajan made the sale.

“Was she satisfied, when she got to the roof?” Anita glanced up at the thick greenery. The little house and shop were in a good location, despite the closeness of the area. The shop was part of the compound wall running around the empty plot of land, which had become a dumping ground for trash of all sorts. An abundance of plants grew despite frequent trash fires late into the night.

“She wanted to know about bathing facilities,” he said.

“Yes, she would want to know that.”

“I assured her we have a regular supply of water. Did she not see the tank on the roof?”

“Did she understand that's how you get water here?”

“Yes, yes.”

“But?” Anita marveled that neither one of them, boy or tourist, had grown frustrated with the negotiation. Usually the foreigner gave up and walked away, but this one seemed to want the room. It was, after all, well situated if tiny.

“She said there's an odor from the trash.” The boy's shoulders sagged. “And the fires are too close to the house.”

"Oh! That is a consideration." Anita handed over the few rupees she owed and stowed the incense in her cloth bag.

"No! No! The fires are not near. I'm very careful."

"Yes, of course, you are."

"I showed her. She didn't believe me so I showed her." As though still feeling he had to prove his point, he jumped up and came out of the little shop, leaving the window open and its packages of inventory on the counter. He hurried to the compound gate and pushed it open, waving to Anita to follow him. "See what I mean? I keep the fires over there."

To satisfy the boy, whom she'd known since he was an infant, Anita stepped into the compound and admired how well he'd placed the fires, away from anything that could catch a spark. She had to admit to herself, however, that life next to a steadily burning pyre of trash might become too much, and the foreigner may not have been able to get this across. But the family wasn't going to stop burning trash. That was a fact of life in the resort.

It was too bad because it could be a lovely spot, Anita thought as she scanned the poorly tended greenery. And despite all the hotels looming over it on the steep hillside above, no windows looked down on it. The sightlines gave it added privacy. The compound wall also marked the narrow lanes that zigzagged through the resort. It was an attractive piece of property. Anita returned to the canal walk.

"She didn't take the room, did she?"

He flicked his fingers in disgust, clucked his tongue, and shook his head. "She is still looking but she may return. She wants quiet and solitude." He lowered his chin and looked at her.

"Have you never thought of selling?"

Once again, the boy gave his repertoire of images of disgust. "Lawsuit," he said. "Since before I was born. It could go on until after I am dead."

Only ten years old, Anita thought, and already wise to the ways of the world.

Four

Deepa shifted the heavy cloth bag from her left hand to her right as she turned the corner into the lane. She paused just long enough to catch the quick turn of Crocker Dawes's head as he glanced back at her. He wouldn't wave, or do anything else more noticeable, and she appreciated that. Still, neither one could stop from glancing back at the other. Thirty-five years was a long time.

The lane narrowed and she pressed against the compound wall to let a gaggle of boys run past. In their now-dusty school uniforms, blue shorts and white shirts, they hadn't yet exhausted their energy for the afternoon. They shouted and hooted and jumped over protruding rocks. Deepa walked on and turned into another lane, following this one until it crossed still another lane, widening out. When she saw the man up ahead she shifted the cloth bag into her left hand, holding it out at her side as though it were heavy.

Bhadar strolled along the lane, his stiff khaki shorts and white vest announcing his role as neighborhood guardian, whether the neighbors wanted one or not.

"Haven't you got a job to go to?" asked Deepa before he could open his mouth. He'd been making his presence known in the area far too often for anyone's tolerance.

"I'm doing my duty." He all but sniffed at her. "Why so many provisions?" Bhadar circled her, moving far enough away to avoid an accusation but close enough to be positioned when she opened the compound gate. "You were speaking to that man again."

"Are you following me?"

"You were seen."

"And I saw many others also. I see you. You are here where you do not live. You have no relatives here. No work here. Why are you here?" She held both bags in her left hand and worked the gate key out of her purse slung across her chest.

"You know why I'm here."

"Bhadar, no one here is going to hire you as a private guard. If we want one, we'll hire a Gurkha—we know them and they have training."

She pushed the key into the padlock and turned, slipping it off and into one of the cloth bags. She gripped the gate, holding it in place so he couldn't push it open and follow her in.

"We have an agreement." Bhadar stood erect, like the soldier he pretended to be. "No foreigners are to be coming here, in the village. They are welcomed in the resort area but not in the private areas where we live."

"I made no such agreement." She pushed open the gate just enough to slip inside, holding the planks tight against Bhadar's threat.

"Your daughter did." Bhadar was more battering ram than manipulative politician, hardnosed and pushy rather than sly and sneaky. But he was always annoying.

"My daughter does not live here." Deepa swung inside the compound and held the gate almost closed. "And in her neighborhood both foreigners and Indians live on the same lanes."

"The IT world is different." Bhadar studied the gate, as though he might find a flaw to exploit. Deepa pushed it the last few inches and heard the latch click into place. The iron works were old but still serviceable. She rested the bags on the ground and pushed the hasp through on her side.

"You don't live here," she said. "And you are not making anything better." She gathered up her cloth bags and turned to the house.

Bhadar grabbed the top of the gate with both hands and stuck his head over. "I am not alone in my thinking, Deepa Nayar. You should know that." She ignored him, not even turning around to acknowledge his threat, but the hiss of his voice followed her to the veranda.

Five

The young man scuffed along the lane, tugging on the rope. The goat resisted. Neither man nor goat was willing to alter the pace, which left both frustrated. Anita watched this unresolved conflict through the open office window and wondered if it would ever get easier. The animal had taken up residence in the hotel compound after Anita rescued it from a hungry leopard in the hills. She shivered whenever she thought about the end of that night—two people dead, two injured, one gone missing perhaps forever, and a goat lucky to be alive.

"Is it that awful animal again?" Auntie Meena leaned out the window and watched man and animal begin the precarious journey down the steps to the back compound. One or the other always seemed in danger of tumbling to the bottom and landing with a cracked skull.

"That is a very lucky animal, Auntie. Shiva would frown on us for abandoning it." Anita returned to the grocery list from Cook. "This is quite a long list."

"Are we not doing all we can to bring comfort to our guests?" Auntie Meena shuffled sheets of paper, which, Anita noticed, were blank passport reporting forms, while she tried to look busy.

Anita nodded. "It is our duty to offer whatever comfort and accommodation we can. But all this?"

Auntie Meena managed to convey deep outrage at the suggestion that her purchasing decisions were open to question.

As if, Anita thought, anyone else's opinion would ever matter in Hotel Delite.

"Everything about these guests seems off," Anita said. The tour group had intrigued her from the beginning.

In late August, a travel agent in the States sent a reservation request for eight individuals, later changed to six. They would stay for one week. They would require a car for some of this time. Anita had set about booking Joseph, their driver, and car for this period, lining up a second car for other guests. December could be a slow month, but it looked like this year it would be one of the better ones. She was delighted. And then came the special requests.

Each guest would require a separate room.

Each guest room would be cleaned top to bottom every midmorning. Since this was always done anyway, Anita didn't think about it except to wonder what sort of hotels the tour groups had been staying in that prompted the leader to ask about this.

If there were farm animals nearby, could they be kept at a distance? Anita made arrangements for the goat to be tethered in a private yard during the day, returning in the evening. She had no idea what she could do about the other meandering animals.

One guest wanted a steak. Could a vegetarian nation provide this?

"Where is this vegetarian nation?" Auntie Meena asked in all seriousness.

"I think he means us," Anita replied, hoping the tour leaders would organize a reading list on India before they left the States. The special requests went on, and for the most part were the usual minor ones from foreigners—no powder washing soaps, certain breads were not to be served, and no peanuts. But the last one struck her as odd.

Could Hotel Delite provide genuine French pastries?

"Are we doing this?" Auntie Meena asked when she read the last request. "They will be stale by the time they arrive here from France." Suddenly, she looked up with that expression Anita knew well. Her aunt had an idea. "They can purchase them in the airport in Paris."

"Paris?" Anita repeated.

"Yes, yes, Paris. They are selling genuine pastries in Paris, isn't it?"

"They're not arriving from Paris," Anita pointed out. "They're arriving from Greece."

"Oh, oh, oh." Meena began to cool herself with a sheaf of paper. "Very great problem, Anita. Very great problem."

But Deepa Nayar, who kept an exclusive clientele for her European dishes, including pastries, solved that problem. Anita arranged for her to deliver twelve pastries to Hotel Delite every morning for a week, expecting to have to persuade her but she agreed with alacrity. The problem solved, Anita didn't give the pastries another thought until the morning of the tour group's arrival.

"Auntie Meena," Anita said in a thoughtful tone, "how many people ate the pastries this morning at breakfast?"

"I am not knowing this, Anita. Why am I knowing this?"

"You know everything, Auntie."

Afraid to admit she might be slipping, Auntie Meena faded down the hallway and into the kitchen. She returned a moment later, looking as thoughtful as Anita had sounded. "Only three people are eating these pastries in the morning, and you and I are two of them. But one guest is eating again this afternoon. He is taking tea in the parlor, and is asking especially for these."

"Which one is this?" Anita asked.

Auntie Meena peered at the registration book, running her finger along the rows of colored blocks. "Ah, this one, with the peculiar name."

Anita leaned over to read it. "Crocker Dawes. Perhaps I shall ask him this evening about his love for these pastries. Are the tour members in the guest dining room this evening?"

"And that is another thing that is peculiar," Auntie Meena said. "Why are they requiring the guest dining room to themselves on their very first night, and this night alone? They are not taking the pleasure of the terrace and the beauty of the palm trees overhead and the ocean views. And this one with the strange name is speaking Malayalam." Meena's eyes opened wide as she recalled the surprise she felt when the foreigner leaned over the registration desk late that morning, his palms pressed together, and said, "Namaskaram. Ivite tiriccuvannata enikku valare santosham."

"You must have been pleased, Auntie."

"Pleased? I am so startled I cannot welcome him properly," Meena said. "Only later am I thinking his speech is peculiar. And he is having a very peculiar accent."

"All accents sound peculiar," Anita said, still thinking about the pastries.

"His grammar is most correct," Auntie Meena said, "but he is saying he is returned. I am knowing from tour leader that no one is coming to India a second time. How he is learning this language I am not knowing? Peculiar."

"Perhaps you should ask him. Things are less peculiar if you understand."

Auntie Meena shook her head. "They are foreigners. It is their nature to be peculiar."

"And we are peculiar to them," Anita said.

* * * * *

The murmur of conversation hung at the doorway to the guest dining room. Instead of the bursts of laughter or eruptions of congenial objections, the voices were low and words seemed to flow haltingly. It was an unusual mood for an evening meal among friends.

Anita waited for one of the guests to break into song. She had once spent an evening on the front desk listening to college songs, beginning with "High Above . . . Cayuga's Waters." By late in the evening, she'd heard so many songs ending with "Fight fight fight" that her nerves were jangled and her head ached. There was none of that unrestrained exuberance tonight, however. Anita paused in the doorway, hoping to get a sense of the guests' mood before entering. But she couldn't wait forever. She didn't like the feeling of eavesdropping for its own sake, and that was what this was becoming. She straightened her shoulders and walked in.

Kenneth Maxinter sat at the head of the large center table, at the far end. He was unlike the usual sort of guest Hotel Delite attracted. She rarely saw a man in a silk shirt and linen slacks with gold necklaces in her dining room. His hazel eyes expressed the delight he must feel in being the center of attention, and she imagined that his charm could dominate a room if he so chose.

As he lifted his glass to make a toast he spotted Anita, but instead of pausing to acknowledge her arrival, he began his speech. It went on longer than she thought it would, and after a few minutes (she was sure it was at least three) she wondered if she looked as awkward as she felt. She was used to standing by in the gallery while tourists stared at her photographs and asked unanswerable questions, but this was different. She was obviously waiting.

"And so, to the trip of a lifetime!" Kenneth lifted his glass even higher, nodded to the others around the table, and drank.

This, Anita thought, was a bit dramatic. She scanned the faces of the other guests, and noted their quiet agreement with the toast. And yet, no one seemed enthusiastic. Nearest to Anita, at the near end of the table, sat Larry Forche. If the evening was special for Kenneth, it wasn't for Larry. He had relaxed enough to wear khaki shorts and a blue-striped cotton shirt, but he could be going anywhere—to the beach, shopping, or dinner. He lifted his glass a few inches from the table and turned to the woman on his right, Sandra Stover, with a puppy-dog look of hopefulness.

Anita couldn't tell if Sandra was paying attention to Larry. She was wearing a different blond wig, and she wore makeup, despite the heat, skillfully applied. Anita wondered if she'd been swimming, and the wig was to hide her unmanaged hair, but then decided probably not. Her cotton dress was belted at the waist, causing the blouse and skirt to billow out. She twirled the stem of her glass but never lifted it from the table. She must have felt Larry staring at her because she glanced at him. She didn't smile, but her mouth twitched and she returned her attention to her wine glass.

Opposite Sandra sat Angela Deetcher, who lifted her glass straight up in the air, lifting and drinking with a formality that seemed almost military in its precision. She nodded approval of the toast, but it didn't elicit even a smile. Anita tried not to stare at her, but Angela wouldn't have noticed. Her look was fixed on the man beside her.

Crocker Dawes was the last one to lift his glass, as though he questioned the point of the toast. Tall and thin, he stretched out his legs under the table, and even leaning back in his chair, his fingers could dust crumbs from the white cloth. He set the glass down, rested his left wrist on the edge, and with his right hand mopped the sweat from his face with a large plaid handkerchief. He'd been out in the sun, not just today, but for several days previously. He had the complexion of a man who liked to be outdoors despite his coloring, but his temples seemed pale, as though the sun didn't penetrate there. He brushed back his red hair with his left hand and unself-consciously brushed his fingers together, as though afraid he'd picked up dust. This was the man who had ordered the special pastries and spoken Malayalam to Auntie Meena. He raised his glass and turned to Kenneth.

"Well said, Ken. Well said. The trip of a lifetime." He tipped his glass, letting a few drops of white wine fall, unnoticed, onto the white tablecloth.

"Glad you appreciate it, Crocker." Kenneth nodded in acknowledgment and then lowered his glass. "Not bad." He indicated the wine. "Especially for a country without a history of wine making."

"Is it Indian?" Sandra asked. She didn't look interested in either the question or the answer. Indeed, her question didn't seem to be addressed to anyone in particular, and her look settled on no one.

Anita took the opportunity to step in and after a general greeting provided information on the growing wine industry in India, the labels that Hotel Delite usually served, and suggestions on other restaurants to try if they were interested in more of this.

"You have reserved a car for the rest of the week," she said. "Will that be adequate? We're able to provide a van, if you think you'd be more comfortable."

"No, no, the hotel car is fine." Kenneth waved away her concerns but she noticed that he didn't consult any of the other tour members. She wanted to say five of them would be cramped in a regular car, and a van would be much better. The increase in cost was little, but the greater comfort was worth it. But she didn't get a chance to say that. She didn't get a chance to say much of anything. Indeed, Anita wondered if anyone in this group got a chance to say much of anything. Kenneth Maxinter was as much a showman as he was a tour leader. But she had seen what she wanted to see. She made appropriate noises, wished everyone a good evening, and retreated to the office.

* * * * *

"You are working, at this hour?" Auntie Meena leaned over Anita's shoulder as she typed into the computer. "Who is going to Athens?"

Anita spun around in her chair. "No one is going to Athens. This tour group is coming from Athens and I want to know more about them."

"Anita! I order you to ignore them." The minute she said this, Auntie Meena realized the problem. Her face went blank, she opened her mouth but couldn't seem to think of what to say. "I am not meaning this in the way it is sounding."

Anita smiled. "How do you mean it?"

"You are understanding me." Not daring to say anything more, Auntie Meena tugged on her sari and twirled out of the office to the registration desk. "Ah! Mr. and Mrs. Allbret."

Anita leaned around to peek through the doorway and saw the older couple stop and chat with Meena. Her aunt always enjoyed this kind of interaction with guests, the older and feebler the guest was, the better because they gave the least amount of trouble and were often the most appreciative of the attentions a hotel staff could provide. Since it was nearing nine-thirty, Anita knew that Auntie Meena would remain on the desk saying good night to Hotel Delite guests and visitors from other hotels as they left the terrace dining room. This part of the resort retired early.

Not expecting anyone in Athens to reply immediately, Anita shut down the computer and rocked the office chair back and forth. She listened to the voices inside and outside the hotel rise and fall, murmurings that burst into laughter and comments before subsiding again into private thoughts. Evening layered over the hotel regardless of how the guests felt. Occasionally, one or two went off to enjoy a late-night party at another hotel, and later Sanjay would rise from his mat to unlock the door for them. But not tonight, it seemed. The two men from Australia, Gene and Ron, strolled up to the desk.

"So, Mrs. Nayar," Gene began. The taller of the two, he most often began conversations, but after a few moments, Ron interjected a question or two. He was the quiet, astute one, and Anita enjoyed watching him query the waiter Moonu every morning about aspects of Indian life. The two men left early every morning for a hike through the area, and they managed to cover, in Anita's view, quite a lot of territory. They walked into the city of Trivandrum, rode buses into the hills and walked back, or hiked up and down the coast. Unaffected by the heat apparently, they wore full hiking boots with woolen socks, which they washed themselves in their room.

Ron didn't mask his curiosity, pinning his attention on Meena. "We heard someone talking about this place where everyone walks up a hill to a temple, and it's open to everyone, all religions and all nationalities. Is that around here?"

"Ah, Sabarimala," Auntie Meena said, relieved at finding herself on firm ground. She wasn't as confident as Moonu in answering questions about the entire subcontinent. "Yes, it is very holy. Most beautiful."

"Have you been?" Gene typed the name into his mobile.

"Ah, not since I was a child." Meena looked uncomfortable, and looked to Anita for help, giving her niece a desperate come-and-save-me look.

"I think we have a guidebook that includes sites that non-Hindus can visit." Anita came out from behind the counter and led the way to the hall bookcase. "Males of any age can visit Sabarimala when the temple is open, but only young girls and old women can visit there. You'll see fathers with their daughters but not their wives. I went as a child, and so did my aunt." Anita pulled open the glass-fronted door to the bookcase and shifted a number of books until she found the one she wanted. She handed it to Ron.

"Evening." The greeting came from Angela Deetcher. She and Sandra Stover came down the hall, chatting with each other until they reached the bookcase. Sandra held her palm in front of her as she fingered the loose spices Indians sometimes ate at the end of the meal, provided by the restaurant at the door, like mints in Western countries. Unlike some restaurants in the area, however, Hotel Delite did not follow the North Indian practice of serving a mixture of spices at the end of every meal. Some guests asked for the mixture of licorice, cloves, fennel, and other spices, and the waiter explained that it was not the custom in Kerala. This version was called Mukhwas, and sold mostly in North India. The two women had picked up little packets of the spices from the plane or airport. They maneuvered past Anita in the narrow space, and continued to the stairs. Behind them came Kenneth Maxinter.

"I think we should put off the journey until later in the week, nearer the end," Larry said. He trotted behind Kenneth, trying to hold his attention, but the tour leader was more interested in the bookcase and Anita, and then in the two young trekkers, Ron and Gene. Ron reached for the slim volume Anita held out and began turning the pages.

"Thinking of hiking in the hills, are you?" Kenneth edged in between the two men, his hands resting in his pockets. "Some great walks up near Ponmudi. That's where the maharajah used to go in the hot season. Lovely hills, nice trails. I think you have to have a tribal guide to go very far, but I hear it's worth it. I'm thinking of taking the group up there if you're interested in joining us."

Gene and Ron glanced at each other so swiftly and discreetly that Anita guessed they'd had other encounters with travelers trying to loop them into a group. But the greater surprise was Larry's reaction.

"Ah, Kenneth?" Larry looked from the tour leader to the two young men. "I don't remember that being on the agenda. I don't think Sandra could handle—"

"Optional," Kenneth said, making an abrupt half-turn to silence Larry. "Let me know if you're interested. Could be fun." He didn't wink. Instead, he lifted both eyebrows in a query, tipped his head, and gave a half smile. "Let me know." He waved and turned around to the staircase. Larry followed, hunched over and torn between dampening any interest the boys might have in the invitation and following Kenneth to continue their earlier conversation.

Auntie Meena watched the tour leader walk away and then turned her curious gaze on the two younger guests. "You are wanting a trip into the hills?" She was prepared to assist her guests even if she had doubts about what was wanted.

"No, thanks, Mrs. Nayar." Gene took the guidebook out of Ron's hands, and waved it by his face. "We'll look this over. Looks pretty comprehensive, right, Ron?" Ron nodded agreement, and the two backed away, heading to their own room. They seemed relieved to escape so much attention.

"Good evening, Mr. Dawes," Anita said. Crocker Dawes had lingered in the hallway behind the others as Kenneth intercepted the two trekkers. When the two young men escaped and the other tour members reached the top of the stairs, Crocker moved to the bookcase and began poking through the offerings. Anita heard doors open and close on the second floor, voices fade.

"Retiring?" she asked.

"I guess so," he said after backing away from the books. He slipped his hands into his pockets, his lips pressed shut as though he were afraid of what might slip out. He took a deep breath, smiled, and said, "You must have a pretty long day."

Ah, thought Anita, a guest in need of conversation. "Yes, very long, but we get breaks during the day, don't we, Auntie."

"Oh, yes." Auntie Meena glanced at Anita, as if to say, See, some guests are quite thoughtful.

"How early do you begin?" Crocker asked. "You must be up at six to make breakfast, all those pastries."

Oh, yes, thought Anita, the man who ordered the pastries. "We're not making them. They arrive very early in the morning, by five-thirty or so."

"Oh, the baker's boy delivers them?"

Hmm, thought Anita. "No, the baker herself is coming. She brings these breakfast sweets herself. Sometimes her daughter comes, to help out. We are most appreciative." She took note of his expression, not sure what to make of it, and wished him good night as he turned to the stairs. When he was gone, she turned to Auntie Meena. "What was it he said to you in Malayalam when he first arrived?"

Meena frowned as she tried to recall the conversation. "He is saying that now he is returned here he is very happy. Valare santosham."

"Now he is returned," Anita repeated. "I wonder when he was here the first time."

This was the moment when Auntie Meena would normally launch into her ready lecture on dialects of Malayalam, which Anita had neglected to learn because she was, after all, corrupted by having an American father. Her mother could be forgiven for making this error but her father was, well, outside the ritual acceptance. Hence, Anita needed education on the finer points of being a Malayali. Anita readied herself for this one but before Auntie Meena could begin, both women started at the sound of a door slamming.

"Ooh! I am thinking there is distress up there." Auntie Meena raised her eyes to the ceiling and then turned to listen as someone clattered down the stairs.

Sandra Stover hurried down the hallway. "Oh, dear," she said to the two women. "Larry Forche seems to be unwell, some kind of stomach upset. A little diarrhea, I think. Do you have anything?" Anita headed into the office. She could hear Auntie Meena reassuring Sandra that this sort of thing happened occasionally, and it was not to be worried about. Anita returned with a remedy, and told Sandra to check in with her later if things worsened. If necessary, there was a good clinic nearby. Sandra hurried up the stairs.

A door opened and closed, then another. Meena looked up, and pursed her lips, listening. "It is falling quiet now, isn't it?" Letting her worries fade, Auntie Meena picked up the thread of the earlier conversation. She tugged her sari into better shape, ready to assert her views. "But you are not understanding Mr. Dawes properly. He is having dialect of far far north. You are not recognizing this."

"Why is it, Auntie, that anytime a foreigner speaks Malayalam, it sounds so strange to you that you insist he learned it in the north of Kerala, where all Malayalam is influenced by border languages?"

"I am not saying this," Meena said, lifting her chin and trying to peer down at Anita over her nose. This was physically impossible because Anita was so much taller, but she did her best. “I am having very well-tuned ear.” And with that, she turned her head to one side and then the other, as though she were an antenna on the roof of Hotel Delite.

Six

Long before daylight on the following morning Anita climbed out of an autorickshaw onto a path leading to the top of a small hill. The mountains signaling the end of the Western Ghats floated above a sea of mist, and below the layer of white small houses faded away in the valley. Anita wanted a very particular photograph. She followed the narrow path, more a trail made by wandering goats, onto the top of the mound. Here she had spotted the sun discovering the vale some weeks ago while on a ride back from visiting friends, and she knew then it would make a photograph she would be proud of. In the center of the mound she set up her tripod and camera, and waited.

There was a dampness and coolness in the air that rarely reached as far south as the resort. Also a quiet, a different sort of quiet. Anita pulled the shawl tightly around her shoulders and paced across the scrubland. Farther up, the road turned and ran past a forest of deciduous trees, and after that tall thick shrubs crowded the verge. She often sent tourists on a drive into the countryside so they could see something more than tourist shops and city streets. Some enjoyed the discovery of another corner of India, one that most people didn't see, but others came back unimpressed. She tried to assess the current crop of hotel guests and identify any who might appreciate such a side trip.

The two trekkers, Gene and Ron, might like the idea of driving deep into the hillside and walking back to Trivandrum, but no one else seemed a likely prospect. Larry Forche couldn't seem to answer a question or greeting without turning to Sandra Stover to see what she would say or think. He followed her everywhere, and even if she didn't seem to mind, she didn't seem to care either. Angela Deetcher was an independent sort but she might appreciate some of the lushness of the countryside, the opportunity to encounter exotic birds and village life. Kenneth Maxinter wanted to visit the high-end hotels, so Anita arranged a car for him for later in the week. Crocker Dawes seemed to be interested in visiting the area but not one to need suggestions. She was dying to ask him when he had first visited India. Meeting a foreigner who spoke the local language was unusual.

The fog settled and thinned, light outlined the mountain ridge against the morning sky, and Anita dove for her camera. She began taking shots before the morning sun seemed to be where she wanted it, just in case, always just in case. When she felt she'd taken enough, she headed back to the resort. The autorickshaw left her at the top of Lighthouse Road and she strolled down the hill to the hotel. She enjoyed this time of morning and didn't hasten her step.

At this hour most of the people out and about were hotel and restaurant employees heading off to work and preparing for the day. A fruit seller scurried past her and farther down the hill turned down a tiled lane to a hotel. Anita passed the lane to the temple and stopped to look down into the courtyard. A small temple sat at the far end of the plot, where the land sloped down a hill. The ground had been scooped out, leaving tall walls on which sat hotels and houses. Anita worried the land would sink and cave in during the monsoon, but so far that hadn't happened. Out of the corner of her eye she spotted a tall figure.

Crocker Dawes was hard to miss. He paused at a lane that ran along a compound wall, and glanced down at a piece of paper in his hand. Anita tried to recall if there were any early morning yoga or meditation classes in this area. She thought she knew all of the teachers in the resort, even those that popped up over night with signs that insisted they had been professional teachers for generations.

But the foreigners were astute about evaluating teachers. Some of the Americans came with their own expertise. Still, Anita liked to keep an eye out, just in case. When a tourist felt cheated by a restaurant, hotel, fruit seller, shopkeeper or anyone else, everyone in the resort suffered. Seeing Crocker Dawes here at this hour reminded her that neither she nor Auntie Meena had given the tour group the introductory lecture, as she thought of it. But she needn't have worried about Crocker. He spoke to someone out of sight, seemed satisfied, and stepped onto the lane. Anita continued on her way, reminding herself to ask him what class he had attended. She was surprised he'd managed to find something at this hour on his second day in India, even if he had been here before.

Over the years Anita had taken to using the tourists meditating on the shore as a barometer of the day to come. If there were more than one or two foreigners sitting cross-legged, it would be a good day—not too hot and not too wet, with perhaps only a brief shower in the evening. If there were many tourists on the beach and on the rocky headlands before six o'clock, it would be an excellent day and foreigners would engage in many activities. If there were no tourists meditating on the rocks or on the beach, it would be a bad day—very little activity. If tourists walked the beach before six in the morning, it would be a very bad day, with too much heat, and hoteliers would wonder if they should close until the fall season.

* * * * *

Anita was confident she'd captured the image she wanted, and headed straight to her own suite well pleased with herself. She didn't re-emerge until noise from the parking area drew her out. She greeted the guests milling about the hotel car.

"We're waiting for Kenneth," Larry told her. "I'm sure he said he was coming with us this morning."

"If he were coming he'd be here by now." Sandra leaned against the back of the car, arms crossed, a sour look on her face. But then she winced, and turned away, and Anita wondered if she felt unwell.

"He almost missed the flight," Angela said.

"I don't remember that." Larry looked worried. "Perhaps that's what the argument was about last night."

"What argument?" Angela said.

"Oh, I thought I heard Ken having an argument in his room with someone."

"I don't remember that," Sandra said.

"Yes, yes, of course, you do," Larry said. "I think you mentioned it."

"I did?"

"Didn't you say something about it, Angela?" Larry turned to the other woman.

"Did I?" Angela frowned as though trying to recall.

"At this point I don't think what happened last night matters," Sandra said. "I just want to get going."

"You settled on this plan yesterday?" Anita said, to get oriented.

"In tedious detail," Angela said. "We talked about it to the exclusion of almost everything else."

Sandra gave her a quizzical look but before she could comment Larry jumped in and said, "Yes, yes, we did. You remember, Sandra. We commented on it while we were walking around that lovely island."

It was hard to tell if Sandra did remember because right now she was looking at Larry Forche as if she didn't even remember him. "You commented on how lovely the island was," Larry said.

"Did I? Yes, it was." She began to nod, once or twice and then with a little shake of her shoulders. "Yes, I do recall. Thank you, Larry." She gave him a sweet smile, but she didn't look convinced.

"But right now we want to get going," Angela said. "Waiting is pointless."

"Of course, of course," Anita said, stepping in now that she thought she understood the problem. "You're off to the museum and then to the Taj Hotel for lunch, is that right?" The others agreed. "Then I can assure you that when Mr. Maxinter comes down, I will see that he meets you at the Taj if he is not in time to catch you at the museum. I will send him in a taxi." She glanced at Joseph standing off to the side, a rag in his hand to give the tourists the impression that he was polishing the car instead of eavesdropping.

Anita's was not an ideal solution but it was a solution, and the three guests mumbled agreement and climbed into the hotel car.

"Gone," Anita said unnecessarily to Ravi at the hotel desk.

"Do you know how long they were standing there arguing?"

"How long?" Anita guessed the guests could have spent a good half hour at that disagreement.

"Almost two hours." Ravi hunched over the papers he'd been working on at the counter.

"Two hours?" Anita stopped in the office doorway.

"It is agreement in this tour group not to be chasing after others," Ravi said when he saw Anita's expression. "They are having privacy understandings. This is what they are saying."

* * * * *

Later in the afternoon Auntie Meena slid into the office chair opposite Anita, tipped her head back and closed her eyes. "Not a word, Anita, not one word. Peace is coming to me." Her eyelids fluttered shut. "I am listening to the tourists meditating on the roof and I am thinking, perhaps this is wise. Perhaps I must seek out the tourists' guru and speak to him."

"Perhaps you could take a nap," Anita said.

Auntie Meena's head snapped forward and she opened her eyes to glare at Anita. "You are not to be mocking. These foreigners are very calm, are they not?" Meena leaned forward. "Well, are they not?"

"Certainly, Auntie, they are much quieter than some. They are almost stately, well, some of them. But you have our family guru, yes?"

Meena rocked her head from side to side, murmuring agreement. "This is so."

"And your astrologer."

"Ah, yes, very wise man," Meena said, as Anita knew she would. Auntie Meena worshiped her astrologer, who had advised her mother, various other relatives, and, Meena hoped, would some day be Anita's advisor, if both of them lived long enough.

"Then, it is well." Anita returned to reading the accounts book and comparing it with the document produced by the computer. Auntie Meena liked the prestige of participating in the modern world, but she wasn't sure she trusted it. When it came right down to it, she preferred the comfort of the old ledger, heavy, bulky, and filled with neat letters and numbers in ink. Each ledger became an old friend, and she was known to run her fingers down the spine with gentle affection. And trust. Definitely, with trust.

"But they are so calm." Meena seemed caught with this idea and gave a deep sigh.

"That reminds me," Anita said. "There's a new class of some sort, I think, along the lane near the temple. Have you heard of this?"

Auntie Meena shook her head. "Another one?"

"Perhaps Pema knows." Anita turned to the woman now standing in the office doorway. Pema shook her head; she hadn't heard about any new classes. Anita reminded herself to ask Crocker Dawes about it, and continued, "We are commenting on how calm the tourists are this week. Do you find it so, Pema?" Pema, now head maidservant, cleaned all the rooms every day with little help and had definite opinions on the various guests. The job had once been Poota's, but she was prone to elephantiasis, and when her legs swelled she could do little. Pema was young, energetic, and Poota's niece. It kept the job in the family but it meant sometimes Pema was doing everything alone.

Pema shrugged. "This group is tidy and neat. They are not eating in their rooms, only this little bit, and this makes the work easier. And they are not doing their laundry, and this also makes the work easier. And only one person to each room upstairs. Very easy."

"But?" Anita peered into the wastebasket Pema was taking to the midden to empty.

"Why does there have to be a but?" Auntie Meena slid forward on her chair and stuck out her chin. "You must not make her dissatisfied." Auntie Meena also had a desperate fear of losing her staff, since good workers were becoming harder and harder to find. Besides, she knew both maidservants well, and had grown fond of them. "You are not dissatisfied, are you, Pema?"

"No, Amma. I am satisfied." Pema gave Auntie Meena a sympathetic look.

"But there is one matter, yes?" Anita turned to her aunt. "There is something otherwise she would not be standing in the doorway without her cleaning equipment holding a wastebasket and a pair of shoes. Am I right?" The shoes were covered in dirt and little twigs. It looked like someone had taken a hike into rough and wet territory.

"Where is your cleaning equipment?" Meena began calculating how much it would cost to replace everything.

"Upstairs in the hallway."

"There, you see, Anita?" Meena preened. "No problem at all."

"Why is it upstairs?" Anita asked.

"I cannot get into room six. The door is locked."

Anita looked at her aunt. "Did Mr. Maxinter go out after all?"

"I did not see him," Meena said.

Ravi confirmed that Kenneth Maxinter had not left the hotel, or at least had not left his key at the desk and Ravi had not seen him go out.

"Then he must be here," Anita said.

"Perhaps he is unwell," Pema said.

"Why did you say this, Pema?" Auntie Meena was ready to pounce.

"I leave the foreigners to their own habits, but I think I heard a moan when I knocked on the door earlier this morning."

Anita stood up, glancing at the clock. It was past two in the afternoon. The three guests who had gone off to tour the city and have lunch at the Taj had not returned, and Crocker Dawes had not reappeared all day. "I'll check, just to be sure." Anita took a master key and headed up the stairs.

"You must not make much of nothing, Anita." Auntie Meena grabbed her sari skirts and hurried after Anita.

"You may be right, but I want to check, just to be safe."

"I will apologize to him for our rude interruption of his rest," Auntie Meena said as she followed. Pema deposited the shoes and dustbin on the floor behind the counter, and followed them upstairs.

Anita rapped on the door of room six, but heard nothing even after several attempts to rouse Mr. Maxinter. She stepped away from the door and turned to the next room, room five, opening it with her master key. She crossed at once to the balcony, went out, and leaned over the parapet to peer into the other room.

"What is it?" Auntie Meena asked.

"We must go in." Anita unlocked the door to room six and all three women pushed into the doorway. Kenneth Maxinter lay curled up on the bed, his right arm dangling over the edge. Anita knelt by him, felt along his neck, looked for a pulse, and gasped.

"Gone?" Pema said.

"Gone." Anita stepped back from the inert figure. She was used to seeing dead bodies but here was a dead foreigner in her hotel in the middle of the tourist season. This was certainly a tragedy for Mr. Maxinter—to die so far from home. But it was also a tragedy—or at least a threat of one—for Hotel Delite.

"No no no. Not possible." Auntie Meena stared at the limp form, shaking her hands as though she had touched something bad.

"I'm afraid it is possible." Anita shook her head. This was not going to be a good day at all.

"Oh, Shivayashivoo! What horrible deeds have I ever done to justify this?" Meena clasped her hands together as if in prayer. "Whoever will come to Hotel Delite after this?"

"Tourists are modern," Pema said with a slight curl of her lip. "They do not care about something like this."

"But it is terrible!" Auntie Meena began to look frantic, on the verge of panic.

"It is a holy thing for him," Pema said, her hands clasped in front of her, a knowing smile on her face.

"What nonsense are you talking?" Meena turned to the maidservant, her hands stilled, a look of incomprehension spreading over her face. "The man is dead in my hotel!"

"Is it not better to die here than in States, away from the holy rivers and the many places Vishnu has seen fit to bless?"

Auntie Meena struggled to believe this, but her penchant for worry overcame her good sense.

"Perhaps, Auntie, it's not as bad as it seems." Anita leaned over the dead man.

"He is not dead?"

"He's not officially dead, Auntie. As far as the law is concerned, he is still alive. Only a doctor at the hospital can say he is dead, his soul returned to the Atman."

"This is true?" Auntie Meena grabbed Anita's arm.

"This is true, Auntie."

"But we must take no chances."

"At least it seems to be a natural—"

But Auntie Meena was no longer paying attention to her niece. She began praising Shiva for his greatness, his kindness to his devotees, his magnificence and munificence, and begging him for patience.

"Patience?" Anita wondered aloud.

"I must call my astrologer. He will remove the *aavi* before it transforms into an evil, angry spirit. We must hurry."

Meena dragged Pema from the room.

Seven

"The astrologer has come." Auntie Meena brushed past Anita to greet a man in a long white mundu and white shirt carrying a small black leather briefcase with a bulge at one end.

"The rock," Anita thought. Along with the necessary prayers and incense, he'll draw the *aavi*, Maxinter's soul, to the rock and carry it off to the cremation ground. Her aunt wouldn't rest until the rite was completed and the danger of an evil spirit lingering in Hotel Delite averted.

Anita loved her aunt dearly but sometimes the sudden eruption into their lives of her various beliefs threatened to overbalance Anita's sanity if not Meena's. When the ambulance drew into the parking lot, Anita hurried out to stall them. Over the next hour the driver and assistants were happy to accept cold drinks and conversation with Joseph, the hotel driver, while Meena and her astrologer proceeded with the rites in Maxinter's room. Now the only question was whether or not Maxinter's body could be removed before the return of the guests.

Under Anita's orders, Ravi kept watch at the top of the hill to waylay the hotel car if the other tour members should arrive before the body had been removed. The minute the door slammed on the ambulance, Anita closed her eyes and gave an audible sigh of relief. She reached Ravi on his cell, telling him it was safe to return to the hotel.

"We have good luck today," Anita told her aunt when the astrologer wandered into the dining room for a cup of tea and the ambulance with its cargo maneuvered up the narrow lane to Lighthouse Road.

"Yes, my astrologer is most reliable." Meena fanned herself with the end of her dupatta.

Now all Anita had to do was figure out the best way to tell the guests. She felt stranded in the parking lot, trying to decide what to do next. Ravi hurried down the hill and back to his place at the desk. Anita followed, wondering aloud how to gather the guests to give them the news.

"Mr. and Mrs. Allbret are having dinner in Trivandrum," Ravi offered from the other side of the reception desk. A few years younger than Anita, and something of a younger brother in her view, Ravi offered a welcomed stability when things became difficult, as he termed it. Auntie Meena often turned to him, aware that his mother had died when he was a child and therefore feeling it her duty to fill the gap.

"How do you know this about the Allbrets?" Anita asked.

"I am listening as they are departing at noontime." He waggled his head and smiled. "And she is wearing very fragrant perfume." Ravi was proud of his excellent sense of smell.

"And why does this matter?"

"Because Mr. Allbret is buying this for her for special occasion. He is telling me this." Ravi grew thoughtful. "But he is not as happy as I am expecting. He wonders if salesman is correct about the happy effect of this fragrance. Still, it is very loving, isn't it?"

Anita agreed that it was. "In that case, I will block off the parlor and usher the others into that area and tell them there. I must have tea ready for them. Can you tell Cook, Ravi?" Ravi jumped to pass along the order while Anita kept her eye on the parking lot.

When the hotel car arrived, Anita was ready. She stepped forward as the car with its three passengers pulled into the parking lot and Joseph shut off the engine. Unlike other foreigners who had stayed at Hotel Delite, however, none of the tourists opened a car door. Each waited for Joseph to get out and open all three doors.

Larry emerged from the front passenger side, and Sandra and Angela from the rear seats. All three looked exhausted but not displeased with their day. And, to Anita, it seemed to have been a long one. They had departed at midmorning and were returning only now, at almost five o'clock.

"Welcome!" Anita crossed the hall to greet them. With a few soft words and quick and intentionally confusing phrases she ushered the trio into the parlor. Behind them came Auntie Meena, who felt it her duty to be present during the reporting of the tragic event of Kenneth Maxinter's death. Moonu arrived with the tea tray.

"Oh, how nice!" Sandra leaned over the teacups. "Just the thing." She lifted her hand to the scarf over her head and seemed to shift her wig into place.

Sandra poured herself a cup of tea and then took a chair by the window overlooking the terrace and out to sea. She leaned on the chair arm as she seated herself. Angela also poured herself a cup and spooned in sugar. Once again, Anita noticed, Larry kept his eyes on Sandra. And so did Angela. Anita began the unpleasant task.

"I thought tea here would help with what I have to tell you," she said.

All three faces turned to her.

"And what is that?" Sandra said. She sounded weary but also businesslike.

"I'm afraid there's been a death," Auntie Meena said, standing beside Anita, delivering the bad news because she was the owner of Hotel Delite and it was her duty, and because she was Anita's aunt and still harbored the belief that an unmarried woman had to be protected from the harsh realities of life, and that included delivering bad news.

"Oh, that's too bad." Angela stirred her tea and walked to a chair to sit down. "Isn't it?" she said to Larry and Sandra. Both nodded and murmured agreement. Anita tried not to show her surprise at this casual response.

"Yes, we are finding Mr. Maxinter this afternoon." Auntie Meena tried to look compassionate but only managed to look uncomfortable, which she was. She clasped her hands in front of her and gave the others an expectant look, perhaps giving them permission to express their sorrow.

"You mean Crocker, Mr. Dawes," Larry said.

Auntie Meena and Anita glanced at each other. Meena turned aside and said in Malayalam to Anita, "Are they having as much trouble telling each other apart as they have telling Indians apart? Do they not yet know each other well enough?"

Anita took a moment to consider this and then said to the guests, "We're quite certain it's Mr. Maxinter. We have his passport and other identification."

Sandra's teacup slid from her lap and crashed on the floor. Larry moved to wrap his arm around her. Anita could hear him murmuring to her but it didn't sound like words of comfort for the death of a friend. His whispering sounded too intense to be soothing. Angela rested her teacup in its saucer.

"Well, that is sad and a very great surprise. Ken, you said? And you're quite sure?" Angela commanded attention, stopping Anita in her path toward Sandra.

"Yes, we're sure," Anita said.

"Well, very sad, and not expected, but life can change in an instant," Angela said. "Yes, quite a surprise." She deposited cup and saucer on the table. "I am going upstairs to rest." She stood and went up the stairs, without a single look back at the others remaining. Pema appeared to clean up the broken crockery and spilt tea, and Anita moved to sit by Sandra.

"You're distressed, Mrs. Stover. May I call a doctor? Or, I can take you to the clinic. It's not far."

"She's quite all right," Larry said. "I'll take care of her."

Anita would have been happier if Sandra had said something, offered her own assurance that she could manage. "Could you tell me, Mrs. Stover, one thing before you go?" She waited. "Why did you think it was Mr. Dawes who died?"

Sandra and Larry glanced at each other. Sandra shook her head.

"I was confused. That's all. I'm tired." Sandra raised a hand to her wig and patted it along the side.

"Yes, she's tired," Larry said. "Please, we'd like to be alone." He helped her from the chair and led her to the stairs, and this time he was murmuring words of reassurance, promising all would be well and he would never leave her. She barely seemed to hear him.

* * * * *

Anita unlocked the door to room six where she had discovered the body of Kenneth Maxinter curled up on his bed. She had ordered the room locked but a police official had already called, releasing the room for rental. Auntie Meena was delighted, but Anita was not. She pushed open the door and stood in the corner of the room. The astrologer's rite left a lingering fragrance of sandalwood incense mixed with the smell of saltwater and something else. She leaned over the bed, sniffing, capturing just a hint of a man's sweat. Maxinter must have been sweating near the end, lying in his clothes.

The medical men had been careful, and the room looked little different from the moment the guest had entered the previous day. There were no signs of a struggle, and no signs that he had thrashed about. Anita had found him lying on his side as though he had died in his sleep. And yet she felt uneasy. An inexplicable death would be bad for business.

One of the casement windows let in a breeze that ruffled a curtain and an envelope sticking out of a book on the desk. Anita closed the window and picked up the book, a journal. She read the first few pages but found nothing interesting. The opening section recorded passport numbers, plane ticket numbers, contact information, and document numbers. The following pages recorded sites the man had visited on the tour so far. He had enjoyed Copenhagen, and Athens less so.

Nearby on the desk sat a mobile and a small packet of spices and seeds that airlines plying the Asian routes often provided with a meal. This one had the name of the airline the tour group had taken. Nearby sat a teacup that Maxinter apparently had filled with the spices and seeds, to enjoy after dinner in his room. South Indian restaurants didn't provide this mixture, but Anita knew people could buy it in the shops. She would have to return the cup to the dining room.

Anita flipped through the journal again. On one of the notes near the end of their stay in Athens, Kenneth Maxinter noted that “Georgio left us today.” That would explain the reduction in the number of guests, she thought. And since it happened near the end of their stay, Maxinter didn't think to let Hotel Delite know. Or perhaps he asked the Athens hotel to forward the information. She still hadn't heard from the Greek hotel, and wondered if it mattered.

The envelope slipped a bit between the pages and Anita pulled it out and turned it over. It was addressed to C.J. Dawes, with an address in the States. She lifted the flap but the envelope was empty. She would have to give it to Crocker.

These thoughts meandered through her mind, but left her right where she began: this tour group was decidedly odd. Why were Sandra and Larry so calm about the announcement of a death of one of their own but surprised to learn it was Kenneth Maxinter? Why did they think Crocker was the one who had died? Why was Angela neither surprised nor engaged in any way? And where *was* Crocker Dawes?

Anita relocked the room and returned to the registration desk, where Auntie Meena sat perched on a stool staring at the registration book. In the office Anita pulled out the file for current guests and read through the names. She saw what she expected.

"I'll tell other hotels that we have two rooms available at discount. It's important to fill them." Auntie Meena smiled the brittle smile of the desperate who hope all is well, now that the obvious, large crisis has passed.

"Let's not rent room six yet," Anita said, joining her aunt at the counter.

"Why not?" Meena was immediately on alert. "The astrologer has done the necessary. It has been released by the authorities. There is no problem, Anita, no problem at all." She saw the expression on Anita's face and buried her own face in her hands. "Not again. Oh, Shiva!"

"I'm curious about one or two things, Auntie," Anita said, trying to soothe her aunt.

"What is that?" Meena nodded at the teacup.

"The digestive the group picked up on the airplane, I think. Mr. Maxinter had it in his room."

"Throw it away. But not just now. Stay." With a panicked look on her face, Meena nodded to the man coming toward the doorway. "It's the other one, the one they can't tell apart from the man who died."

Anita slipped the journal and cup onto the shelf under the counter, out of sight. So far Auntie Meena had managed to conduct herself like someone who often found dead bodies in her hotel, as though this were a problem easily managed. But Anita knew, from long experience, that Auntie Meena was beginning to unravel.

"Why do Americans all look so innocent, so boyish, even when they're old?" Meena asked. It was a question Anita couldn't answer but one that captured her imagination as well.

Crocker Dawes, Anita thought, looks like the typical American tourist—large, healthy, filling the space around him. But in terms of features, he looks nothing like Kenneth Maxinter. And even if the two men did look alike, that wouldn't explain the confusion of the other tour members.

But even more curious, she thought, as she watched Crocker Dawes approach, his smile radiating good will and good cheer, was how much healthier and more cheerful he seemed since his arrival. In less than two full days, he looked like a new man. Her mind wandered to various explanations, and she recalled an ayurveda clinic located not far from the lane where she'd seen him walking that morning. But could anything have had such a profound effect in so short a time? She would have to find out, gently, after she got through the current business of announcing the tour leader's death. She readied herself for one more explanation.

* * * * *

Crocker Dawes walked through the door to Hotel Delite like a man who had just won the lottery. He had a broad smile on his face, and he walked with a robust swing of his arms and shoulders, almost skipping up the few steps to the doorway. His red hair streaked with gray brushed his forehead pinked by the sun. With his shirt sleeves rolled up to his elbows and his jaunty walk, he made Anita think of a scene from a movie set in Florida. He seemed so youthful and alive, so sensuous and virile that she lifted her hand to her hair, tidying up a few loose hairs. And yet she knew he was in his sixties. She composed herself and reported Kenneth's death.

"Ken?" Crocker leaned forward. He sounded surprised and, well, skeptical. "You're sure you mean Kenneth Maxinter? My height, a little younger, white hair? The tour leader?"

"Yes, Mr. Dawes, that's the man I mean." Anita stepped back to get a better look at Crocker Dawes. Over the years she'd had to deliver all sorts of bad news to guests—a mother had to be conveyed to a hospital when her daughter nearly drowned, a friend had to donate blood to save his traveling companion, a wife had to watch her husband succumb to a heart attack, and more. But this group had the most unexpected responses to, well, unexpected death.

"I sure am surprised," Crocker said.

"I can see that." Anita frowned, studying him.

"I mean," Crocker said, beginning anew, "he didn't seem sick or anything. How did it happen?"

"He appears to have died in his sleep. He didn't come down for the trip to the museum and lunch today with the other tour members, and no one saw him all day. The maidservant wanted to get in to clean the room but no one answered her knock. I checked in the afternoon and found him." She again offered condolences but Crocker wasn't listening. He seemed to be thinking it over.

"How ironic," Crocker said. "He seemed so healthy." He shook his head with a smile.

"Ironic?" Anita repeated.

"You never know, do you? You just never know." He rested his hands on his hips. "I thought Ken was an okay guy. Didn't know him long, but he seemed okay. Too bad. Really. You just never know." He went on in this vein for a few more minutes, giving Anita the chance to size him up. He too seemed like an okay guy, with an innocent charm and open and unguarded expressions.

"I have yet to remove all his belongings," Anita said, "but I did find a letter addressed to you in the States."

"To me?" Crocker frowned, slipping his hands into his pockets. He seemed perplexed. Anita pulled out the envelope.

"Yes, this one." She held it out to him. He took the envelope and held it between his fingers, staring at it, his expression changing from confusion and curiosity to surprise, sadness, and then amusement. She felt she'd never forget watching his face change, so mobile and revealing, like clouds scudding across the sky, changing every moment with shadows of varying shapes, patches of blue and gray, until sunshine breaks through and burns it all away, leaving only clean bright blue.

"It's empty, of course."

"Yes, it is." Anita waited. "Why did you say, of course?"

Crocker Dawes stared at Anita, as though she were a perfect stranger and he could look her over and marvel at the way she was put together, as though she had some odd facial arrangement and he wanted to examine and understand it. "Thanks for saving this for me."

"Who's C.J. Dawes?" As he opened his mouth to reply, she said, "I know it isn't you. I record all the passport information for our guests."

"Ah," he said, and smiled. "So you know my middle name doesn't begin with the letter j."

She waited.

"C.J. Dawes is my ex-wife. It's a long story."

"Most marriages are." Anita nodded to the envelope. "But this?"

"It's just an envelope, I'm happy to say." He stuffed it into his pocket. "Very glad to say."

She decided to try another tack. "Who's Georgio?"

Crocker blanched. "How do you know about him?"

"Did you know him?" Anita ignored his question. "Another member of your tour group?"

"Yes, he was on our tour." Crocker straightened up. Anita could feel the temperature dropping. "He decided to leave us in Athens." He rubbed his closed lips together. "He loved it there, and that is where he wanted to remain. So he did." He backed away as he spoke, and excused himself before Anita could ask anything more. She still didn't know why the others assumed at first he was the dead man, nor how he learned to speak Malayalam and when he had been here for the first time.

Really, the more she learned about the people on this tour, the less she knew. She was glad to lock the door and close out the day.

Eight

Life at Hotel Delite seemed to settle down enough for Anita to feel she could leave early the following morning for another photo shoot. She still felt off balance after Kenneth Maxinter's death and the stress from dealing with the authorities and the other tour members, so a few hours away was especially attractive. She photographed and walked and photographed some more, savoring the solitude and fresh dawn air in the hills. When she felt she'd been away long enough, she steeled herself on the drive back for more of the craziness that came with running a hotel. As the autorickshaw coasted down Lighthouse Road, Anita decided to reward herself for the success of her outing with one of Deepa Nayar's special treats. They had been an added expense but Anita felt the need of something a little different.

All the way into the kitchen Anita imagined sitting with a pot of fresh coffee and a plate of still warm pastries. She found Pohty, the cook, standing over his pot of fermenting rice and lentils, preparing to make idlies.

"You are searching?" he said.

"I went out to photograph," Anita said, "and I have been salivating for a little pastry with jam on the long drive back, but I see I am too early for the day's quota."

"There is no quota for today."

"No?" Anita spun around. "But the guests—"

"The guests are not requesting." Pohty had black wavy hair neatly trimmed, and his mustache was, as always, impeccably shaped. He was not yet stout, but he would be, filling out his torso with bowls of rice. His bare feet moved silently through the kitchen. He was a graceful man and was firm with anyone who interfered with his work or muddled his direct orders.

"Not requesting?" Anita tried to absorb this. She had gone to some trouble in tracking down Deepa. The high-end hotels paid her so well for her special baking that she had no need to expand her clientele. But she had been agreeable, and, as Anita recalled, oddly not very surprised at the request.

"One is wanting black coffee and light toast. She puts a little butter and jam and eats it in small nibbles." He lifted his eyebrows in disapproval.

"And the others?"

"Ah, the others. The woman with the changing hair and the man who follows her about are ordering but not eating. Such waste," he added under his breath. "But the one who died, ah, he is the one who is ordering and eating. He likes his food."

"That leaves Crocker Dawes, the guest for whom we went to all this trouble. Are you telling me now that he does not like the pastries? What is he eating?"

"Nothing." The cook turned to her and waited for her to react.

"Nothing? But . . . All right. Where is he going for breakfast? You have that sly look that tells me you think you have found out a secret."

Pohty chuckled. Despite his reduced status and circumstances after cutting off relations with his caste, though Hotel Delite paid him well and treated him well, Prakash Pohty never succumbed to pettiness. He had nothing bad to say about others, except Moonu, the waiter, who bore the brunt of the cook's rough affection. "We cooks know each other. He has found—hmm—a companion."

Anita felt her good mood sinking and a rising disappointment in Crocker Dawes. She thought him above the impulse to latch onto a young Indian woman for a one or two week fling. And she would have thought any young woman who worked in the area knew better. "Well, don't tell Auntie Meena."

"She already knows." He returned to his mortar and pestle.

"What? I saw him on a lane yesterday morning." She recalled his tall figure so out of place at that hour and in that place.

"Did I not say he is finding another place to eat?"

"And where is that?"

"Ah, that would be telling. Isn't that an English saying?"

"Yes, Pohty, it would be telling. So, please, tell me."

He shook his head, then pushed a basket along the counter to her. "Here." He pulled off the cloth covering the remains of yesterday's order. "Still fresh enough." Having solved what he regarded as Anita's problem, finding breakfast, he turned to preparing coconut chutney to accompany the idlies.

* * * * *

In the office Anita settled in front of the computer with her pastries and coffee. She had tried to contact the registration clerk at the hotel in Athens where the tour group had stayed. All members of the tour had stayed at the same hotel, according to their registration documents, and from there flown directly to Trivandrum. The Athens hotel seemed quite busy, and she had received a number of emails promising to address her request later. She glanced up at the clock. Athens was about three and a half hours behind Trivandrum, which meant that it was not yet three o'clock in the morning there. She logged on and emailed the night clerk, hoping he might be bored enough to answer, if he was awake.

The letters spread out across the screen, corrections pushing the line further and further along, until Anita was confident she had phrased her question in such a way that the other hotel clerk would not consider it an accusation, a veiled insult, or anything else. She hit send, and waited.

Sanjay came around the corner and leaned in through the office door. "Very quiet this night," he said. That meant it had been a good night, and he'd been able to get some sleep. He hefted the bed roll onto his shoulder and headed out the back door. She heard him going down the steps in the early morning quiet, and then the door scraping over the cement floor in front of the servants' storeroom.

She broke off a corner of the pastry and savored it, deciding that once in a while this was a reasonable treat but she wouldn't like it as a steady diet. She felt the craving for a dosa coming on and began to think about lunch. Perhaps she'd ask Pohty for an egg later. The computer pinged and she felt a little burst of delight at the return address. The Athens night clerk was awake and at his computer. She opened the email, and was pleased to see the message was a long one. She read it through.

Six guests had arrived at the hotel in Athens almost two weeks ago. They set about enjoying themselves, seeing the sights and, for one of them, revisiting old haunts. It was unclear to Anita which of the guests most loved the city, but one told the night clerk during the second day of the visit that he'd never been happier than when he'd lived in Greece. That was Georgio Panelli, who spent some of his childhood living with a grandmother outside the city. According to the clerk, he returned almost every evening after a long walk and sat up talking with the clerk late into the night, sometimes even until dawn. The clerk liked him, but found the late night talks very tiring. And then Georgio decided to leave the tour, and let them go on without him.

This was not unusual in Anita's experience. Tour groups split up all the time. There was often someone who didn't like the other members, couldn't get along, ran out of money, or got sick and wanted to go home. It wasn't rare and it wasn't common, but it happened often enough for Anita to no longer be surprised.

"So early?" Auntie Meena whispered as she came into the office, the sound of her sari brushing against the chairs like the memory of a song. She glanced at the camera. "Ah, yes. Perhaps you are finding a job." Auntie Meena still hoped Anita would turn out to be normal in some way, a way that was understandable to a conventional middle-aged matron.

"I'm talking via email to the clerk in Athens." Anita wiggled the mouse to wake up the page.

"Ask him why he is not warning us of the dip in numbers for this tour." Still exasperated over the loss of revenue, Meena turned her attention to the pastries, then leaned closer. "Not fresh." She stood up. "Where is Deepa this morning?"

"Not here. We aren't having another order. The guests aren't eating them. These are from yesterday."

"Not eating?" Meena made a face.

"One guest in Athens decided to stay there," Anita said. "Let me finish this."

"And did he get his money back?"

Anita shrugged. "Did they pay us a deposit?"

"I suppose we shall have to negotiate this deposit for the missing one and the one who has died." Auntie Meena closed her eyes, muttered a few prayers, and headed for the kitchen. "I must have breakfast before it all begins again."

Anita silently agreed and continued reading. She reread the email three times. Two lines bothered her the most. She reread them.

"We understand how you feel about the numbers being inaccurate. I was very concerned that six arrived here when we were expecting seven, but there was nothing we could do. You know how it is. We adjusted the deposits. We can't afford to lose business, with our economy being what it is."

So, the tour had been even larger at the outset, before it reached Athens and then Trivandrum. But the last line sent her heart racing.

"I liked Georgio. We all liked him. He spoke enough Greek to be passable, and he loved everything about our country. And you know it is hard to like Greece right now. We were all so sorry when we heard his body was found at the beach."

Anita couldn't say how long she stared at the email, reading it again and again, trying to make sense of it. After some time, she sent an email thanking the clerk, offered sympathy and hopes that the economy improved for him and his hotel, and signed off. She didn't like what she had read at all.

* * * * *

Auntie Meena trusted Ravi, the young desk clerk, with managing just about every aspect of the hotel, and this quality of trusting him, among other facets of Meena's personality, intimidated Ravi almost to the point of catatonia. Still, he managed a smile whenever he took his place behind the counter and Meena retired to the office. At least, she was supposed to retire to the office. This morning, she didn't.

"We are having most attractive sunset last evening, isn't it?" Auntie Meena straightened a pile of newspapers stacked at one end of the counter, made available every morning for the guests to enjoy. Ravi stared at her supple fingers straightening the folded papers, each digit slipping among the folds separating and smoothing them out. If asked, no one would testify to recalling Auntie Meena ever showing any interest in sunsets, sunrises, rainbows, sunny skies, or anything else that happened outside Hotel Delite and which she did not have some control over.

"Very nice, Amma." Ravi managed a sickly smile. Perhaps her odd comment was a prelude to a criticism, one he had not anticipated. From the hallway Anita watched this exchange and could guess the thoughts tumbling through Ravi's mind as he tried to catch up with his employer.

"Ah, Anita." Meena smiled at her niece. "Going out, I see." She beamed. But Anita was nothing like Ravi. She didn't for one moment attribute her aunt's strange behavior to her own conduct; instead she sensed something was up. Anita rested her camera on the counter and pulled out her small calendar.

"I have a few minor errands to carry out in Trivandrum, but first I have a few things to do here."

"Nonsense, Anita." Meena inched forward. "You are telling me and I am doing them."

Both Ravi and Anita stared at Meena, then glanced at each other. From the upstairs came the sounds of buckets and mops clattering, doors opening and closing.

"You've rented room six and sent Pema to clean it, haven't you?" Anita was at once alert. She dashed up the stairs and stopped Pema just as she was dragging her cleaning equipment into the room.

"But Anita Chechi, your aunt is ordering this." Pema dangled a rag from one hand, and pulled on a mop with the other.

"Not yet. Not yet." Anita ushered the maidservant out of the room and closed the door. She should have known. Auntie Meena had not wanted to wait even a few hours to rent the room as soon as the astrologer had cleared it. Anita had to implore her aunt to wait until the police reported that Kenneth Maxinter had died of natural causes, but Meena insisted there was no sign of unnatural death. The astrologer was effective in all his work.

Still, she had nodded and looked away, and Anita had taken that as acquiescence, of a sort. How wrong she had been.

After sending Pema away, Anita returned to the room and set about examining it, just in case she noticed something that might be useful later. Kenneth Maxinter might well have died of natural causes, but there was so much that was odd about his death that Anita felt unable to let it go. At the small table desk, she pulled out the chair and sat down. She'd already taken the journal, she recalled, and left it down at the counter. She'd have to reclaim it.

The desk drawer was empty, and the only other paper on the desk belonged to Hotel Delite, a small notepad with several blank sheets. She swung around and looked at the rest of the furniture. The small table between the twin beds had no drawer and no shelf. The two comfortable chairs sat next to each other, without a table. Anita turned to the closet, and here she was rewarded with a suitcase and a few items of clothing on hangers.

The clothing was the expected—a few cotton shirts and two pairs of shorts hung up alongside a pair of nice slacks. The suitcase, unlocked, contained more clothing, a cell phone charger, a cell phone, and a manila envelope. Anita sat down on the bed, opened the envelope and let the contents spill onto her lap—three envelopes, empty, and each one addressed to a different person in the States. Inside were four sheets of unused matching stationery.

Anita picked up the cell phone and punched it on, checking to see if Kenneth Maxinter, the presumed owner, by some good fortune hadn't used a password, but no such luck. She shook the cell in annoyance, and went in search of Pema. The maidservant could pack up the dead man's property and leave it in the store room, to be returned to his family if they wanted. At the very least, the police would return for his contact information for his next of kin.

Nine

Deepa Nair snapped a wet towel and hung it over the line. The midday breeze lifted the towels and lungis, before leaving them to droop again to the red dirt below. A bright blue lungi with threads of green and gold brushed against the face of a small child playing with a doll on the ground. The cotton fabric rose again, behind the child, framing her head and dark hair. Deepa's heart clenched. To see Uma, her little granddaughter, happy and healthy at play sent little sparks of joy through her, but to see her sprawled on the dirt below laundry hanging on the line forced her to peer through a larger frame. If a tourist from the resort were passing by, he or she would probably stop to take a snap.

The houses along this lane lay quiet in the heat. Deepa could hear a motorbike starting up and driving away, or a neighbor calling out. Once in a while a tourist, having lost the pathway to the beach or seeking a shortcut to the hotels down below, wandered to the end of the lane, found it blocked, and turned back. She rarely thought anything about it, but when days passed and she saw no foreigner, she guessed Bhadar or another was redirecting them to the main road.

When the American Crocker Dawes had first knocked on the compound gate yesterday morning, she stood inside the house waiting, listening to the knuckles rapping on wood. She thought about letting him wait until he gave up and went away, but even if he did leave, she knew he'd return today, and then tomorrow and the next day. She should never have answered his letter. She was not used to ambivalence—her life had never allowed enough freedom for such a feeling to arise.

"Amma!" The little girl skittered into the kitchen and out through the front door. She knew the sound of her mother's scooter.

Deepa's daughter rode in, parked next to the veranda, and stepped off. She unpacked a carrying tote from the pillion seat and leaned down to kiss her daughter as the child wrapped her arms around her mother's legs. Deepa went out to meet her, took the bag of vegetables and other goods into the kitchen, and began unpacking the bag.

"I have brought all the spices you asked for, Amma," her daughter said. "What are you making?" Her daughter inspected the pots and pans on the counter and stove, smiled curiously, and turned to her mother. "It is a secret, isn't it?"

"A little one, Mallika." Deepa patted her daughter's cheek and finished putting away small packets of folded paper.

"Is this something different for the hotels?" Mallika asked. "You are making a savory?"

Before Deepa could answer, her granddaughter waggled her head enthusiastically.

"He is liking it!" Little Uma's eyes widened with excitement as she delivered the important news. Mallika looked from her daughter to her mother. Deepa rested her hands at her waist and met her daughter's questioning expression.

"The owner is coming here to taste it?" Mallika was both delighted and startled. "But, Amma, this is so wonderful. You are not making and hurrying to the restaurant, the restaurant is coming to you. It is great, isn't it? You are having even more success. I am telling you, we can find investor and get a professional kitchen."

"No!" Deepa raised both hands and took a step back. "No, Mallika, it is enough. What I have is enough."

"But this is an important client, isn't it?" Mallika nodded to her mother's sari, a traditional Kerala one, white with a purple border. This was far nicer than anything Deepa usually wore at home and nicer than anything she wore in the kitchen when making her pastries.

"Can I not present myself well for anyone?" Embarrassed that she had revealed so much, or rather that little Uma had observed so much, Deepa brushed down the wrinkles in her sari, composed herself, and smiled at her daughter. “It is enough. I am satisfied. Now, you go. You cannot be late. I have an understanding boss,” she said with a wink, “but you do not.”

“As long as I am returning with some sort of specialty, it is all right.” Mallika patted her daughter's cheek. “What shall I take this time?”

Deepa turned to a basket on the table and tipped it toward her daughter. “This is very fine.” She wrapped a few items in newspaper and handed them over.

“He will be surprised to have this in the middle of the day. I am only bringing them in the morning when I am helping with deliveries,” Mallika said.

“He is a good boss,” her mother said. “It is harmless to be generous.”

“He wants you to cook for him. He is willing to fire his cook and hire you.”

Deepa pulled a face and shook her head. “I cannot give up my business. My clients are expecting me every morning.”

“Lucky people.” Mallika slipped the package into her tote. “Are you teaching anyone these things?”

Deepa shook her head. “Never. Let them learn on their own. This is my business.”

“You taught me but I don't make them as you do. Something is missing.” Mallika walked out to the yard and turned her scooter toward the lane. Deepa followed her and her granddaughter onto the veranda.

“You're coming tomorrow evening, aren't you?” Deepa ignored her daughter's comment. Uma climbed onto the front of the scooter, and wrapped her little fingers around the handlebars. Mallika climbed onto the seat and locked her knees around her daughter.

“Tomorrow,” Mallika said. “And perhaps you'll tell us your secret.”

“Perhaps.” Deepa smiled at her daughter. Mallika had come late in Deepa's marriage, late at least for an Indian woman, and she would have gladly waited even longer if she'd known her daughter would be so perfect, so beautiful. And now she had Uma.

Deepa remained on the veranda long after the blue and white scooter had turned the corner at the end of the lane and headed down to the main road. She continued to stand, lost in her own thoughts, when she noticed a neighbor walking by, watching her staring down the lane. Deepa shook herself and reached for a reed broom, turning her back to sweep the veranda until he had passed by. When he was gone, she set the broom in the corner and returned to the kitchen.

She had little left to do, but a few things had to be just right. She studied the four chairs in the front room, chose one, and carried it outdoors. The side yard was divided into two parts, with a palm-leaf screen as a separator. She placed the chair by a table and stood back to examine the arrangement. She next added a folded-up banana leaf and, just in case, a few pieces of cutlery. She couldn't be certain what would be needed.

From this position in her compound she could see the front yard, the gate, and the trees and plants along the compound wall, but the foliage blocked much of the view. People passing by could see someone was in the side yard but not much more. The arrangement offered both privacy and modesty, but not secrecy. Deepa was pleased as well as relieved.

The airmail letter came over two years ago, and at first Deepa didn't know what to make of it. Some of her neighbors made friends with the foreigners who visited the resort every year, becoming regular guests, and they sent or brought with them small gifts for their Indian friends. But this letter was different. When Crocker Dawes left India so many years ago, she never expected to see him again.

Unlike some of the other villagers who had worked with the Peace Corps volunteers and later with NGO workers, she had not hoped to hold on. She had overheard an Indian guide telling the American young people, "Don't forget them. They've been your friends." But over time, for one reason or another, the foreigners drifted out of the villagers' thoughts and lives. Letters continued for a while, and sometimes Crocker included a few unusual stamps in his airmail letters. But over time his thin blue envelopes became less frequent, and her replies shorter and more delayed. She married soon after Crocker and the others left, and her husband couldn't understand why she should correspond if there was no benefit for him and their future children. Postage was expensive. Eventually the letters stopped.

The American was easy to lose in the layers of memory, merging into the shadows of the past, dulled by the years and the seismic changes in her country. Once in a while an Indian returning from the States would mention having met a group of former Peace Corps or other NGO volunteers, and good wishes would be exchanged. But even that had stopped years ago.

And then a letter—*the* letter, as she thought of it—arrived two years ago, and Deepa was transported to a time before Mallika, before her husband, before the death of her parents, before everything she regarded as her life.

Deepa dusted and wiped down the chair and table one more time. By the end of the afternoon the entire area would know she had given lunch, properly of course, to a foreigner at her home. It wouldn't take long for her neighbors to figure it out. Most of the older people knew about the foreign volunteers who popped up in villages and cities, but until now none had any reason to connect her with them. Why should they? That was thirty years ago. Most surprised would be Mallika. Now she would grasp why her mother understood western cooking as well as she did.

Deepa looked up at the sound of a light rapping on the wooden gate. Crocker Dawes towered over the compound wall, his smile abashed but as warm and as enthusiastic as the first time she'd met him, all those years ago. She went to open the gate.

Ten

Ravi propped his elbow on the counter and rested his head on his palm. A few years younger than Anita, he counted himself fortunate to have found a steady job at Hotel Delite. His position made him so secure that he was given to maudlin thoughts about his future. From his perch behind the registration desk, he watched the world passing him by, and it made him philosophical.

"Why are foreigners not happy?" he asked Anita as she came down the hall.

"Some of them are, Ravi." Anita never gave his dark side much serious thought. He was at heart a happy person, but he gave way to gloom when he was bored. He seemed incapable of genuine misery.

"It does not seem so." He gazed out the front door at the tourists in the parking lot. He looked from one to another as the two hikers and the young couple in room three debated on whether or not it was worth it to share the taxi for the day. One hiker kept referring to it as a hop-off, hop-on arrangement, and the husband in the couple frowned. His wife seemed bored. "They should ask Joseph. He is giving good advice." Ravi felt sorry for Joseph, who never seemed to be consulted about transactions like this.

"Are they still here?" Anita walked behind the desk. She clutched the large envelope from Kenneth Maxinter's room to her chest, trying to sort out what it might mean. She glanced out the doorway.

"It is never easy for Joseph. So much backing and forthing, isn't it?" Ravi sat up straight and rearranged the book in front of him. "No one leaving and no one arriving. Meena Amma is not happy with two empty rooms. When are you saying she can rent room six?"

"Soon." Anita leaned over to peer under the counter. "I left something here. Ah, here it is." She drew out the journal and the small cup of spices and placed both on the counter. After a moment of reflection, she went into the office and drew out the passport registration forms for the tour group.

"Ah! You are adding this to the menu?" Ravi reached for the cup. He made a little gasp of pleasure when he spotted the spices and tipped the cup over just enough to let a few pour into his open palm. "I like this idea very much. Betel leaf is very bad for you. This is very good."

"Ah! Ravi!" Anita burst through the door. "You didn't eat any of that, did you?"

But of course, he had. She watched him chewing and then watched him recognize her fear. He glanced at the spices, at her, then gulped. "No, no, you are alarming me for no reason. I know these spices. Fennel and star anise and cloves and the others. It is all right with me."

Anita watched him closely, but when he showed no signs of reaction she smiled. "Yes, of course, you're right. I'm overreacting. But you must promise me that if you feel at all unwell, you'll go straight to hospital."

"Yes, of course. But it is all right. You are wrong about these." He nodded to the spices and flicked his fingers in disgust at the idea that there could be anything wrong with them. "Is Meena Amma agreeing to add these?"

"Auntie Meena won't want them on the menu. Too foreign for her."

"Even so I enjoy this." He glanced at the parking lot again. The foreigners seemed to have come to a decision and all four of them piled into the car. Joseph slid into the front seat and gave Ravi a final look, a plea for rescue perhaps. He started the car and headed out.

Ravi nodded to the spices. "Where did you get these?"

"I think the tour group got them on the plane on the flight from Athens, as part of an Indian meal. I found these in Kenneth Maxinter's room. And I think I saw Angela Deetcher with some."

"Ooh." Ravi sounded disappointed.

"No one from the tour group is in the hotel still?"

"All gone out," Ravi said. "Mr. Dawes departs for a meal somewhere, and Angela Deetcher is seeing museums and attending a lecture, and the couple who are not a couple are having a meal on the Promenade."

"They told you this? They're a couple?"

"They are telling me they are taking lunch together." Ravi smiled. It was remarkable in Anita's mind that all sorts of strangers were willing to tell Ravi just about everything and anything, and all because he sat behind a hotel registration desk. Sometimes, she had the feeling he could ask anyone anything and get an honest answer. She would have to test the theory sometime.

"And Auntie Meena?"

"Probably in hiding—from you," Ravi said. "Or in mourning for the loss of income."

Anita threw a star anise at him and left the hotel.

* * * * *

Anita hoped an afternoon in her photography gallery would give her time to think but the longer she sat, counting tourists passing on the lane, the duller she felt. When she should have been drawing in the foreigners and inducing them to part with modest sums of rupees, she stared at an empty concrete wall until Kanjappa, who owned the bookstore across the lane, called to her not once but three times.

"You are distracted," he said. "Times will improve."

Anita shrugged. "I'm distracted by something else."

"Ah!" He said, nodding with exaggeration. "The one who died, isn't it? There is some question there?"

"I find questions without answers." She pushed herself up in her chair. "It's very confusing. Odd bits here and there obscure the man's death."

"And Auntie Meena?" Kanjappa tilted his head to one side. He was a young man who loved his bookstore, despite having another job at the insistence of his family. He had a sweet nature and had at once adopted everyone on his lane as members of his extended family. Anita thought him dear and Chinnappa thought him annoying. But then, Chinnappa, the tailor next door, thought everyone was annoying, even his customers.

"Ah, Auntie Meena! She is worried something will come of my questions." Anita waved to him as he ducked back inside to help a customer.

"We saw you pass the restaurant." The announcement came from Larry Forche. "I waved but you didn't see me." He stepped up onto the low platform and began to admire the photographs on the back wall and then turned to the bins. "Come and look, Sandra. They're wonderful."

Sandra glanced across the lane from the doorway to Kanjappa's store. Under the deep eaves, safe from sudden showers, stood a tall bookcase stocked with paperback novels in various European languages. She looked tired, but greeted Anita with a warm if weak smile. "Larry is in love with everything he sees."

"Not everything." He gave her a smile and moved on to another bin of photographs. "But this is a wonderful country, isn't it? You just walk along and pluck fruit from the side of the road, sit down at a table and a waiter rushes over with a glass of your favorite juice, stand on a street corner looking lost and half a dozen drivers show up to help." Sandra glanced at him over her shoulder and giggled.

Anita had to agree with Ravi's tacit assessment: they were a charming couple even if they insisted they were not. She began moving bins around so Larry could examine the contents more easily. She wasn't as interested in selling as she was in enjoying the company of two people who seemed to be nice to have around and to know.

Anita offered Sandra a canvas chair, and she settled down to enjoy watching the tourists pass by. She wore a scarf over her blond wig, and was properly dressed in white crops and a pink patterned blouse. She looked like she belonged in an ad for a California resort, not on an Indian beach. Perhaps that was why she found the kaleidoscope of tourists so interesting—because they were so different from what she was used to.

"Do you enjoy travel?" Anita asked.

Sandra raised her face to Anita's and gave her a quizzical look. "I'm not sure." She turned to call to Larry, who appeared at her side.

"We were looking for a tailor when we saw you go by, so we thought we'd follow you and ask you, didn't we, Sandra?" He looked down at her for confirmation. She shook her head, but in a gently chiding way.

"If you're looking for a tailor, then, I can recommend my neighbor, Chinnappa." When Sandra agreed, Anita called the old man over, and stepped back as he and Sandra discussed a pair of silk slacks and matching blouse. She seemed taken with his attention to her requirements and when he returned to his shop to pull out sample bolts of silk she stood up to follow.

"I've never had anything made specifically for me," Sandra said. "Something I should do before—" she broke off as she stepped down onto the lane. Before she went into the shop, she turned back. "Don't stop what you're doing, Larry. I'll be fine."

Anita waited to see how Larry might take this polite dismissal. With his hands clasped in front of him, his shoulders drawn up, his face creased into a life-altering smile, he nodded mightily. Then he turned to Anita, "Thank you, thank you so much for suggesting him."

"No mention, no mention," Anita said. What on earth was going on with them? She led him to another bin of photographs and began talking about the images, slipping in a question here and there. "Have you been friends a long time?"

"Oh, yes," Larry said. "At least it feels like it. In a good way." He stayed her hand to admire the photographs of a temple nearby. "Do you believe in reincarnation?"

The question startled Anita and she strove to answer it sincerely, but soon realized he wasn't interested in her beliefs.

"I do. I didn't before, but I do now." Larry rested his hand on a group of photos. "It has helped me more than I can say." Embarrassed at his admission, he again flipped through photos in the bin.

"Are all of you on the tour friends from home?"

"Not friends exactly." Larry shifted away from the bin and looked at her over his shoulder. "Kenneth Maxinter wasn't our friend, exactly. He ran the tour for us." He was on the verge of telling her something and looked past her, over her shoulder, to see who else might be within earshot. "It must seem odd to you that none of us on the tour feels sad at Kenneth's death."

"I assumed you didn't know him well."

"We knew him well enough, but not like friends." He began to finger the photographs again, and Anita cast around for the right question to get him to talk. She sensed he wanted to but didn't know how to begin.

"How did you meet?" The question may have been too direct, Anita thought, when Larry jerked around and stared at her. Then he laughed.

"I lived in New Jersey, where I was born—even in the same neighborhood." He swallowed hard. "I moved up to Massachusetts when I was—" He shut his eyes. "I met him a few years ago there." He turned away. "I like your work." Whatever he had been going to say was brushed aside, and his polite demeanor, evident from the moment he arrived at Hotel Delite, reasserted itself.

Anita thanked him for the compliments as he scuttled out of the gallery and into the tailor shop next door. She listened for a little while, as Chinnappa and Sandra carried on a halting negotiation for the new outfit, and then heard all parties wish each other well. Larry and Sandra walked back toward the Promenade. Just before they disappeared from view, Larry turned around and stopped, looking back at Anita. He gave a sudden sheepish grin and hurried after Sandra, now out of sight.

*****

In late afternoon, tourists straggled up from the beach, sandy and sweaty and rimed with salt from a swim in the ocean. Some would take a nap, some would log on to a computer in a café or their room, some would indulge in a long, cold shower. In a couple of hours, as dusk thickened, they would appear on the Promenade, strolling past restaurants with touts trying to entice them in. Before that happened, however, Anita wanted a few images she'd been thinking about most of the day. She closed up her shop and stepped into the lane.

Her thoughts had lingered on Larry and Sandra, and their desultory manner of touring the resort. As courteous and polite as they seemed, neither one evinced any real enthusiasm. This was so unlike other visitors that Anita couldn't get it out of her mind. No matter how she examined the idea, she feared that here were two guests who didn't enjoy the tropics. They found no beauty in the landscape, no sensuous discovery in the food or art, no pleasure in the friendships offered. It made her sad. And then it made her curious. Why were they here?

Anita walked down a lane, crossed to another, and found a path leading up the hill. She continued on almost to the top, and there turned and followed a narrowing lane running between private homes. She continued to walk away from the beach, the canal, the crashing waves, and honking taxis. Life grew quieter, with a stillness held in place by the heat resting on the palm leaves and low shrubbery.

A young mother with two little girls in tow approached, and Anita stepped onto a boulder to let them pass. She had made friends with some of the families in the outlying areas, homes lying concealed from anyone visiting the resort, in the hope of easing any tension created by a Hotel Delite guest wandering away from the resort, getting lost, and offending someone who might otherwise help. Few families living along the coast had managed to hold onto their property, and had to accept multi-story hotels looming over them. Those who lived farther back from the ocean and deeper in the hills watched and waited, and gritted their teeth.

"You are going the wrong way," the mother said in English. "Other side you are finding."

"It is the old estate I want," Anita answered in Malayalam.

"You are not wanting a lost guest on the other side?"

Anita shook her head, but thanked her for offering the help. She was glad to find that her forays into the neighborhood were bearing fruit, even though she didn't need the help right now. Perhaps a foreigner from some other hotel had wandered into a garden, to take a photo of the goats or perhaps the flowers. Anita never got used to the affection foreigners felt for the wandering goats, even following them around to get the perfect snap.

In the small cluster of homes a radio played softly, one person called out to another, a goat bleated and chickens squawked. The quiet felt cleansing, and that was one reason she walked through here. At the hotel, she listened to the waves crashing, the autorickshaws buzzing, taxis honking, visitors laughing and chatting.

The lane came to an abrupt end, leaving the walker to look down on the remnants of an old estate. The ground fell away, falling almost straight down to a ripple in the land, not enough to be called a valley, and then rose again on the other side. Halfway down the center of this open area lay the abandoned estate, with its crumbling brick walls and carved wooden gate. Remnants of once luxurious shrubs traced the outlines of a garden. Anita stepped onto the top of an old stone wall against which villagers had built their homes. She walked along the stone wall, which was just wide enough for one person, to an old dirt staircase, which led down to the estate. She made her way down.

From the far end of the bowl, within hearing distance, an elderly woman watched her. She circled the brick wall and gate, sighted her camera at various locations, and took a number of shots. The wall built atop a row of boulders and outcroppings turned to accommodate the landscape, and here the workmanship was notable. It was hard not to admire the skill, since the bricklayer must have known that most people would never see his work and the beauty he created would be admired by few.

"The old way." The woman stood with her arms crossed over her chest as Anita approached. She turned to acknowledge the other woman, took another few shots, and then walked toward the house, which stood on a platform a good ten feet above her. The woman pointed her to a path through the rocks, and Anita found herself in a yard with a goat tethered in anticipation of milking and a few chickens annoying each other.

"I saw you coming," the other woman said. Anita had never spoken with this woman before but had seen her on a number of occasions. "One guest is lost?"

"I had no call," Anita said. "I came to photograph."

"Ah." The woman waggled her head. "He knows his way then." The woman adjusted the dishcloth hanging over her shoulder in lieu of an upper garment to cover her choli, or blouse.

"Do you mean someone from Hotel Delite?" Anita continued to be amazed at how much the villagers knew about the tourists.

She gave an affirmative head shake. "Going that way." She waved her hand along the lane that passed in front of the house and Anita wondered that anyone from the resort would find his way out here. The difficulty of the lanes alone would discourage most people.

"But not lost? Not asking for directions?"

The woman shook her head. "You are coming for this?" She nodded to the camera. "Then he is knowing someone." She shrugged and turned away. Anita thanked her for taking the time to let her know, and took the lane indicated. She didn't like doing this, since it meant she was walking through private yards, but the lane was a well-worn path that everyone had to use, and if she didn't take this path, she would have to return to the old estate and climb the stairs to the other side.

Anita walked along, for the most part ignored by the homeowners whose property she crossed, until the lane widened and she found herself one coconut field away from a wider lane. But instead of starting up the hill, she stepped back, behind a shrub. The women who had assumed she was tracking down a lost hotel guest had been right to think so. Up ahead, emerging from the gate of a small house halfway down another lane, was Crocker Dawes, and behind him stood Deepa Nayar. They talked for a minute or so before Crocker stepped into the lane and walked toward the main road. Deepa held the gate open long after he turned a corner and disappeared from sight. And the expression on her face was not that of a woman who had been asked for directions by a strange man.

Eleven

One of Ravi's last tasks of the evening was lining up the room keys on the registration desk for guests to collect when they returned. Ravi tapped each one, as though warning it not to fall out of order. He stepped back to admire his handiwork just as Anita slipped behind the counter. She scanned the keys, pulling each one toward her.

"Mr. Dawes is not in this evening?" Even though she had run back to the hotel, she hadn't expected to arrive before him but she had hoped to arrive before he went out again. "When did he go out?"

"This morning," Ravi said. "He has been out all day. Probably photographing the goats."

"You mean he hasn't returned yet?" Anita fell back with a sigh of relief.

"Why is this important to you?" Ravi gave her a skeptical look.

"You don't like our goat, do you?" Anita distracted him by focusing on one of his pet peeves. She had insisted that Hotel Delite keep the goat rescued from a relative's home in the hills when a leopard had tried to haul it off for a meal. Auntie Meena disliked the animal, and Ravi thought it a nuisance, and Sanjay took everything in stride. But Brij, dear sweet Brij, the laundryman, loved all animals, and adopted the creature at once.

"Ah! Just now coming is the man you want." Ravi nodded toward the door. There, striding down the lane, was Crocker Dawes, carrying a small paper bag.

"He must have gone shopping along the way."

"Along what way?" Ravi asked.

Anita wondered how much she should tell him. "I saw him earlier, in the village area, but he didn't see me. So, you are not to say anything."

"I am never saying anything," Ravi said, stepping away from the counter.

He had two great fears—Anita and Auntie Meena. His one goal in life, when he thought about it, was surviving these two women.

"Soon I am leaving," he said.

"Good idea." Anita hopped onto the stool. She swept up the keys and slid them below the counter just as Crocker Dawes came through the door. Ravi took the opportunity to escape out the side door.

"Good evening!" Crocker Dawes marched up to the registration desk with a smile as wide as his shoulders. "You have a lovely hotel, Miss Anita, just lovely."

"You're very kind to say so, Mr. Dawes. We think so too." Anita cast around in her mind for small talk to keep him engaged. "And you know a lot about India too. You speak Malayalam?"

His confused expression held a hint of suspicion, so Anita went on before he could withdraw.

"You didn't eat in our restaurant this noon so I'm guessing you found a superb Indian restaurant on the Promenade." When he blushed she knew she had guessed correctly. He wasn't yet ready to tell anyone where he had gone for lunch, and whom he knew well enough to visit at home for a meal.

"I had a wonderful meal," he said.

"I'm glad, and perhaps because you're familiar with India already you could help me with a small matter."

"Of course if I can." He leaned forward, placing his bundle on the counter and growing serious. "Just tell me what it is and if I can help I will."

"You're very kind." Unfortunately she had no idea what to ask him to help her with.

"Yes?" he said.

At that moment she caught sight of Ravi sneaking by the open window and heard the goat. "It's about our goat."

"You have a goat?"

"Yes, didn't you know?" Anita perked up. She could talk about the goat forever, or, at least for several minutes until she thought of another way to approach him. "I rescued the goat from a leopard in the hills. I think this goat is very lucky, and we must keep such a lucky animal."

"Any animal that found itself living here would be lucky indeed."

Oh dear, thought Anita, I hope he's not always this fatuous. "Yes, yes, indeed. I am glad you think so. It's very encouraging. We were asked to keep farm animals away while the tour is in residence."

"Understandable," Crocker said.

Anita decided to let that pass. She didn't see how it was understandable at all. There were animals all over the country.

"What is the problem?" Crocker asked, again.

"It's a little problem, well, perhaps not really a problem. A question perhaps."

"And?"

"Yes, a question." She smiled up at him and took a deep breath. "Anyway, I'm thinking this. Usually tourists like the goats. You see them on the road above? Tourists see them and follow them and photograph them. So, I was thinking, perhaps I should let my goat wander about and when the tourists see the goat they'll come into the hotel to photograph the animal."

"You're not thinking of letting the animal inside the hotel, are you?"

"Oh, no, just the parking lot. There." She nodded to the area outside the doorway, where just then Joseph was sleeping in the front seat of the hotel car. She must remind him that it didn't look professional and he had other places for napping. "And maybe this lane. Do you think that would trouble the goat? All those cameras clicking at him?"

"People use their cells now, so the most you hear is the pfft pfft of the button on the cell."

"Pfft?" Anita repeated. She never used her cell for a photograph. That's what her camera was for, but she had to agree he was right. Everywhere she went she saw tourists pulling out their mobiles and taking snaps.

"But goats are pretty placid creatures, and these guys around here look pretty good."

"You know something about goats?"

"Well, I had one when I lived here."

"Oooh! You lived here. In Trivandrum?"

"No," he said, blushing. "In the countryside, up in the hills."

"Ah, yes, a good place for goats." Anita wondered why someone would blush when admitting they had lived in India before. "And why were you living here? With your parents?" He didn't give the impression of having lived here with a diplomatic family, but she'd been wrong before about people.

Crocker gave a deep good-hearted laugh. "No, Miss Anita, I assure you I was not with my parents."

Curiouser and curiouser, thought Anita. She leaned forward with what she hoped was a look of innocent expectation, and waited. Crocker knew he was cornered, and because, she guessed, he was brought up to be a gentleman, he had to say something.

"I was with an NGO, building infrastructure back in the early 1990s, sort of like the Peace Corps." He seemed both proud and embarrassed.

"Oh, I see. What was your task?" She had seen one of the schools a group had built in Tamilnadu, still in use though needing a new roof. .

"I persuaded the villagers to build latrines with me," he said, standing up straighter, his hands resting on the counter. "It was the best year of my life."

* * * * *

Anita's efforts to elicit information about Crocker Dawes's activities during the day failed miserably, and he could not be stalled any longer. She listened to his footsteps fade up the stairs. It was nearing the hour when tourists went in search of an evening meal, taking to the Promenade to choose a restaurant or heading to a place already selected in one of the high-end hotels. Mr. and Mrs. Allbret came by the registration desk and slid their key across to Anita.

"We found the most attractive place at the top of the hill on the other side," Mrs. Allbret began. "The wall hangings are amazing, and the carpets. Well, I just had to take my shoes off and walk across barefoot." She blushed.

"Going native, she is." Mr. Allbret smiled at his wife.

"We spent the day wandering through the museums, all four of them." Mrs. Allbret looked surprised at the realization. "We couldn't decide which one to leave out so we visited all of them."

"We should be tired," Mr. Allbret said.

"Yes, we should be." Mrs. Allbret turned to give him a questioning look. He shook his head.

"I'm not tired. Not at all."

"If you say so, dear." She turned back to Anita. "The restaurant decor is so beautiful. The whole place feels just so Indian."

"How nice." Anita was used to the unexpected reactions of foreigners to all things Indian. This was one of the mildest, and her reaction had been tested for neutrality. It worked. And it opened a door. "You seem to enjoy the same things. That's always so important in a marriage, I think. Though I'm not married," she added. "How did you first meet?"

Mrs. Allbret looked startled at the question but her husband jumped right in. "At a sales conference."

"We aren't in sales," Mrs. Allbret hastened to add. "We were with different companies making presentations on products that the chain of boutiques might carry. I was demonstrating new scarves that my company imported from Asia, India too, and Jim, here, was demonstrating—what was it you were demonstrating, dear?"

"How quickly they forget," he said. "I was trying to sell them on smalls made of wire, like little egg baskets, flower holders, things like that."

"That was almost twenty years ago, wasn't it, Jim?"

"Yes, it was, Lucy. Almost twenty years."

The two gazed at each other, in love but not like lovebirds. There was some other message being shared between them. Anita turned to busy herself with the keys, uncertain about what their attention to each other meant.

"We always wanted to see India," Jim said, "and we knew it had better be sooner rather than later."

"So here we are." Lucy brightened right up but Anita thought there was an implicit message between them. She considered this as she watched them wander up the lane, select an autorickshaw, and head out for the evening.

Talking with the Allbrets had been easy. They felt no unease at being asked somewhat personal questions, the kind that were usual in tourist hotels where people became instant friends and certain questions were allowed—where are you from, how long will you be here, have you been here before, do you have friends here, that sort of thing. Anita had pushed a little deeper, knowing that most foreigners had learned after the first day or so to expect some of these more personal questions.

Over the years Anita overheard some of the hotel staff as well as Indian guests ask foreigners what faith they followed, what god they worshiped, how many children they had, how many brothers they had, how did they get permission to travel alone (this always to women), does the father know she is here (this always to a woman), and the like. But so far Anita hadn't even been able to get any of the tour members alone long enough to ask if they were enjoying their trip. Her brief conversation with Crocker Dawes this afternoon had been as much as she'd been able to accomplish.

"One table." Auntie Meena interrupted Anita's reverie. "Only one." She leaned on the counter and looked through the doorway. The sun would be setting soon, and guests would come to sit on the terrace to enjoy the beautiful if quick drop of fire into the sea.

Anita jumped down from the stool and went for the key to the guest dining room. The tour group had asked for the right to use that room for dinner and Auntie Meena had agreed. "It's inconvenient. Who made the request?"

"Miss Deetcher. She is having unpleasant afternoon, she is telling Moonu, so she is wanting quiet." Auntie Meena pushed herself away from the counter. "Why?"

Anita knew she meant "Why me?" But for her, this could be just the opportunity.

"Don't worry, Auntie. I shall attend to her, and Moonu will be free to work on the terrace."

"You are so good, Anita." Before she could continue, Auntie Meena paused, grew suspicious, and leaned toward her, studying her face. "You are up to something, isn't it? Tell me the truth." She clapped a hand against her breast, closed her eyes, and began to mutter prayers. "It is that man's death, isn't it? Why can't you let him die in peace?"

"Why are you so suspicious, Auntie?"

"Why? Because I know you, Anita. Because only now we have a dead body. Because you find murder where there is only Lord Yama's call. Because my karma is terrible!"

"Nonsense, Auntie. You have very good karma. Am I not here helping? Do I not bring guests here from my gallery?" Anita saw her aunt blink and decided it would be better to coast past that one. Auntie Meena wasn't known for supporting Anita's forays into the world with her camera, and after her one-woman show in Trivandrum, and the role a former male friend played in it, Auntie Meena was even less enthusiastic than she had been. "You have very good karma, Auntie. Hotel Delite is popular and prosperous. So I'll prepare the dining room for one."

And, she thought, I will have an opportunity to talk to one more person in the tour. Angela Deetcher is the least approachable of the tour members, but alone in a dining room she will have to talk to me.

* * * * *

Anita held the dining room door open for Angela as she came down the hallway, her thin form moving carefully down the center, past the office, small kitchen, and the side door. Though she kept her attention fixed on the floor, she managed a quick side glance at Anita before stopping a few steps inside the room and looking about. She had the place to herself, and as this became clear to her, Anita thought she stood up straighter, lifting her chin and relaxing her shoulders.

"Perhaps you would like a table near the window," Anita said. "There's a small puja this evening on the beach and you'll be able to see most of it from here."

"A puja?" Angela repeated the strange word, drawing out the first syllable. "I think I read about that. Kenneth suggested various books for us to read, and Georgio—" She stopped in midsentence. "That would be fine." She walked across the room, steadying herself as she went by lightly touching a chair or table corner with her fingers.

"Is Georgio on another tour?" Anita already knew this was the man who had stayed in Athens and later been found dead but she wanted to know what Angela would conceal or reveal. Anita held out a chair for her, but she didn't look up.

"Not exactly." Angela sat down and placed her small cotton purse on the table. "He decided to leave us in Greece."

Anita placed a menu in front of her, and wondered if she knew what had happened to him. This was one of the strangest tours Hotel Delite had ever hosted. She stepped to the front of the table and began reviewing the special curries available. As she spoke, the guest held the menu with both hands, neither nodding nor looking up. When Anita finished, Angela dropped the menu onto the tablecloth.

"I'm going to be fifty-five tomorrow," Angela said. "You probably know that." Through the window she had a view of the compound and beach beyond. "Is it true you saved a goat from being eaten by a leopard?"

Anita said it was.

"I asked about taking an elephant ride but the tour operator said I needed at least two other people to make it worthwhile. They wouldn't bring out the elephants for only one person. I offered to pay for all three, but he said no. I think the offer made him uneasy. He didn't smile at all. The other vendors smile at us." She continued to stare through the window.

"Perhaps they're hoping you'll bring the other tour members," Anita said. "That's the way it usually goes."

"Yes, I suppose it does."

The silence lengthened but any question about dinner was met with silence.

"I was thinking of going to a botanical garden," Angela said. "I don't need an entire group to do that, do I?"

Over the next few minutes Angela ordered a mild vegetable kurma and rice, after a clear soup. Anita took her time adjusting the table setting, hoping to draw out her guest, but had no success. She was about to withdraw to think up a better approach when Angela rested her hand on Anita's.

"Do people change when they come here?"

"How do you mean?" Anita asked, trying not to show how startled she was by the other woman's touch.

"I mean, do people behave differently, in ways they never have before?" Angela's eyelashes fluttered, as though she had something in her eyes. Her shoulders twitched, and she took a deep breath and withdrew her hand. Before Anita could answer, the woman continued. "It's just that, we're all different now."

"Different how?"

Out of the corner of her eye Anita saw Moonu approach and she waved him away with a slight lift of a finger. She couldn't take the chance of losing the opening Angela had given her. She reached out and repositioned the small vase of flowers.

"I valued privacy and solitude above all else, the chance to be alone." Angela recited this as though unsure she had in fact felt that way.

"I suppose you get used to being in a crowd here," Anita said. "No one's ever alone in India. There's always someone around."

"Yes, I suppose." Angela was being polite, and Anita had the sense she hadn't been listening at all. "We seemed such friends when we started out." Angela unfolded her cloth napkin and draped it across her lap, smoothing out the edges. She was searching for something, Anita could tell, and wanted to speak but the words were slow to fall into place. "We were friends."

"I'm sure you were."

"We trusted each other."

"Of course. Friends do."

"We couldn't have known." She kept smoothing the napkin in her lap, running her fingertips over it, pressing it down on her thighs. "I'm not sure the others do know. Crocker, for instance."

"Mr. Dawes seems quite happy with how his visit is going."

Angela looked up, her expression quizzical. "Yes, he does, doesn't he?"

"Didn't he expect to enjoy himself?"

"Not like this." Angela took a deep breath and looked at her table setting. "I'm hungry."

"Of course." Anita collected the second setting and turned toward the kitchen.

"Not that way."

"No? You don't want your meal?"

"Yes, of course, I do. But for me being hungry isn't usual."

Anita waved to Moonu in the doorway and he appeared a moment later with a bowl of soup on a tray. He served her and stepped back. Anita was often grateful for the loyalty of the hotel staff, but this evening she was especially appreciative. Moonu had lingered in the doorway to catch the order and hurried to get it ready before he returned to his duties on the terrace. She would have to thank him.

Angela tasted the soup. "Very nice. How is it made?"

Anita went over the recipe as Angela took small sips. The spoon rose and fell, rose and fell, without a single drop falling from the spoon into the bowl or onto her lap. She was delicate in action as well as in appearance.

"Before we left Boston, we tried the foods of the various countries we were going to visit," Angela said. "I didn't think I could enjoy a curry but Georgio ordered for us in the restaurant and he seemed to know how to choose."

"What did you order?"

"I don't recall exactly, but no meat and no chicken. But fish seemed to be all right, and vegetables of course." She smiled with what could only be called the satisfaction of accomplishment as she laid her spoon on the plate. "That was quite good."

"What other foods did you try?"

"Greek, of course. The English food and the Danish food weren't so different, so those meals were easy for us."

"You'll find a wide range of foods here, from all over the world."

"Fusion it's called, isn't it?" Angela said.

"That too."

"It was so easy to look forward to this trip," Angela said.

"Is there something I can help you with?"

Angela shook her head, and just then Moonu arrived with her dinner, setting out the serving platters and removing the soup. "I'd take a photo but it would be pointless."

"May I ask why?" This so astounded Anita as to drive out her sense of caution.

"What?" Angela took a startled breath and shook her head. "No reason, really." She picked up her napkin and snapped it once, then placed it again in her lap. "But it is hard. Really, it is hard. I'm only fifty-five but I do feel different here."

Anita pulled out the chair opposite. "If I may," she said, and sat down. "Perhaps I can help."

"I doubt it," Angela said. "It's the nature of the tour, I suppose."

"I don't understand." Anita willed the other woman to talk. Her comments were both confusing and disturbing.

"Considering where we met." Angela turned to the window again, her confusion finding rest in the small cluster of men and women performing puja on the beach.

"Where did you meet?"

Angela tipped her head and stared at her. "Of course, you wouldn't know." She left off reworking the napkin. "We met in a support group."

"Oh." Anita leaned back. Of course, she thought. That's why they're friendly but not really friends.

"All of us were in the same group. It was larger at the outset but our numbers dwindled, as it were." Angela's attention drifted to the beach again. "It was Kenneth's idea."

"He was the organizer?"

Angela nodded. "It was an idea that came up when he was sitting in. I can't remember why." She frowned, thinking back. "Anyway, we talked about taking this trip." Again, silence fell. "The trip has changed all of us. I can feel it. It's changed me and—it's changed all of us." She waited for some time before picking up her fork and beginning to eat. She thanked Anita for her sympathies and ate in silence. After a moment, Anita rose and stood near the door, going over the conversation. When Angela finished eating, she rested her fork and leaned back in her chair.

Moonu cleared the plates and Anita brought a dessert menu. "I think I can help you find a good tour of botanical sites in this area."

"Yes, that would be nice." Angela spoke without enthusiasm and fingered the menu.

"People often find a trip to Asia bringing out unexpected discoveries. I'm not surprised that you feel this trip has changed you, but I always like to know more. It helps us with other visitors. We like to be of service."

"You're very sweet. Do you know that?" Angela gazed up at her.

"How has the trip changed you?" Anita asked, trying to stay on track.

"Have you seen Crocker Dawes?" Angela grinned, the first time Anita had seen anything like genuine amusement in her. "He's feeling like the young volunteer again. And now that he's rediscovered the girl who worked for them when he and his friends were here, well, you can see what that's done to him."

"He does seem happy." Anita tried not to show her surprise, but she felt that little ping in her chest. Lots of puzzle pieces floated down to fill in empty spaces.

"He was never that happy before, not even when we started talking about this trip." Angela looked down at her fork.

"He said he built latrines while he was here."

"The best year of his life." Angela nodded.

"Did he tell you that?"

"Oh, yes." Angela looked out the window again. "They seem to be finished, the people on the beach."

"What would you say was the best year in your life?"

"Oh, there was never any doubt about that, right from the first." She smiled up at Anita. "The best year of my life was the year I spent as a student in Australia. I would have spent my life there if I could." She paused and again brushed unseen wrinkles from her napkin. "I was on a fellowship provided in part by a pharmaceutical company, so I couldn't stay. I owed them five years of research after I returned and received my degree. I'm a chemist."

Anita's mind raced. She recalled the tour's full itinerary, but especially the two locations that the Indian government wanted—where had they arrived from and where would they depart to.

"What's in this?" Angela held the menu, pointed to an item, and looked up.

Startled, Anita brought her attention back to the laminated sheet. She described the recipe for payasam. "Would you like to try that?" She was never confident her recommendations would be well received, particularly by people who never ate spicy or different kinds of food.

"I had some in Boston. It was delicious. I'll have that." She handed back the menu. "Georgio was right. He said I'd like Indian food and I do."

Twelve

The evening hours closed in around Deepa like a silk shawl, softening the sound of engines starting up and the cries of children chasing goats or each other. She needed this time of the day, the small lull between timings. Even when there were disagreements, moods seemed to ease at this hour. She lifted her head at the sound of her daughter's motor scooter coming down the lane. She loved that sound, and when she thought about Mallika moving to the Gulf States to be with her husband, taking little Uma with her, her heart seized and she gasped. But she pushed aside the inevitable, and hurried out to greet her daughter and granddaughter. She barely noticed the stream of smoke threading its way into the night sky.

Mallika puttered in and parked her scooter. Uma jumped off and ran to greet her grandmother. When Deepa looked up at Mallika, she was shocked at the look on her face—grim, and angry. The young woman's hands were clenched at her sides. She turned from her mother and pulled open the gate, marching outside. Deepa followed.

Standing in the center of the lane, Mallika pointed to a spot near the end of Deepa's compound. There, pushed up against the white-washed stucco and baked-brick wall was a pile of brush on fire, smoldering with little flame but steady smoke. Someone had swept the land and mounded the debris against the wall, burning it there instead of farther down, where an empty plot stood without a compound wall, where neighbors often burned trash or tossed refuse.

"It is an insult." Mallika whispered but the feeling in her words shouted.

Deepa took a few steps closer, as if to get a better look. Then she knelt down and pondered the smoking pile. She found a twig along the edge, and used it to tease out a slip of burning paper, which she then dusted with sand, putting out the fire. She studied the fragments.

"Have you seen this before, Mallika?"

"Why do you think I have?" She leaned forward like a palm tree in a typhoon, a single form bending into the wind of change and resentment. Deepa looked up at her.

"Your conversations with Bhadar have encouraged this. That's why it matters."

"Why would you think Bhadar has anything to do with this?" She gripped her sari skirt and leaned over her mother. "This fire is an insult to us."

Deepa picked up the paper and stood, knocking the paper against her sari skirt to dislodge any dirt or ash. She read the announcement on the paper aloud and handed it to her daughter. "This is Bhadar's announcement of his goal of a purified village, free of foreigners and others he doesn't like. He was passing these out last week."

"That means nothing." Mallika stepped away, her hand blocking the paper.

"This is Bhadar's doing because you have encouraged him." Deepa was about to say more when she spotted little Uma standing in the gateway watching them. She smiled at the little girl, not wanting to alarm her. "Come, let us eat. You have to leave soon. You can't be driving around late at night."

"People are very unsettled, Amma."

Deepa paused. "It's true we live with so much change now. But we sought this ourselves. And how we react to it is on us, no one else." She pointed to the purse still hanging across her daughter's chest. "Would you give up your cell phone? Your job? Your scooter? Would you live my mother's life?" Deepa picked up Uma and gave her a kiss. "I've made something special for us."

"But, Amma." Mallika stared at the smoldering debris. "What of this?"

Deepa shrugged. "What of it? It will burn itself out. Like everything else in life."

Thirteen

Angela Deetcher stood up from the table and thanked Anita for dinner. She had eaten a three-course meal and looked ten years younger at the end of it. As if to prove the visible change went deeper, she strolled to the parlor and then to the window overlooking the terrace and diners below. She waved to someone and seemed to exchanged a few words before heading upstairs to her room. When Anita heard a door close, she went into the office. She couldn't ignore this much of a change in a hotel guest.

"So much working at this hour?" Auntie Meena came into the office with a chit and a handful of cash. "What are you looking for?" she asked after giving the change to Moonu.

"I had a very interesting conversation with Miss Deetcher." Anita pulled out the reservations file for the tour and flipped through the few sheets of paper inside. Meena peered over her shoulder.

"Such an interesting itinerary, isn't it?" Auntie Meena said. "Oh, the joys of travel! Such freedom they are having! And look how varied their interests. It is a journey by committee." She clucked perhaps approvingly—it would be hard to say—and went out to the registration desk.

Indeed, thought Anita, the itinerary was interesting at the very least.

London
Copenhagen
Athens
Trivandrum

Saigon
Sydney
Tokyo

Anita reviewed the few other pieces of correspondence before putting the file away. She did the same with the file on the computer before shutting that down.

"You're right, Auntie. It does look like a tour organized by a committee." She joined her aunt at the counter. "It's very unusual."

Auntie Meena slid the key across the counter to the young couple in room three and wished them a good night as they left. "They are enjoying themselves. See how red he is."

"He'll be in pain tomorrow." Anita followed the couple down the hall and suggested a bowl of ice to the husband, to ease any discomfort from the sunburn. When he accepted, she gave the order to Moonu and returned to the front desk.

"Ah, our guests return." Auntie Meena began to preen as she prepared to greet Sandra Stover and Larry Forche.

"All our guests return every evening, Auntie." Amused, Anita tried to guess what seemed so special about these two to Auntie Meena. "Let me guess. You see romance, yes?"

"Oh, yes! So much romance." She gave Anita a loopy grin. "Are you not seeing this?"

Anita watched the couple stroll down the lane running by Hotel Delite and passing farther along by the beach before ending in a pile of rocks that locals considered a misarranged series of steps and foreigners took as a sign the lane had ended. When Anita's goat escaped the compound, it often chose that spot from which to survey its domain.

Larry seemed to have a lot to say to Sandra, and every few words he turned to her with an eager smile. Sandra never looked at him directly, paying attention to where she put her feet on a lane that was always kept clear of debris or animal droppings. They were similar in age but different in personality. Larry didn't mind dressing casually to the point of sloppiness, all the more noticeable next to Sandra's meticulous presentation. Her outfits always looked perfect, more suitable to an ocean liner than a beach resort. This evening she wore a blonde wig with more curl, and her makeup, again, was flawless. When they entered the hotel, Larry seemed almost fey.

"Your key, madam." He handed Sandra the key to her room. "And the key to my heart." He held his key out to her, and she let herself laugh. She glanced at Anita.

"Pay no attention to him." Sandra said it with a smile, and Auntie Meena went from shock to blushing.

"Did you enjoy your evening?" Anita asked.

Larry launched into an enthusiastic report of dinner in a small restaurant. "Practically on the sand!" He seemed unable to accept the nearness of the beach to hotels and restaurants. "And the size of the beer bottles!"

"We didn't have any of that," Sandra was quick to add.

Anita didn't even have to count to three before she heard the expected defense from Auntie Meena.

"Oh, but Kerala is having the very best beer. You are to be assured of that."

"Do you like it?" Larry asked.

Anita thought Auntie Meena would choke.

"My aunt doesn't drink alcohol. Most Hindus don't," Anita explained. "But we are very proud of what we make."

"Ah, yes. It is local pride." Auntie Meena waggled her head and smiled.

"I'm sure it's very good," Larry said.

"Miss Deetcher enjoyed a very fine meal here," Anita said.

"Very fine." Auntie Meena agreed without a moment's hesitation.

"And we had a nice chat about where she spent the happiest year of her life," Anita added. Larry and Sandra glanced at each other before looking away. Larry took a small step back and Sandra began to turn.

"How nice!" Sandra said, the first to recover.

"It seems to be the topic of the day," Anita said. "Crocker Dawes told me this afternoon that he'd spent the best year of his life building latrines. Here in India!"

Larry and Sandra reacted as she expected, and she almost felt sorry for putting them on the spot. But she reminded herself that a man had died in Hotel Delite, and she had to know how it happened and why.

* * * * *

There was no question in Anita's mind that Auntie Meena would confront her about the guests' reactions, so she went into the office, resigned to the confrontation. Auntie Meena followed her.

"What is this about latrines?"

"Did you not wonder how Mr. Dawes learned Malayalam?"

"In school." Auntie Meena followed Anita to the desk and watched her switch on the computer. "He is a man who builds latrines?"

"Poor Auntie! You are shocked." Anita smiled up at her. "He was a volunteer with an NGO."

"Oh, oooh, oh." Meena fanned herself with the end of her sari and fell into a chair. "Oooh. I suppose that is all right." Her face sagged. It was clearly not all right but she continued to struggle with it.

"And Miss Deetcher spent the best year of her life in Australia," Anita said.

"Ah, she is a woman of taste." This report made Auntie Meena feel much better and she began to relax, unpleating and smoothing out the wrinkles she had put in the pallu of her sari. "We must make an effort to attract such people." Meena sat up straighter in her chair. "Perhaps she will become a regular, visiting every year and enjoying fine accommodations and friendship. We are like a family for our regulars, aren't we?" This idea pleased her.

"I doubt Miss Deetcher plans to return, Auntie."

"You are too negative, Anita. Positiveness is important."

"I think she has other plans. Like dying."

"Anita!" The gasp was so loud Anita expected Moonu to appear at any moment asking what is wrong, who is dying, should he call the ambulance? "You are toying with Lord Yama!"

But Anita wasn't listening. She was reading an email from the hotel in Athens, an unexpected follow-up from the manager's earlier reply. If she needed confirmation for her suspicions, here it was.

"Listen to this, Auntie." Anita began to read.

Is funny you are thinking about numbers. Here we are expecting seven guests and getting the six. You are expecting six and you are getting five. In Copenhagen, cousin working there is telling me hotel is expecting eight and getting seven. Guests are staying behind. Very confusing for us. Not our best season and slow to replace guests. Hope you can rent room asap.

Anita stared at the screen, reading the email again and again. Despite the awkward English, she got the point, but needed time to let the implications sink in. She turned at the sound of Auntie Meena's little gasp.

"They are leaving guests at stops and not taking them along?" she said. "Mr. Maxinter is abandoning his flock?"

Anita started to laugh, but the humor faded. There was nothing funny about what seemed to be happening here. "No, Auntie. I don't think that's it exactly. I don't think Mr. Maxinter was leaving people behind. It's something else."

"I am relieved." Meena began fanning herself again with the end of her sari.

"I think it's worse." Anita pulled her chair around, glanced out at the desk and listened for a moment before settling back. "These guests are choosing not to return home. They're ending their suffering."

Auntie Meena reacted as Anita expected her to. Her hands went to her mouth, her face blanched, she muttered a prayer, and then flashed a look of determination. "I am calling my astrologer again. He is coming to see each one. Perhaps there is more to know. They are not to go forward in life without sound knowledge. He has purified Hotel Delite, hasn't he?" Meena struggled to keep the tears from her eyes. "These are our guests. We are helping them. It is our duty. My astrologer will know what to do."

Anita rested her hand on her aunt's knee. "You are good, Auntie. Indeed, you are good. But I think there are other things we can do."

"What? What? Tell me!" Meena leaned forward, almost bumping Anita's forehead with her own.

"Nothing dramatic, Auntie. Something quiet, I think."

"I don't understand this. If there are illnesses, why are they here and not at home under the care of a doctor?" Meena lost her agitation and now looked perplexed. "Yes, we are having excellent medical services. But if I am dying, am I leaving my doctor?" Anita knew this was true—Auntie Meena was loyal to those she looked to for help and could not believe any one of them would fail her. She might fail her doctor by dying, but her doctor would not fail her by giving her a false diagnosis.

"Suppose you were given a diagnosis of perhaps a year or two to live. What would you do, Auntie?" Anita had put the pieces together in her own mind, but this puzzle must look bizarre to anyone else. She could easily have gotten it wrong.

"Oh! Such sorrow." Auntie Meena leaned to one side, propped her head up with her hand and lost herself in daydreams.

"Do you know what you would do?" Anita asked again.

"Oh, yes, I have always known, since my husband died," Meena said, avoiding Anita's eye. "This is our family's ancestral land, but there is also land in the hills, and I have many happy memories there. If such medical news comes to me, I am going to the hills where husband was born and visiting dear sweet sister-in-law, Leela. She was a sister to me. I would call her home. And your mother." Meena leaned to the other side of her chair and reached out to touch Anita's face. "Your mother, my dearest sister. Even your father I would call."

At that Anita had to laugh. "You would forgive my father all his sins? Even his birth? You would want only to be with those you loved in a place where you were happy."

Auntie Meena reached out to turn the computer screen so she could see it more clearly. She read through the list of cities on the tour, and counted out loud the number of guests at each one. "So here we are having five guests. And one is dying. Just as in the other cities."

"But not the one who was supposed to," Anita said.

"What?" Auntie Meena was alert again, throwing off sentimentality. "What do you mean not the one who was supposed to die? How do you know this?"

"Do you remember when I told the group that we had a death? They were very calm until I announced who it was. They thought it was Crocker Dawes. They were shocked when I told them it was Kenneth Maxinter." Anita paused. "His death was not planned, at least not by him."

"Oh!" Auntie Meena shut her eyes against the very idea. "What have I done? How can my karma be so awful? I am a simple woman. A simple woman. Truly Shiva forgets me."

* * * * *

Few guests in the resort area stayed out later than ten o'clock in the evening, and most retired to their hotels before then. The restaurants grew quiet, with few orders after nine o'clock. Bus schedules thinned out, the sound of taxis or autorickshaws faded, and the lines of these vehicles disappeared, each one taken to shelter for the night. Hotel Delite rented space to one or two private taxis, and Anita didn't even look up when she heard the gate being closed after they drove into the parking spots. Sanjay, the night guard, stumped down the stairs and into the hotel.

"Just waiting for the two hikers," Anita said.

Sanjay waggled his head and left his bedroll propped in the corner of the parlor, where he would spread it out and sleep. He went down to the terrace to get something to eat from the lower-level kitchen and let the guard dog out of his kennel, a sweet black mutt that romped and slept and snuffled through the night.

Anita put the hikers' room key on the counter and gathered up the old newspapers. She stacked them onto the shelf under the desk. When they bumped up next to something she bent down to clean out the area. She pulled out a book and a teacup. "How could I forget these?"

She dipped her fingers in, separated the spices she preferred, and drew out a small collection of fennel, anise, and cloves. She popped these into her mouth, following Ravi's earlier example. A taxi drove down the lane and parked next to the compound wall. Before the night guard could reach the gate, two passengers climbed out of the taxi, loped into the hotel parking lot and waved to the guard on their way down the stairs to the front door.

"We're late, aren't we?" Gene said to Anita when he reached the counter.

"Not so late." Anita reached for the key.

"We got lost," Ron said. His face was bright red, as though he'd spent the day on the beach, but Anita recalled they had asked about buses into the hills.

"Did you have a good day?" She wanted to ask more but didn't want to appear nosy. She was also very tired.

"We got lost," Gene said. "We took a bus that was supposed to take us up to some botanical garden but I guess it was the wrong one. When we realized our mistake, it was too late. The driver said the next bus came sometime—we couldn't understand and no one at the village could explain to us. So we walked down. We got into the eastern edge of the city about nine, and we knew we couldn't walk another three hours, so we found a taxi."

"It cost a fortune," Ron said. "But at least we're here."

"We may have to cut our trip short by one day," Gene said, looking at Ron, who nodded, as though this were a topic they'd already discussed and agreed upon.

"Anyway," Gene said, turning back. "We saw lots of countryside."

Anita laughed. "I hope you found that pleasurable."

"He did," Ron said. "He's an amateur botanist."

"Ah, you have come to the right place," Anita said, but Gene wasn't paying any attention to her. He was peering into the teacup. "Would you care to try this?" She tipped the cup toward him.

Gene frowned and looked up at her, his brow furrowed in a question. "It looks like those seeds I've read about."

"What seeds are those?" Anita asked.

"I read this article about suicides in Kerala."

"Oh, yes, we have a high rate of suicide, unfortunately," Anita said. "It's very sad. But these are seeds for digestion." She looked down into the teacup, but this time she looked with Gene's comment in mind. "Which ones?" Gene pointed to a small black seed, about the length of a thumbnail with a jagged edge, as though it had been cut in half.

Anita couldn't have said how her thoughts had shifted, throwing together images that should not have been shoved together, but in her unsettled thoughts odd forms began to cohere.

"It looks just like the seed from that poison fruit."

"Otalam fruit," Anita said. "It is called otalam."

"Why is it in the cup with the other spices? Can you eat it if you separate it from the fruit?" Gene asked.

"No, I don't think so," Anita said.

"So, why is it here?" Ron asked, leaning closer.

"I'm sure it's just a mistake—we're not used to these after-dinner offerings." But Anita wasn't sure at all. She wrapped her fingers around the teacup and drew it toward her lest anyone else think about trying the spices.

Fourteen

The following morning Anita sat in the waiting room of the Anandabuddhi Hospital trying to identify the variety of smells assaulting her while she waited to be summoned to the doctor's office. She could almost see the aromas, a series of colored ribbons undulating toward her, so distinctive were they. They seemed to match the variety of persons come for medical care.

"Good morning, Anita Missi." Dr. Premod greeted Anita as she was ushered into an office. The doctor held the edge of a chart against her midriff and motioned Anita to a chair on the other side of a large desk. The doctor's green sari, the uniform of her profession in this hospital, was immaculately cleaned and pressed, and smelled of lavender, which Anita added to the swirl of fragrances and odors filling her nostrils. "It is nice to see you in good health. I've become accustomed to seeing you only in dire circumstances."

"But not this time." Anita smiled. "You've examined the item I brought you? Was I right about this?"

"Yes, you're correct." Dr. Premod studied in the States, and received her degree from a well-respected medical school. Then, to the surprise of many but not to those who knew her well, she turned down a position in Chicago and headed home to India. Here she worked long hours in an expensive private hospital, and then spent additional time at small village clinics. No one but her family knew that except Anita, who ran into her once in a while in the most unexpected places. "How are you feeling?" the doctor asked, a note of suspicion creeping into her voice.

“You can relax, doctor. I'm feeling just fine. For once I didn't eat the poison, fall into the ditch, get bitten by a snake, or any one of a number of things I've done in the past. Forgive me for being so flippant. It's relief at avoiding what I know could have been certain death.”

“Certain death indeed. And an unpleasant one.” Dr. Premod slid into the chair behind her desk. “How did you find the seeds? And you also have the fruit?”

“I found the seeds mixed in with spices that were in a teacup in the room of the man who died in Hotel Delite,” Anita said. “I took the cup intending to leave it in the kitchen but got waylaid and left it on a shelf beneath the registration desk. I pulled it out later and one of the guests, an amateur botanist, saw the seeds, and recognized them.”

“You were lucky, Anita.”

Anita agreed: she had been very lucky. “I put the seeds aside to bring to you, and then later, just before we locked up for the night, Sanjay, our night guard, brought in that.” She nodded to the plastic bag of mashed fruit.

Dr. Premod reached out and rested her hand on the bag, squeezing the contents with her fingertips.

“Sanjay released the dog from its kennel for the night, and he saw the dog and goat playing with something. He went to inspect what it was, and he wrapped it in newspaper and brought it in to me.” Anita remembered the guard's initial delight at the animals' game but his subsequent concern. “At first he worried someone was throwing trash over our compound wall.” Anita looked at the mashed fruit sitting in the plastic bag. “But then he recognized it. Not mango.”

Through the open door Anita could see an orderly pushing an empty gurney, and doctors' aides in blue saris passed farther down the hall. This part of the hospital was quiet with a subdued tone to every activity. There might be a crisis, but it would be quiet.

“So you brought it here for an official identification.”

“I was sitting in the office trying to make sense of what has been happening to our tour group.”

“And eating.” Dr. Premod sat up straight. For her this was a relaxed posture, unconscious and natural.

"When I first brought the cup of seeds down to the desk, Ravi noticed and ate some, but he must have taken a few of the others, the ones he recognized."

"Then Ravi was lucky too."

"I noticed one of the guests had a small packet of the after-dinner digestive spices that some airlines include on the dinner tray." Anita paused before listing them. "Star anise, licorice, cloves, fennel."

The doctor interrupted her. "And a few halved otalam seeds for good measure."

Anita nodded. "Yes, otalam."

"We might as well call this the suicide plant." Dr. Premod took a deep breath. "Do you have this tree in your compound?"

"No, that's why Sanjay was concerned. I've seen the tree in other parts of the resort but I never thought much about it. So many of the plants in our area are toxic to one degree or another. But we know that and we avoid them."

"Otalam grows wild along our coast," Dr. Premod said. "The flowers are quite pretty, unfortunately. It can grow in salty swamps, so I would expect to find it in this area."

"But the seeds are bitter, yes?" Anita asked.

"They are indeed, but the taste can be hidden when the seeds are added to cooking and once mixed in with spices they are unnoticed and palatable." Dr. Premod spoke precisely, watching Anita. "The oil in the seeds acts like digitalis, disrupting the heart rhythm."

"So the victim might not even know he's been poisoned, just that he feels like he's having a heart attack?"

"That's possible. Doctors don't think to look for evidence of otalam unless they are given reason to do so. It's possible some who are thought to have committed suicide or died of heart ailment are actually murdered."

"Is this speculation?"

Dr. Premod shook her head. "No, not at all." She glanced across the room at a file cabinet, as though mentally locating a scientific paper in its drawers. "A research team in France has been investigating otalam and has documented over five hundred cases of fatal otalam poisoning in Kerala alone.

They're now thinking half of Kerala's plant poisoning deaths are the result of cerbera, from otalam seeds." Dr. Premod leaned toward her. "I must know where you got this. Did you buy it?"

"We had a death in Hotel Delite," Anita said. "It appeared to be natural, and the body was taken away. I thought it seemed odd, for a few reasons, but I couldn't find anything concrete." She exhaled slowly. "I searched the room and found nothing."

"Except this cup of spices?"

"I took the spices and a journal from the victim's room."

"So now you suspect the death of the hotel guest was not natural," the doctor said. "I must report this."

"Yes, please do." Anita held up her hand as Dr. Premod reached for a pad of paper. "The other guests also had little bags of spices, which I am told they received on the plane."

"Has anyone else fallen ill?"

Anita shook her head.

"I'll alert the authorities to this matter." Dr. Premod picked up a pen. "It is terrible to think this is an act of random killing."

"I don't think it is," Anita said. "In fact, I'm almost certain it isn't."

* * * * *

There is something comforting in returning home after an ordeal, touching familiar objects and feeling the welcome of one's own place. These things—settee, table, chair, lamp, pillows and coverlet, photos tacked to the wall—are inanimate, mere junk to strangers. But to Anita they had taken on some of her consciousness, shaped her vision, and carried the promise of security in the familiar. She fell onto the settee and stared at her private suite, her glance moving from object to object as she tried to absorb the shock of coming so close to dying by an accidental, unlucky clasping of the fingers. These two rooms over the garage had been her home for years, taken for granted until this night, when it was a refuge, a blessing, her own. She and Ravi had been lucky, but there was no guarantee anyone else would have been.

In the quiet of Hotel Delite typical of late evening, as night took over the resort, she could have lain on the floor of her office all night, passing the point of possible recovery. But such an ending was not to be. Sanjay had arrived early enough to spend a little time with the guard dog and goat, watch them play, and recognize that something was wrong. The hikers had returned to find Anita at the desk, and one was educated enough to recognize the seeds in the spice mixture.

Thanks to Dr. Premod, Anita now had confirmation someone had murdered Kenneth Maxinter, and she knew how. But she suspected something even worse, even more macabre and bizarre. An entire tour group was moving around the world with the sole purpose of diminishing its number, one member dying in each location visited. By the time the tour ended in Tokyo, no one was expected to be left—except the tour leader, Kenneth Maxinter.

But someone had interrupted that plan.

"Why are you visiting Dr. Premod?" Auntie Meena appeared in the doorway to Anita's suite over the garage. She hadn't knocked, called out, or given any warning. Abandoning all of her normal behaviors, Auntie Meena stood over Anita sprawled on her settee. "What is happening? You are ill?"

"I've been resting, Auntie." Anita plumped up the pillows behind her and stretched out her legs, resting her feet on a footstool. "I need to think."

"No, I forbid it!" Meena looked aghast. Her right hand went to her breast and her left arm flew away from her body. Not for the first time did Anita think her aunt should have been in films.

"You forbid me to think?" Anita gave her aunt a quizzical look.

"Please, Anita." Meena collapsed onto the edge of the settee, reaching for Anita's hand and crushing it between her own, kneading her niece's fingers until Anita began to wince. "I am having so much fear for you. Why are you going to Dr. Premod?"

"I had a few questions. It's nothing."

"It is not nothing. Sanjay told me he found this otalam in the compound, and the animals playing with it." Meena shut her eyes. "It is dangerous, Anita, this love of murder you have. Please give it up."

"There is no danger for me now. I know Kenneth Maxinter's death was not an accident. I know how he died." She pulled her right hand out of the crucible of Meena's fear.

"But I am afraid."

"Nonsense. You can't be afraid, not someone who runs a hotel practically by herself." Anita smiled, giving her aunt a moment to bask in the compliment. She gathered Meena's hands and held them still. "Besides, I need your help."

"Me?" If Meena was shocked at the discovery of otalam fruit in the compound, she was almost catatonic at the idea of confronting a murderer herself. "But I am timid and foolish and and . . . " She bobbed back and forth, as though trying to pump out another adjective.

"But you are someone who likes to engage our guests and get to know them." Anita smiled, and as she expected, Meena couldn't resist the warmth that flowed whenever she spied an opportunity to mother her guests.

"They are so lost, so far from home." Auntie Meena had never been much of a traveler herself. Though her husband had been a pilot, she had always covered her eyes when watching his plane take off. "They need my support, isn't it?"

"Exactly, Auntie. Exactly. They need to talk about their families, the ones they have left behind. They need to talk about their lives and share what they care about. They need to talk to someone who cares about them. Can you do this?"

Auntie Meena adored her niece, but even her affection had its limits. "This is spying, isn't it?" She glared at Anita with a suspicious glint in her eye.

"Investigating, Auntie, investigating. Gathering information that will help us understand motives."

"Well . . . " Auntie Meena struggled against the idea of violating standards of good behavior, but then, to Anita's surprise, she sat up straight, a new look in her eye. "So I am watching and learning and following, yes?"

"Following?" It was Anita's turn to look suspicious. "I didn't say anything about following."

* * * * *

A mix of foreigners filled the narrow lane stretching back from the beach. They shifted a few feet in either direction, back and forward, as they watched two monkeys grab small bananas from the hands of two young Italian women. The monkeys ran along the six-foot-high wall banking up against a two-story hotel with no windows on this, the back side. The workers in the restaurants and shops lining the other side of the walk watched with both amusement and apprehension. No one in the four-table restaurant, open-air grocery, tailor shop, or gift shop liked monkeys. The owners considered them thieves, but tolerated them, since the creatures entertained the foreigners.

Kurup, the owner of the small grocery store, draped towels over the crates of fruit nearest to the cement walk, and stood guard among them. He watched the tourists in the lane, and others who wandered into the store. Inside, his oldest son waited on customers among tables covered with fruits, boxes of cereal and sweet biscuits, and various toiletries. Anita knew he wasn't guarding inventory against only the monkeys.

"Any success?" Anita asked when she reached him. She watched the monkeys but without enthusiasm. She didn't like the animals, and felt their invasion of the resort was a bad sign.

"Not coming for two or three days," Kurup said.

"But as soon as you turn your back, he'll be here." Anita commiserated a few more minutes before moving on. The occasional shoplifter, for whatever reason, was a thorn cutting deep into the vendors' profit. No one wanted to prosecute a tourist or fellow worker, but the small vendors who were preyed on couldn't afford to indulge a thief. Anita turned a corner, walked on, and came to the herbal shop.

Guru Vasant sat deep in the gloom behind his offerings, the sun's rays reaching the bottles and baskets arrayed in front of him. They stood on three tiers, rising up to his chest, so that he peered over them at prospective customers passing by. His bright white khurta absorbed enough light to alert others that someone sat behind the shop's wares. And his hearing or perhaps his intuition was so good that he knew, without opening his eyes, if someone had stopped in front, stepping closer to the display. He opened his eyes just enough for Anita to notice.

"Welcome, Anita Missi." He smiled his enigmatic smile and opened his eyes to greet her. She was glad his smile didn't display his betel-stained teeth.

"Greetings, Guru." Anita examined the offerings. "You are growing in popularity."

The laconic Buddha figure tipped his head in acknowledgment.

"One of my guests made a purchase here."

"And your young friend, Peeru, came yesterday to inquire about this." He gave her a wiggle of his dark eyebrows.

"So he did." Anita held up a basket of cinnamon sticks and asked for a few grams.

Guru Vasant took the basket and began to weight the sticks. "And I am telling him what the guest had purchased."

"So you did."

He held up the number of sticks of cinnamon, named the price, and Anita agreed.

"Did she mention if she is enjoying her stay here?" Anita held out the rupees.

Guru Vasant held the sticks in his hand while he considered the question. When he had made a decision, of sorts, he dropped the spice into a paper bag made from folded newspaper with a coir rope handle, and held it out to her. "She is not complaining about Hotel Delite."

"I'm glad to hear that." Anita reached for the bag.

"She is gracious."

"I'm glad to hear that too. After all, if she bought a sleep aid, then I worry she's having trouble sleeping at the hotel and perhaps there's something I can do to make her visit more relaxing. We like to accommodate our guests, as I'm sure you know."

Guru Vasant tipped his head again in acknowledgment and offered an agreeable smile. "I am telling her to use this herbal remedy sparingly."

"Always good advice." It was the right thing to say, but she knew this was not the ordinary advice. "Did you give her any other words of caution?"

He settled back on his high chair, closed his eyes and began to hum. He hadn't yet dismissed her as a customer because he hadn't given her a little card to slip into her bag, as he was sometimes known to do. He seemed to like the additional interaction with customers and never failed to add this little moment. Anita had a small collection of business cards, which she left in a basket at Hotel Delite for guests to peruse. She waited, convinced he had something more to say.

"She is most particular about spices," he said, "examining each basket carefully, taking out a sample of several and studying it. Then she is putting it back. She is most careful to keep her hands visible, to reassure me perhaps. I am at first concerned that she means to take a few and not pay, but she is most careful. I am made to relax by her conduct. She is honest. She is examining and learning about spices."

Anita considered this. "Did she ask about any in particular?"

"I am not having every one and she is asking about one that is prepared—licorice. She is describing and I am showing her the prepared spices." He leaned back and rummaged around the shelves hidden behind the display tables. "This one." He held up a bag of spice mix popular in North India.

"Did she buy this?"

He shook his head. "Only the sleep aid. But she is interested in learning, she tells me. And I am believing her. She is not seeking to buy but to understand."

"Did she ask any other questions?"

He let his eyes close as he thought back. "Her conversation is casual but it is particular. She is asking where these come from and I am telling. She is asking if these are things people can collect on their own."

"And what did you say?"

He shrugged. "I am suggesting this is not a good idea because taking from someone's garden is stealing." He smiled as he stifled a laugh. He grew serious. "She is asking again if these are dangerous in great quantities. I am saying all foods are dangerous in excess."

Anita examined the baskets and bottles a second time, methodically going across one tier and then the second and third. It was possible that Angela Deetcher had come here first looking for something to add to the spice mix to poison Kenneth Maxinter. When she found nothing here, she turned to the poison fruit.

"Did the foreign guest say what she was looking for? You said she was interested in learning."

"Indeed she was and perhaps still is," he said. "But she was looking, just as you are."

"And what am I looking for?"

"Ah! I cannot name it, but I expect the good doctor in the hospital can." He smiled again, and this time a few of his orange-tinted teeth appeared between bright red lips.

"So you have heard."

The herbalist shrugged. "You are going by autorickshaw, isn't it? Autorickshaw drivers talk. Do we not follow the vicissitudes of our own?" He stopped smiling. "Ah, I see I have said something significant."

"Indeed, Guru Vasant, you have." Anita folded the bag, so she could slip it into her purse. "Have you heard of anyone here suffering from otalam poisoning? Perhaps you can tell me how many of these trees we have in the resort. I know of three but I think I've been walking past others without even noticing, and I'm hoping that you have noticed."

"I can think of several in this area," he said, and began counting them off on his fingers.

Fifteen

The minute Deepa Nayar stepped into the dining room, with little Uma hanging onto her grandmother's hand with both of hers, she was convinced she'd made a mistake. The sign outside said Meals Ready, and the lunch crowd filled most of the first floor. When she inquired at the cashier's desk, the man sent her and Uma upstairs to the second floor. This too was crowded, but in a booth along the opposite wall she spotted Crocker Dawes before he spotted her. He was the most noticeable person in the room, the only foreigner and far too large for the booth. Even though he hunched over reading the menu, he loomed over the table, his shoulders rising far above the seat back, his graying red hair blending with the color of the painted walls.

He must have sensed she was there because he glanced up and caught her eye. He slid out of the booth and stood. In a flash she felt again the strange sensations of almost thirty years ago, the amusement and surprise she'd felt when he did such things as a young man. She hoped Uma wouldn't notice and repeat every little thing she saw and heard.

"I'm glad you came," Crocker said. "And you too." He leaned forward and addressed the child in Malayalam, the local language, when he noticed her staring at him wide-eyed and open-mouthed.

Crocker spent several minutes reminiscing about the food he'd eaten in Kerala years ago and then ordered a sadhyam meal after Deepa had ordered for herself and Uma. Despite Deepa's self-consciousness, the waiter didn't bat an eye. He just took the menus and walked away.

"This is very strange for me." Deepa turned to English after a lull in the conversation. She wondered how long they could talk in Malayalam about the changes in the city of Trivandrum, the traffic lights and high-rises, the air-conditioned shops and the new roads, the crowds of people and the new bus station.

"No stranger than it is for me," he said.

She was surprised at how much English she retained, and attributed that to working in an environment where English was heard daily. She had rarely spoken it after she married, and now she struggled to find the right word when a foreigner asked for anything more complicated than basic directions.

"I was sorry to hear about your husband," Crocker said. She looked at him. "Well, maybe not. I mean . . ." He blushed a deep red, the splotches spreading upward from his throat to cover his face. She'd been told long ago that people with red hair had trouble with the sun and color in their faces, and she'd never understood what that meant until she met Crocker Dawes, and here she was, learning about that oddity all over again.

"I understand." Deepa looked down at Uma, who had been following the unintelligible exchange with curiosity.

"I suppose you were surprised to hear from me after so many years."

The food arrived and whatever she was going to say was forgotten as she saw to Uma's meal as well as her own. The child lost all interest in the two adults and propped her chin on the table, as her tiny hand made little balls of rice and vegetables, and popped them into her mouth. The meal was a good one, fortunately, Deepa thought, or she and Crocker would have had even more difficulty bridging the years.

She found the thali tasty and acceptable. The small bowls of vegetables were not as good as her own, but the avial was quite passable. The chutney was also passable, but the lime pickle was quite good. She wouldn't have felt the need to apologize to a guest for the meal.

"Why did you stop writing?" she asked halfway through as she came to feel more comfortable.

"I never thought I'd get back here." He ate like an Indian, leaning on his left forearm, his left hand resting on the edge of the table and pointing inward, and using his right hand to mix vegetables and rice. "India seemed so far away back then."

"But not now?"

He shook his head. "Not now. Plane fare is cheaper for one thing."

She acknowledged this with a dip of her head. "So you can travel back and forth as desired." When he didn't answer, she looked up and found him staring at her.

"Not writing sooner was a mistake. Stopping our correspondence was a bigger one."

"A married woman in India cannot have a male correspondent in America." She softened this with a smile, but Crocker remained solemn. "Why did you come back after so many years?"

"I came to understand what really matters to me."

"You are not married now."

"No, my wife and I divorced about ten years ago." He looked at his now empty plate. Then, without a word, he rose and walked to the end of the room where he washed his hands in the sink. When he returned, Deepa slid out of the booth and did the same, taking Uma with her. A waiter cleared the thalis, leaving three small bananas for dessert. Crocker ordered tea.

"We were friends then," Crocker said when Deepa again faced him across the table.

Yes, thought Deepa, we were friends only, because you were such a careful person. He is still a careful person, she thought. Though his legs were long, he made sure to place them so that he didn't bump her knees or put a foot on top of hers. He had always been careful around her, determined, as he once told her, not to put a foot wrong. She smiled at the memory.

"Do you remember what I told you back then?" he asked. "You're smiling."

"You told me many things."

"About being friends."

Deepa did indeed remember, and she could see that he knew that. He leaned back against the booth, his hands resting in his lap. The waiter brought tea and set down two glass tumblers. Uma began to peel her banana, her glance going to Crocker every few seconds.

"I remember." She watched her granddaughter eat the banana.

"Perhaps you didn't believe me."

She lifted the tumbler and took a sip of the creamy, sweet liquid. "I didn't understand at first, and I had no one I could ask to explain it to me. Back then we did not have the same kind of girl friends as women do in America. I learned that from seeing my daughter's Facebook page. It is different, isn't it?"

"What did you not understand?"

"That you were telling the truth." Deepa ran her finger along the rim of the cup, smoothing out unseen wrinkles.

Crocker winced, but he closed his eyes against the pain, and when he opened them again, he gave her a warm look. "Yes, I was telling the truth. Perhaps too enigmatic. I was immature, Deepa. A boy out to save the world by building latrines."

Deepa began to laugh. She leaned forward, lowering her chin, and her shoulders shook. Uma transferred her gaze to her grandmother. "And the old men in the village took it all very solemnly. They wanted latrines."

"Well, they got them."

Deepa and Crocker gave themselves over to the memory and laughter. Uma gave both adults a skeptical eye and decided the banana was the only object worthy of her attention.

"You told me you could not be romantic unless you meant to stay," Deepa said. "And it was not a ploy."

"No, not a ploy."

"And you tell me in your letter that you are returning to stay," Deepa said. "And yet, as I look at your face, I see it does not make you happy."

"I never stopped thinking about you, Deepa." Crocker placed his hands around his tumbler. "Very sentimental. I told myself I was romanticizing a teenage friendship, though we weren't teenagers then. At least, not both of us. I put the thought of you and India aside and went about my business, but the memory always came back. And then . . ."

"And then . . . ?"

"And then I got sick."

Deepa stared at him. Yes, that was the change she sensed in him. She noted his skin and eyes, the tilt of his head, the lack of sheen in his hair. "Is that why you have come, to say goodbye?"

He closed his eyes and took a deep breath. "Yes. But I intend to enjoy my life right up to the last minute." He glanced at Uma and leaned forward. "I was diagnosed with cancer. It was slow-moving, inoperable, and then it decided to speed up." He gave her a rueful smile. "Unreliable disease, but it's the one I've got. So I joined a support group for people with a terminal diagnosis."

Deepa looked down. Without even realizing it, she reached out and placed her hands, both of them, over Crocker's as they lay curved around the tumbler.

"I don't know how we came to it but we got this idea that we should travel to the places we loved best, and if we weren't going to live, we should pick our spot to die. It's a wacky idea, but, you know, a bunch of us thought it was brilliant. And I was one of them."

"This is the place you loved most?" So intrigued with this, Deepa squeezed his hands.

"I was young and ambitious, and eager to help everyone. And you were so beautiful."

Deepa blushed. "You would have said that about any Indian girl who cooked for you."

"No, I wouldn't have." He watched her pull away. "I don't know how much longer I have but I want to spend it here. With you. That's what I learned in that group."

"We have very good hospitals here, Crocker Dawes." This was the first time she had said his name aloud since he'd arrived, and it sounded as peculiar now as it had thirty years ago. She started to laugh, with little gasps of breath, wanting to stop, not able to stop, thinking this was the first step to hysteria.

"That's how I felt when I decided, giddy and happy and foolish. So here I am. And I feel better now than I have in months."

Deepa put her arm around Uma. Her granddaughter was peering at her, her little mouth puckered into a pink rose.

"Do you understand any English?" Deepa asked her in Malayalam. Uma shook her head no. "Well, you will soon."

Sixteen

Anita climbed out of the autorickshaw and stepped into the shade of the marble entry for the Mandala Hotel. It sat on a bluff overlooking the single piece of undeveloped land fronting the beach. Down below tiny figures filled the parking lot during the day, or wandered across the sand to the small restaurant, the only one on this section of beach and consisting of little more than a tent over tables with a makeshift kitchen behind a screen.

From the hotel guests could see little of this activity, since lush palms, shrubbery, and lattice fencing enclosed the terraces and swimming pool. Anita rarely came here, though she knew some of the staff. For the moment the Mandala Hotel was the fanciest on the beach, but not the fanciest in the resort. Between the northern headland with its world-class grand hotel and the lighthouse on the southern headland, by Hotel Delite, guests had a wide choice of accommodation and services.

Anita strolled along the entry plaza to the Mandala Hotel, admiring the carvings at the top of the pillars at the main door and scanning the plantings for *othalanga maram*, as the poisonous plant was known in Malayalam. At one end of the entry she noted a small oleander bush, a member of the same family and also toxic. She crossed the marble-floored lobby, open to the air on three sides, to the terrace beyond. The pool to her left and restaurant to her right were reserved for hotel guests, but a small cafe off the lobby was open to guests from other hotels.

"Ah, Miss Anita." A tall man in a dark suit approached her and bowed. In his mannerisms he seemed old enough to be her father but he had the smile of a much younger man, which he was. After graduating with a degree in hospitality from a German university, he had returned to India and was now making his way up the ladder in a new hotel chain.

"Hello, Peter." She had met Peter Souza in school, and they sometimes joked about having ended up in the same line of work. He traced his family back to an eighteenth-century Portuguese trader and a large number of hoteliers. "I'm admiring your plantings."

"I am so glad you like them." He had a barely noticeable lisp that Anita attributed to his ongoing efforts to avoid pronouncing English words with a Malayalam accent. He brought each syllable forward in his mouth, avoiding the consonants sounded with a tongue pulled back. No fricatives escaped his lips. "Please come and have a cup of tea with me." He led the way into the restaurant reserved for guests and ordered so discreetly that it arrived just as they sat down and before she even noticed the reason for the waiters hurrying by. He attended to her arrangements of tea and small savories, which she appreciated because, she realized, she was hungry.

"It's nice to see how others do things. I don't think Auntie Meena and I could ever manage this."

Peter smiled as she knew he would. "Nor could I if I did not have a staff to order about." He leaned over as he said this. He was admired by the employees, and those who worked there the longest might even admit to a sense of loyalty. "I am very sorry to hear of the unpleasantness in Hotel Delite." He spoke softly, so that no one passing by could overhear him.

Anita thanked him and chose a number of tea sandwiches. "That's actually why I'm walking about this afternoon."

Peter lifted an eyebrow but his smile remained. He mixed sugar and milk into his tea and stirred. "Someone here in this hotel is involved?"

Anita laughed. "I hope not. And I doubt it." She sipped her tea. "No, it's the way he died. We think he somehow got hold of some seeds from the *othalanga* tree, and they got mixed in with a little bag of digestive spices he kept from a meal on the flight to Trivandrum."

Peter pulled his lips into a little moue. His thick black hair waved away from his face; he shaved off his mustache when he left for Germany a few years ago and never regrew it. His skin was smooth around his mouth no matter how intense his thoughts or feelings. “Yes, we have one here.” He turned toward the plantings just beyond the terrace and nodded. “The blooms are lovely, but yes, the plant is toxic throughout.”

“There are several planted in the area,” Anita said. “I asked Guru Vasant at the herbals shop and he gave me a list of those he knew about. I suppose there could be more, but I wanted to at least see the ones he mentioned to see if there is any chance someone could have gotten the seeds here in the resort.”

“Very wise,” Peter said, but Anita chalked this up to his training. He never said the wrong thing, put a foot wrong, forgot someone's name, or did anything that might break the spell of being the face of the perfect hotel. Unlike me and Auntie Meena, Anita thought.

“But we take precautions.” Peter glanced over the rim of his cup and Anita turned around to look. There, among the shrubbery, was a gardener in khaki shorts watering plants and weeding among them, though it looked to Anita as though the beds could not have been tidier. “The fruit of certain plants is removed at once. You know the *othalanga* fruit looks just like the mango, only smaller.”

“Yes, I did know that,” Anita said. “It is sometimes mistaken for the mango by . . .”

“Yes,” Peter said, his smile changing ever so slightly. “By tourists who think you can pluck your breakfast from a tree while you lounge on the terrace.”

Anita winced. She was glad Hotel Delite restricted itself to potted plants, which Brij and Pema took care of.

“Our gardener and his staff watch over everything. They even count blossoms, I am told.”

Anita wasn't sure she was ready to believe that, but she was glad to hear Peter Souza and his staff took extreme precautions to prevent an accident that could be fatal.

“As soon as the flowers bloom, they are clipped at the end of the afternoon.” Peter took another sip of his tea. “We do not leave them for any length of time, and we watch over every part of any of the plants that are poisonous."

"So you never see a guest going out with a flower pinned to her blouse," Anita said.

Peter closed his eyes, followed by a quick intake of breath. He opened his eyes and smiled. "No, we do not. We provide small bouquets in every room, and we also remove any fruit a guest has brought into the rooms and replace it with a bounty of our own. We want our guests to have all the beauty of our luxurious land without the dangers."

"This must be a huge amount of work for you." Even with a lot of staff, watching over the plants and fruits to this degree meant at least two people dedicated to doing nothing else but assisting the gardener in managing toxic plants or plant parts, and the housekeeping staff had to inspect as well as clean. "Why do you even bother to keep these plants here? Why not replace them with something else?"

Peter gave a gentle and graceful shrug. "They are lovely, are they not? And such plants are typical of the tropics and subtropics, are they not? And tourists expect to see certain things, do they not?"

"The owners," Anita said. "The owners like them."

Peter Souza would never criticize the people he worked for, and, Anita knew, he liked many of those in the conglomerate who visited from time to time. "I think perhaps we are overly cautious, but we want our guests to be happy and healthy."

"And alive when they leave here," Anita said.

"Oh! Most definitely alive." And this time Peter did allow himself a small chuckle.

* * * * *

The entry lane to the Mandala Hotel was four car lengths, cutting in from the main road leading down to the government hotel and the northernmost beach in the resort. Farther north the private resorts lacked safe areas for ocean swimming and relied on saltwater pools for their guests. At the intersection with the Mandala Hotel lane and main road was another lane leading down to the northern end of the Promenade and the row of hotels along the beach. This decline was steep, almost forty-five degrees and even steeper in some spots. But from here Anita had a good look at the resort. She had five more sites to visit, according to the list Guru Vasant had given her. Anita started down the hill and turned left near the bottom.

A dirt lane ran between small shops, modest lodges, and the back entries for hotels crowded between the larger hotels fronting the beach and a row of small shops. Here a tourist could buy a mobile phone or small antiques, leave laundry to be done, have clothing made, buy a snack, or book a local tour. A small temple with a high compound wall crowded among the shops, marking out an island of serenity. Anita heard a bell ring and turned into the temple gate, leaving her sandals outside.

A young priest watched her on her circuit of the shrine, but didn't stop his work. A few women prayed in front of the murti in the main shrine. As she circled around to the front, she noted a small shrub, *othalanga maram,* in the eastern corner, by the office. Another priest, also young, approached her as she bent over to examine it.

"It looks like it's dying," Anita said.

"Dying." The priest repeated this and waggled his head to indicate that she was correct; it was dying.

"What happened?"

"A goat." The boy sighed.

"Goats wouldn't eat this, would they?"

"A goat was brought to be consecrated and it got loose and started nibbling on banana leaves left here, and . . ." He shrugged, and Anita got the gist.

"An expensive accident," she said.

"Owner is very, very unhappy." The boy screwed up his face as he spoke. "Very angry."

"So you're removing the plant?"

"Removing and burning. Elsewhere," he added when he saw her expression. Some plants were just as poisonous in smoke as they were when constituted.

Anita thanked him, made a donation, and left the temple compound. Outside, she crossed one more site off her list.

By the end of the afternoon Anita had crisscrossed the resort and examined *othalanga marams* of all sizes and shapes. She was tired, hot and sweaty, and cranky. So far she hadn't found a single plant with fruit or seeds and began to wonder if

Dr. Premod had erred in her identification, or if she had been wasting her time searching through the resort. Poisonous plants grew all over the state.

Anita had two sites left to visit and followed the canal to a small lane that led straight up the hill to a five-story hotel set into the hillside. Just ahead she spotted Rajan, the ten-year-old who ran his parents' shop while they worked elsewhere. He kept the shallow shelves clean and well stocked with sundries—cigarettes, candies, incense, toothpaste, and the like. He looked bored and sleepy, as only a young boy can.

"No business today?" Anita said, walking up to the counter.

Rajan sat up, looking alert. When he saw it was Anita, he sagged. "Quiet time. Tourists are leaving the beach and readying for an evening meal." He watched a number of tourists pass by on the narrow lane.

"I'm ready for a nap myself." Anita had been walking up and down and around for a couple of hours, and the lack of success was wearing on her. "I'm looking for something but no success."

"What are you seeking?" He sat up, ready to provide whatever was wanted.

"A shrub." Anita paused. "Not something to buy in a shop."

"What sort of shrub?" He was a curious child, always alert to opportunity.

"*Othalanga maram.*"

Rajan flicked his fingers and his eyes widened. "Very bad. You don't want this."

"You know this plant?"

He waggled his head almost violently. "We have one but it's not good."

"Where is it?"

"You want to see this?"

"I want to know where they are in the resort," she explained. "So far I have seen a few but none of them have fruit. A few had flowers, but no fruit with seeds."

"The fruit is bad."

"I know, but I want to see if it is something a person could find here in the resort."

Rajan thought about this, glanced up and down the lane, then pulled down the screen, shutting the shop window. He reappeared on the steps. "This way." He led her to the small gate into the vacant lot, reached over to unlatch it from the inside, and pushed it open. "Over there." He pointed to a small shrub growing against the back of the small two-story building. "You didn't see this when you were here before?"

Anita shook her head, but that was it. She crossed the lot, reached out to touch the leaves and lifted a small mango-like fruit hanging among them. She had not noticed this the first time she'd visited the yard, when Rajan had been concerned about renting the rooms above the shop.

"Poisonous." Rajan flicked his fingers again, this time at the plant.

Anita touched the smooth skin of the fruit, and then pulled it from the branch.

"No, Missi. Don't take this."

She held the fruit, smaller than an apple, but green without the tinge of red that marked the mango. Beyond the shrub the rest of the compound was unkempt, with uneven ground, piles of burnt trash on the rough slope rising to the compound wall that defined the narrow lanes.

"Please don't take that." Rajan nodded to the fruit. Anita walked past the shrub to the compound wall, looked over.

"The ground is lower on the other side of the wall," Anita said. Rajan nodded. She turned around. "Where does that go?" Hidden among the trees, a pile of rotting branches intermingled with trash, was a narrow set of stairs.

"To the rooms above," Rajan said.

"You have two sets of stairs?"

"Two."

"Why do you have two sets?" Anita asked.

"To get to the roof where the water tank is. And for workers when repairs are needed."

"Rajan, you told me a tourist came to look at your rooms above but decided not to rent them. Do you remember?" She rested the fruit in her palm.

The boy nodded.

"Did the tourist return? I think you said she was a woman."

He clicked his tongue and pulled a face. "No, she never came back."

"Did she rent elsewhere?"

Rajan shook his head. "I see her walking, sometimes going up the lane and turning that way, and sometimes going up to Lighthouse Road."

"What did she look like?"

Rajan frowned, and then began a detailed description, beginning with the foreign woman's odd way of walking, with a limp that might have been improved, he said, if she gave up those heavy, uneven heeled shoes and wore sandals like everyone else.

* * * * *

Rajan had been definite that Angela Deetcher, as Anita identified her, had not returned to his shop, at least not while he was there. But she could have just as easily come at another time, when the shop was closed and no one would notice someone slipping inside the compound for a few moments. Nor could Rajan say the fruit Anita held in her hand, pulled from the shrub, was the only fruit produced on the shrub in the last few days or weeks. Anita had examined the plant but she couldn't tell if another fruit had been taken or not. It was frustrating to say the least, and very disturbing. Anita headed for the last remaining shrub on Guru Vasant's list.

The lane twisted up the hill, leaving the fancier hotels below and circling around the few remaining private homes still occupied by the original families. The air grew cooler under the trees, and quieter. The path turned into a narrow cement walkway that ran along the outside compound wall of houses built into the slope. She tended to avoid this area in the rainy season because the walks became slippery, and one misstep would land her twenty feet down on ground covered in trash and rocks.

At the halfway point along the walk, a narrow opening revealed a stairway going up, and the remnants of stairs heading down. Most of the steps were buried now, but the shrubbery near the bottom was thick. Anita could tell from here that Guru Vasant was correct—and a very observant man. Mixed among the plants was an *othalanga maram*, though it wasn't thriving. The shrub offered no flowers and definitely no fruit, and might not last many more years.

Anita sat down on the steps to think. She found it hard to accept the motivation behind this group tour, but the evidence was there. She couldn't ignore it. Kenneth Maxinter had organized a group of terminally ill patients to travel the world to their favorite destinations, and there to let their lives end, each in his or her own favorite place. The tour began in London, traveled to Copenhagen and then on to Athens. She didn't know who had stayed in the first two cities, but she had the name of a man, Georgio, who remained in Greece. That left four tourists alive in India.

Crocker Dawes spent his happiest years in Kerala as a volunteer, and came back to Trivandrum to die, or perhaps to kill himself. Angela Deetcher confessed to Anita that she spent her happiest time in Australia, which left two cities and two tourists—Larry Forche and Sandra Stover. Neither one talked about favorite cities or anything beyond Trivandrum.

But here in India something went wrong with Kenneth Maxinter's plan. Instead of Crocker dying, he was alive and Kenneth was dead. Crocker seemed the least likely person to want to take his own life regardless of his diagnosis, and Anita had seen so little of Kenneth Maxinter that she didn't dare speculate.

At the foot of the old staircase a bandicoot rummaged among the trash before slipping away. The deep silence in this corner of the resort brought with it an equally deep sense of peace, something Anita needed as she imagined the group of foreigners sitting together and hatching their plan. What brought them to this point? Surely not only a terminal diagnosis.

A woman carrying a head load came along the narrow walkway, and Anita pulled in her feet to let her pass. The woman barely acknowledged her as she followed the lane and then turned up hill. The steadiness in the woman's steps reminded Anita of how much was revealed in little things. A few years ago the neighborhood had been plagued by a thief who wore shoes but left footprints that seemed different from others. The thief had been caught because a man recognized that the sores on a neighbor's feet came from poorly fitting shoes. That little detail led to the man's discovery and arrest.

Details, Anita thought. The answer to Kenneth's murder was in the details, the ones barely noticed or dismissed on first sight. Rajan remembered Angela's limp and reluctance to rent the room above the shop despite her many questions and inspection. Auntie Meena ruminated on Crocker's passion for French pastries. Ravi sighed over Larry's mooning after Sandra and Moonu worried about Sandra's near complete withdrawal at every meal. And Anita wondered at Kenneth Maxinter's enthusiasms and outsized personality, so different from the other members of the tour.

Seventeen

The shadows lengthened in front of the goats as they wandered across the road in front of the iron gates guarding the coast guard compound. The animals were restless, waiting for the boys to collect them for the evening milking. A kid nuzzled along the wall, and a foreign woman carrying a cloth bag came around the corner by the medical shop. She didn't try to hide her limp with a slow gait. Angela Deetcher spotted Anita at the mouth of the small lane and the two women nodded to each other. Anita fell into step beside her.

"You've been shopping?" Anita asked, indicating the bag.

"I went to the Connemara Market. I saw it when I came out of Jubilee Hall, so I thought I'd take a look. They have those tiny little shops but they're packed with saris and other things." Angela lifted the bag to show Anita. "I never saw so many saris. There's so much color you can hardly tell which one in a pile you want to look at."

"And you bought one?" Foreign tourists often bought gorgeous silk saris and had blouses made to go with them, the little choli that was almost impossible to find at home, but then the women had no idea how to wear them, how to tie them on and keep them from sliding down. She wasn't surprised when people fell in love with the fabrics and the colors, but she hadn't expected Angela Deetcher to be someone who would buy one. She had fallen fast, and this was only her fourth day in India.

Angela laughed. She seemed embarrassed for a moment, then thoughtful. "No, I don't think I'd be able to wear one. I'd always be afraid of it falling off. I don't know how Indian women manage to work in them, with all that fabric falling off the shoulder and all those skirts." She took a deep breath and continued. "I bought a jacket. It's studded with those little mirrors and embroidered everywhere." She glanced down at the bag. "I don't wear things like that, but I thought, well, why not? Just this once."

"What a good idea! It sounds beautiful."

They strolled along, exchanging mild comments. Anita glanced at Angela out of the corner of her eye, taking in the woman's expression, noting the changes in the tilt of her head, the steady look in her eye, the ease of her step despite the limp. Something had changed her, but what?

"Did you spend the day in Trivandrum?"

"I went in this morning, on the bus." Angela grinned. "Me! On a bus in India." She laughed. "I asked Ravi how to see the people, and he said take the bus. I think he meant it as a joke because after I asked about the time he tried to talk me out of it. But I took the bus. From right here." She nodded to the intersection just ahead.

"You've had a long day."

"I rested in an air-conditioned cafe in one of the modern hotels and then went over to Jubilee Hall for a lecture I'd heard about. Recent research in synthesizing dipeptide structures. Quite good. And not something I would hear about for a while in the states. In English, fortunately."

"I have no idea what that means," Anita said, "but I'm glad you enjoyed it."

They had reached the corner at Lighthouse Road, where the bus picked up and discharged passengers almost every hour. A small teashop on the corner served locals, and the homes along the road leading down to the lighthouse belonged to a variety of families, not all of whom worked in the resort. As they descended the hill the few streetlights began to blink on.

"I tried to get the same bus back but the driver said it only went once, at five o'clock and I couldn't find it, so I took one that went somewhere else." Angela frowned.

That explained, Anita thought, why she was walking down the road instead of riding in a taxi or autorickshaw. But it didn't explain why she had changed so much.

"You saw a lot of the city then."

"I had a wonderful time." There could be no doubt about Angela's feelings for her visit to Trivandrum. "And my leg didn't bother me at all." She glanced over at Anita. "It's been a problem since birth. But shoes for this today are so much better than when I was a girl, and there's surgery for some cases. Children today don't go through what I went through."

They walked on, past the temple lane on the right and the little shops on the left, on past the new high-rise hotels with tiny lobbies because the plot of land was so narrow—little more then the width of a small hotel room—past the restaurant in the open yard of a private home, and past the ayurvedic hotel on the left, where rooms had a view of the beach as well as being quiet.

And all the way down the road Anita had the feeling she was being followed. Once she turned around but all she saw was a gaggle of boys marching down the street, and a trio of women heading to the temple. At the bottom of the hill she parted from Angela. Anita turned right and stepped into a tiny shop and made a display of buying a packet of biscuits. As she stood in the darkened interior digging around in her purse, she studied each person who wandered past.

"Buying or not buying?" the shopkeeper said.

"I'm sorry to take so long, Ali." She asked for sweet biscuits and handed him a few rupees. "I was expecting to see something—or someone."

"Perhaps you are looking but not seeing."

"Okay, Ali. What am I missing?" Anita had known Ali for most of her life. His family had owned the corner shop since it was built, and he or one of his brothers or sons had worked here, each one learning the business until he chose to branch out and try something in another resort or in a city. The little shop had launched a number of businesses over the years.

"We are always not seeing what is in front of us and yet all answers are close to home." Ali smiled and lifted his hand in lieu of a shrug. He was nearing sixty, growing paunchy, and prone to philosophical responses to the most mundane question. He never chatted with tourists, however, foreign or native, and if asked for directions he professed not to know where something was.

"Close to home?" Anita repeated. "How do you know what I'm looking for?"

"I don't," Ali said. "But answers are always closer than we think."

Anita rolled her eyes and left the shop. Really, everyone's a guru now.

* * * * *

Anita reached the front door of Hotel Delite just as an autorickshaw pulled into the parking area. Auntie Meena climbed out, paid the driver, and scowled as he drove away. She never liked paying what she regarded as exorbitant fares, and to her all fares were exorbitant.

"Have you had a bad day, Auntie?" Anita watched her aunt make her way down the stairs to the front entrance, leaning on the railing with her left hand. She looked tired and cranky when she reached the registration desk. "Where have you been, Auntie?"

"Trivandrum." Meena dragged herself around the desk and into the office. She slid into a chair and closed her eyes. She leaned back, resting her head against a file cabinet and letting her mouth fall open.

"Auntie? Are you all right?" Anita leaned over her, placed a palm on her pale forehead, and waited.

"I am well. Just tired." Meena's color began to return, and though she still looked exhausted, she managed to smile. Anita went out to the desk and asked Ravi to order tea. He whispered something to her before heading to the kitchen.

"Ravi said you have been gone all day," Anita said when she returned to the office.

Meena looked up at Anita standing over her. "And what of it?"

"Are you unwell?" Anita sat on the edge of a chair, and peered at her aunt, looking for signs of illness or distress.

"Do not look at me like that," Auntie Meena said, turning away. "I can visit the city if I want, can't I?" And with that Auntie Meena leaned forward and stared at the open window. "Are you helping on the desk?"

"I will if you want, Auntie."

"Yes, it pleases me."

The tea arrived. Anita poured, expecting her aunt to criticize her as she often did, or comment on her untidy appearance, which she also often did, or comment on a recent encounter with the nice, successful unmarried son of a distant relative, which she always did. But Auntie Meena did none of these things. She sipped her tea, looked weary, and pushed the half-full cup away.

"I am tired, Anita. Very tired." Auntie Meena rose and walked to the registration desk. She steadied herself with one hand on the counter, and stared out the door. Anita guessed she was thinking about all the stairs she had to climb to reach her suite on the roof. Normally she headed up without a second thought, but this evening she seemed daunted by the stairs. "I feel old," Auntie Meena said. "All day—"

Whatever she was going to say was lost in the sound of sandals slapping on the terrazzo floor. Auntie Meena was at once transformed.

"Good evening, Madam Deetcher." Like a swan stretching her neck, Meena moved to the counter, as though she'd done nothing more than lounge through the afternoon, reading or visiting friends. She took a step toward the guest and clasped her hands in front of her.

"Good evening, Mrs. Nayar." Angela smiled at her and Anita.

The transformation in their guest was stunning, almost as stunning as the change in Auntie Meena. Anita couldn't believe that only an hour ago she had walked down Lighthouse Road with Angela. Angela's hair seemed shinier, the tailored silk slacks and blouse—in shimmering blue—brought color to her cheeks, and the glass beads on her sandals sparkled. Angela glanced at Anita, and merely smiled as though they shared a secret.

"You are taking a meal tonight?" Meena asked.

"I thought I'd visit one of the seafood restaurants on the Promenade," Angela said.

"Yes, of course. Very good restaurants we are having." Auntie Meena escorted Angela to the door, while Anita watched. Her aunt had to be pleased to see the change in their guest, from dour and dowdy to smiling and fashionable.

"So I've heard. Everyone talks about the restaurants." Angela paused in the doorway. "I'm looking forward to a very good meal." With that she took the stairs to the lane. She limped up them but didn't attempt to conceal the uneven length of her legs made more prominent by the flat-heeled sandals.

Auntie Meena took her place at the desk, a wretched look on her face. "Do I not protect my guests from thieves and tricksters? Do I not provide the safest in accommodations? Do I not give the advice of a loving aunt?"

"She's only going out for a meal, Auntie. And I think she looks lovely."

"Yes, she looks lovely." Auntie Meena looked so grim that anyone would have thought Angela had been dragged out in rags and chains, covered with dirt.

"We should be glad she is happy. She looks happier and healthier than when she arrived, and that is all for the good."

But it seemed her words brought little comfort to Auntie Meena, who, resigned to Angela Deetcher's new-found enthusiasm for life, headed for the staircase. Anita continued to marvel at how much Angela Deetcher had changed. But why did this not please Auntie Meena?

* * * * *

Anita spent most of the evening in the office, catching up on paperwork and mulling over the oddities of hotel guests. Mr. and Mrs. Allbret continued to enjoy their excursions, and reported on their discoveries every evening when they returned. Mr. Allbret easily fell into chatting with Ravi or Moonu and asked numerous questions. According to Moonu, the guest even pulled out a list of them one morning at breakfast. The young couple in room three came and went with exuberance, tracking sand in and out along with groceries for the small refrigerator in their room. Most guests stocked it with cold drinks, but this pair went in for lots of cheese, yogurt, and ice cream. Anita imagined them sitting on the balcony and watching the stars while they ate their ice cream.

"Good evening!" Anita greeted the two hikers as they bounded down the steps. They stopped to wipe their feet on the mat and knock off the sand as well, hitting one shoe against the other, side to side. Auntie Meena found this so charming the first time she witnessed it that she almost reduced their room charge—almost.

"We just walked back from Trivandrum," Gene, the taller one, announced to Anita. "Great hike." Anita expressed admiration but her mind was on something else. Gene looked a little different this evening but she couldn't quite put her finger on it. He had light-colored hair, and had obviously been out in the sun, but there was something else.

"But not so great at night." Ron shook his head. "I don't know how people do it but people can tell how close an approaching bus or car is and they just move off to the side of the road. They never miss a step and never look back to check; they just move aside about two steps before some giant truck goes flying by. I was looking behind me the whole time. It's a miracle we got here."

Gene laughed. "Nice walk, though. You sure get to see how people live."

Anita took this in without comment. She wasn't convinced that how people lived on the edge of the expanding highway could be taken for India as a whole but that didn't matter. She was impressed with the two for even taking the walk. It was 13 kilometers into the city from the hotel.

"We started up at Palayam Junction," Ron said. "Did I get that right?"

"Correct," Anita said. "The junction where you see all three religions—the Ganapati Temple next to the Jama Masjid, and diagonally across is Christ Church."

"That's quite a neighborhood," Gene said. "We wanted to see it because from what you read you'd think the entire continent of Asia is going to erupt in a religious war but then you see those three places—three houses of worship and three religions right next door to each other, and everyone going about their business. Awesome."

Anita smiled. Malayalis were proud of their history of religious tolerance, which required no effort because they thought everyone had a religion and so you were bound to bump into religions different from your own. It was as natural as hair color.

"And then you get reminded that they're not museums." Ron grinned as he reached for their room key sitting on the counter.

"No, not museums." Anita wondered if they'd wandered into the church during a service.

"What he means is that we saw one of the guests here coming out of Christ Church," Gene said, rubbing his index finger over his mouth. That was the difference, Anita saw at once. He was growing a mustache, but because his hair and skin were so light, it barely showed. If it didn't get bushy, he'd just look like he hadn't washed his face.

"The woman who's always wearing a wig," Ron said. "She must've had radiation or chemo recently, still waiting for her hair to grow back."

Anita offered her best hotelier's smile that said nothing, absolutely nothing. She hadn't perfected it to the extent Auntie Meena had but she was working on it. Right now she was trying to figure out when they'd seen Sandra Stover in the church because Anita thought all this time she'd been upstairs in her room.

She glanced at the clock. "There is an evening service on Wednesdays. It begins at six, I believe." She kept a list of houses of worship and service timings for guests, but it had been quite a while since someone had asked for a Catholic service in the city, at one of the larger churches. If Sandra had left the service by seven o'clock or so, then she should have returned by now. Gene and Ron offered a few more words of praise for their walk and left Anita on the desk, wondering where Sandra Stover could be. And what about Larry Forche? Was he with her?

Really, she muttered. These people have been here four days and already they've caused more concern than any other tour group in the last four years. She shut her eyes and rested her forehead on the desk. After a moment she straightened up, took a deep breath, and resigned herself to a long and uncomfortable night sleeping on a mat on the floor in the hotel parlor—just in case Sandra Stover's late arrival involved more than Sanjay could handle.

Eighteen

On Thursday morning, just before five o'clock, Pohty, the cook, turned the key and unlocked the kitchen. The door scraped along the floor and the weak light from the hallway washed over the pale gray and white stone chips in the terrazzo floor. Pohty yawned, huffed, shook his head, but before he could survey his domain he stopped, rigid, in the doorway.

"What are you doing here?" He growled at the man lying on the floor.

Sanjay rolled onto his back, gave the cook a scowl and rolled over. "Waiting."

"Waiting?" The cook stared at him. It was hard to tell how he felt about this.

"I asked him to wait." Anita appeared in the doorway behind Pohty. She had heard him come in and dragged herself up from the mat on the floor in the parlor.

Once the hikers retired for the night, Anita had gone upstairs with a master key and entered Sandra Stover's room after knocking and calling out the woman's name. As she feared, the room was empty, with no sign of where the guest had gone. Mindful of the legal consequences, Anita had done little more than check the closets to make sure no one had hidden a body in one, and then the bathroom, to ensure the guest hadn't slipped on the floor tiles and cracked her skull or had a sudden heart attack. There was no sign of Sandra Stover.

It wasn't unheard of for a guest to stay out all night. Some women struck up friendships with local men and the relationships progressed to intimacy. Since no respectable hotel would allow Indian male guests in the rooms of foreign women, the woman might visit the man's home. Or perhaps they traveled for a few days, to spend time together. The behavior was common enough to be recognized but rare enough to still unsettle some of the hotel owners and others in the resort. But Sandra hadn't seemed the type, and Anita worried when she failed to return.

When Sandra hadn't made an appearance by eleven o'clock, Anita spread out a mat on the parlor floor, taking Sanjay's place. She assigned him to the kitchen area, where he could hear anyone walking past the open window in the hopes of finding a way into the hotel after Anita and her aunt locked up. Other guests who stayed out so late as to find themselves locked out usually walked the circumference of the hotel in search of an open window or door to bang on. Guests were always advised of the night guard in the parlor but some forgot about Sanjay and explored the hotel looking for another opening. If anyone was prowling around the hotel, either Sanjay or the dog romping on the lower level would hear him or, in this case, her.

Anita hurried to explain all this to Pohty, especially her worries about Sandra, as soon as she heard his sandals scuffing along the hallway to the kitchen. The cook lifted an eyebrow, gave her an unnervingly skeptical look, and stepped over the night guard.

"Why are you not asking that man who follows her about?" Sanjay said as he shoved himself off the mat. He held up his blanket and folded it, tucking it under his arm, then shifted the mat and began rolling it up. "Is he not with her always?"

"He was in his room last night," Anita said. "I could hear him moving around." She rubbed her hands over her face; she hadn't slept well and the thought of having to track down a missing guest gave her chills. The last time a female guest had not returned, Auntie Meena and Anita had launched an all-out effort to find her, and they had—in bed with the owner of another hotel at the other end of the beach. The guest was so angry and insulted that she threatened to destroy Hotel Delite's reputation. Only a few well-chosen words, delivered with sweet endearments, had prevented this disaster.

"India changes people," Pohty said.

"When did you become so philosophical," Anita said.

The cook turned to her with a smile. "Is it not good for those who come to find a new part of themselves?" He reached for the tin of rice flour.

Anita had to admit he was right. But still, she had an awful feeling something terrible had happened to Sandra Stover and the hotel should figure it out sooner rather than later.

* * * * *

By five-thirty Sanjay had cleared out of the kitchen, the Hotel Delite guard dog, beloved by goats and crows alike, had been returned to his commodious kennel in the lower compound, and Pohty was once again humming to himself as he prepared dosas for those who preferred Indian breakfasts. Anita rocked a flat-bottomed pot to better distribute the coffee grounds brewing on the open flame. The promise of daylight brushed past the open window while Anita poured her coffee through a sieve into a mug.

"We waited all through the night for our missing guest," Anita told Pohty, "and now I'm worried we'll have trouble finding her. I can't be as optimistic as you are."

Pohty glanced at her over his shoulder, a sympathetic smile tugging at his lips. "The numbers are low for this time of year. Perhaps you should turn your attention to the hotel and let the guests find their own way."

"You know I can't do that." Anita heard the squeak of the old hinges on the wooden shutter and turned to help open it, expecting to see Deepa Nayar with her basket of pastries. "Oh, Good morning, Mallika."

Deepa's daughter, Mallika, slid the basket across the sill. "Amma is unwell this morning. She has worked all through the night and I sent her to bed. She needs to rest. I think she is overworking herself, paining her hands to the bones." She gave the basket a half-turn and lifted the cloth covering.

"Oh, the pastries." Crocker Dawes strode into the kitchen, his large figure reminding Anita of just how small the room was.

"This man again?" Pohty studied the foreigner, while he ground coconut for the chutney.

"Good morning." Crocker managed an uncertain but hopeful smile as he looked from the basket to Mallika and back again. "I hope Deepa is well?"

Mallika gave him as thorough a look as he had given her. "You're the American who came all those years ago?" she said in Malayalam.

"And you're Deepa's daughter." Crocker seemed to skim across the floor toward her. "I've wanted to meet you since I arrived."

"Why?" Mallika asked.

"And you have a daughter," Crocker said, undeterred by her bluntness.

Some understanding seemed to come over Mallika, like a cloud passing over the sun and bringing a chill. Her body seemed to pull into itself, seeking warmth and safety while she struggled against her feelings. "You took a meal in my mother's house." The words drifted out of her, separated like beads on a knotted string.

"Yes. Your mother is a wonderful cook."

Mallika still held the basket between her hands as it rested on the sill. She pulled aside the cloth covering and stared at the western pastries, the special croissants and fruit filled swirls with crosshatchings of melted sugar and the little sweet doughnuts sprinkled with cinnamon. She looked up at Crocker Dawes, his broad shoulders and tall frame filling the room. Crocker gazed at Mallika, and Pohty and Anita stared at the two of them.

"I live not far from my mother. I often help her." Mallika stepped back from the window. "I work in an IT office."

"Yes, your mother told me. She's very proud of you." Crocker beamed at her, a slight flush brightening his cheeks.

"I've received an excellent offer and we will be shifting soon to another place. My mother will come with me."

"Oh." Crocker didn't seem to know what to make of this. "She didn't mention that."

Mallika looked everywhere but at him, as though she'd had a rough day and was just waiting for the bus to go home. After a moment, Mallika turned toward Anita. "This is your order."

Crocker Dawes insinuated himself between Anita and the sill. She reached around him and took the basket.

"I knew your mother when we were both very young," he said. "She cooked for us. There was a group of us here. Building things."

Mallika kept her eyes on the basket, unwilling to engage with Crocker any longer. After taking what she wanted, Anita repositioned the cloth covering. Crocker continued to talk about his first visit to India and how interesting it had been for him and his coworkers.

"Your mother made us feel so welcome, along with all the other villagers, of course." Crocker paused, and his thus far imperviousness to other people's discomfort must have begun to thin because he looked worried as Mallika kept her head down, staring at the ground. She had nothing to say to this, and his disappointment was palpable. "Well, I won't keep you." He stepped away from the window, took the basket from Anita, and placed it on the windowsill. "A pleasure to meet you, Mallika."

She tipped her head to acknowledge the courtesy, reached for the basket, and left. Anita was about to break the awkward silence when she felt a light touch on her arm. She turned to Pohty, who shook his head.

"Well, I'm interfering with your work." Crocker gave a slight bow to Anita and Pohty and took three short steps out of the kitchen.

"I feel so bad for him I could cry." Anita was about to say more when she caught Pohty's skepticism.

"He is with the tour, isn't he?"

"Yes, the Americans."

"Hmm. Don't worry about him. He is a man of good character."

"How do you know that?"

"I listen. I observe." He wiped his cheeks and forehead with a rag, and stuck it back into his waistband. The kitchen was heating up. "Release your sorrow."

"I wish it were that easy, Pohty. He looked so disappointed. Mallika doesn't approve of his seeing her mother again after all these years. At first I thought he . . . I'm ashamed to admit what I thought at first. But he came here especially—"

What exactly did he come here expecting? He was so clear about how happy he'd been here, but surely he knew the past was gone, not to be lived again? Did he not know happiness at home? What did he expect to find here and nowhere else?

* * * * *

Anita opened the parlor windows to the fresh morning air. A small boat with a gaff-rigged sail skimmed along the water a hundred meters from shore, its lone fisherman appearing and disappearing in the rise and fall of the swells. The morning haze softened the outlines of the small craft and the sun breaking through glinted on the wake. Anita watched the boat move south, back to the harbor of the once small fishing village that teetered on the cusp of momentous change, when construction of a deep-water port would begin. But that had been in the planning stages for years, and the village continued to grow into a small city centered around fishing.

The sight of the lone boat soothed Anita after her restless night on the parlor floor. When she looked out on the ocean it seemed calm and easy for sailors, but when she saw the waves rolling into the shore, she felt the pressure behind them, and the crash of water against rock signaled to everyone the ocean's power. The resort might be the most relaxing place on earth for tourists, who saw only the beauty of palm trees, clean sandy beaches, and colorful saris. But the surface is not reality, Anita knew. If Sandra Stover didn't appear by the end of breakfast, Anita would have to notify the police.

"She has not come?" Auntie Meena addressed Anita before she even got all the way through the front door. Anita settled behind the counter and pulled up a stool for her aunt.

"Not come. Not a word to us either." Anita turned to exchange a few words with Mr. and Mrs. Allbret as they headed into the dining room for breakfast. The elderly couple nodded and smiled as one, as though trained as dancers for a performance. They had taken to the resort and now sported discreet shorts and tops in subdued colors. The tropics got to everyone, Anita thought as they shuffled on to the dining room.

"How long can we wait?" Auntie Meena asked. "Madam Stover is frail, is she not? She could have had any sort of accident." She began to twist the end of her sari into a long curl, tightening it as though wringing every drop of water from it. She pulled at it and then shook it out and dabbed at her face. "She is perhaps injured."

"Now, Auntie. We know nothing of the sort." But of course it could be exactly of that sort. She pulled her aunt's hands away from her face. "Go have coffee and rest. I'll attend to this." It was at moments like this that Anita wondered how her aunt had survived for so long, considering all the disappointments fate had strewn in her path. But beneath it all she knew her aunt was strong, and that her strength rose at the oddest but the most needful times. Auntie Meena did as she was bid, and wandered off to the kitchen to order coffee and perhaps one of those peculiar pastries Deepa made so well. Anita watched her go and then leaned on the counter, wondering whom she should call first: police, hospital, hotel security along the Promenade?

The sound of autorickshaws and taxis climbing the hill was the sign of the conclusion of the breakfast hour and the beginning of morning activities. Tourists clustered around autos and taxis negotiating fees and timings before climbing in and driving away. Anita listened to taxis depart, to tourists passing by the hotel window to the path leading to the small beach beyond Hotel Delite, to the guard dog letting out the occasional yelp of invitation to play, and to the first slapping of wet laundry against stone. A woman with jasmine in her hair walked by and Anita momentarily lost herself in the sweet scent from the cascade of white flowers.

A taxi drove down the lane behind a straggling group of bathers and turned into the hotel parking lot. The white car had an insignia on the passenger side door but it was too far away for Anita to read. It must have been important because the day guard, who spent much of his time napping, stroking his gray mustache, or chatting with Joseph, the hotel driver, jumped from his chair and hurried to open the back door for the passenger. Out stepped Sandra Stover.

Anita ran up the steps to greet her and get a better look at the taxi, which wasn't a taxi but a private car belonging to Holy Angels Convent in Trivandrum.

"You are so kind," Sandra said to the driver, a man close to Joseph in age. Joseph seemed to know him because the two exchanged a few quick words before the driver climbed back into the car. Sandra and Anita stepped aside to let the driver back out of the lot.

"Welcome again to Hotel Delite," Anita said, trying to find a way to ask what was none of her business. She decided she didn't need a reason. "We were concerned when you didn't return last night, but I see you are well. Is there any problem I could help you with?"

Sandra wore a light shawl draped over her shoulders, which she pulled close around her. She stopped to study the ocean, now sparkling in the sun. "It is wonderful to be able to appreciate beauty."

Anita motioned to the stairs and indicated that she would follow the guest. Sandra walked down the short stairway and into the hotel slowly but with no real difficulty that Anita could see, leading her to believe that Sandra hadn't been injured in any way. The woman's wig looked still close to perfect, and her clothes were only slightly more worn than the day before. Her skirt looked as if it had been pressed that morning.

"We were very concerned," Anita said again when they reached the reception area. "I even went into your room to make sure you hadn't had an accident." She reached behind the counter and found the key for the guest's room, but she held it in her hand, to prompt Sandra to offer some explanation. "One of the other guests mentioned seeing you at one of the churches."

Sandra's smile faded and she raised the shawl over her head, draping it over and down around her shoulders. "You mean Larry?"

"No, actually, the two hikers who are visiting us."

Sandra smiled and the lines around her eyes softened. "The church at that famous junction, Pala something, is beautiful." In a nanosecond Sandra had morphed from a woman with a secret to a tourist sharing a discovery.

Anita agreed. "Is that where you met the people from Holy Angels Convent?" The convent was not near the church, and yet somehow Sandra had managed to get from the church to a convent at least half a mile away, perhaps farther.

"Yes." Sandra pulled the shawl tighter across her chest and extended her hand for the key. Anita had no choice but to give it to her. At least now she knew the hotel guest with the wig and makeup had been safe in the protection of the convent for part of the time anyway. But what she was doing there was apparently going to remain her secret.

Nineteen

Deepa Nayar tipped the pot until the dhal and water poured into the sieve. She swished the sieve back and forth until the water drained, all the time keeping her back to the door. She could hear her daughter's scooter coming down the lane, and steeled herself for the encounter. After Mallika returned from making her deliveries to Hotel Delite, the young woman seethed with dislike for the American she met, but Deepa refused to be drawn into an argument.

Deepa didn't blame her for her feelings. Mallika was still a little girl when her beloved father died, and grew used to having her mother all to herself. The idea that a stranger, and a foreigner also, should come into her mother's life at this late stage was upsetting. With her husband in the Gulf and Deepa's extended family up in the hills, Mallika's mother was her entire family. But she was a sensible girl, Deepa repeatedly told herself, and would grow to understand.

The blue scooter slowed, gears shifting, as it turned into the compound, the sound growing louder before cutting off. Then came the clicks and thwaps of sandals kicked off and landing on the veranda floor, and the soft slap of her daughter's bare feet inside the house and the brush of cotton cloth along the table. Deepa took a deep breath and exhaled.

Mallika stood up her bag to steady the stack of metal containers. "We must talk, Amma, about that Amrikan."

During the early hours Deepa practiced the conversation she wanted to have, but her initial determination turned into fragile glass, cracking and crinkling under the pressure of her love for her family. She held the bowl of dhal in her hand. "Problems have solutions."

Whenever Mallika looked hard at her, Deepa felt a clutch of love so strong and so deep it hurt. She wanted to avoid the confrontation she knew was inevitable, and hoped that one day her daughter would understand how her life had come to be what it was.

"You sent me with pastries so I would meet this man." She clutched the tote fabric in her hands, twisting the top where the drawstrings pulled tight, and gritted her teeth. Deepa could hear the molars hit each other.

"This one is an old friend, Mallika. A very old friend."

When Mallika understood the point of the errand this morning, an errand she undertook gladly whenever Deepa asked, she found herself face to face with the man she glimpsed a couple of days ago, and heard about from the neighbors, the stranger who came to the house for a meal, in the middle of the day, and lingered long after any normal visit would have concluded. Mallika knew who he must be the minute she saw him in the Hotel Delite kitchen. He didn't behave the way she expected him to, reaching for the basket and picking out one of the delicacies. Instead he began to talk to her.

"Why did I have to meet him? Why did you send me?" Mallika pulled the cloth bag toward her, cradling it against her chest. "He is the one who taught you this foreign cooking."

Deepa nodded. "He and the others. There were four of them."

"I'm glad they left," Mallika said. "We do not need foreigners to build our country."

Deepa laughed, then restrained herself. "They only built latrines, Ammu. We didn't have so much sanitation in those days and they helped us."

"We don't need help. We're a modern nation now."

"Yes, that's mostly true." It was at moments like this that Deepa felt the rift between old and new. Her daughter took such pride in her place in the world as an Indian, a citizen of a free and independent country that had sent a rocket to Mars, had a large army respected worldwide, produced some of the greatest scientists in the world, and was a leader among developing countries. She challenged anything that smacked of patronization and colonialism.

"Back then we had no latrines and we didn't know how to build them," Deepa said. "We had no energy to do so. We were glad to have the help. And some places still don't have them." As a young woman she sat in the doorway with her mother and sisters as her father and the other elders of the village sat on the veranda and discussed at length the virtues of the young foreigners. The foreigners were very young, her father pointed out several times, and how would they know enough? "They were very polite. We appreciated this."

"And now they are everywhere," Mallika said, echoing the complaints of the villagers who had lived in the resort undisturbed for generations, fishing up and down the coast, selling their vegetables at daily markets, and worshipping at the small family shrines that sprawled into little temples open to other villagers. "They wander where there are no lanes."

"Yes." Deepa winced at the truth of this.

"Cousin sister found one in her yard taking photos of the rooster." Mallika's lip curled in disdain.

"And where is the harm? Cousin-sister's husband's brother writes very nice reports of America," Deepa pointed out. "He's making money and just bought a very nice house."

"He doesn't find strangers in his yard chasing his chickens," Mallika said, her body growing tense.

"He doesn't have chickens, Mallika."

"He wants something. But I told him we're moving." She lifted her chin as she held the bag by both hands in front of her, letting it hang down almost to the floor. She was not as tall as her mother, but she had finer, more delicate features, like her father.

"Yes, he wants something." This was the crux of the matter as far as Deepa was concerned. She knew what Crocker Dawes wanted, and she knew what Mallika thought he wanted, but she wasn't as sure that she knew what she, Deepa Nayar, a widow in her late fifties with one daughter and one granddaughter, wanted. "You're moving?" Deepa tried not to smile.

Mallika tried to ignore her mother's question. She'd made up the story to throw the American off balance, but now she looked like a little girl caught in her lie.

Poor Mallika, Deepa thought. She is so proud of her country, so sure of its value and bright future, so confident of her view of the world, that she cannot see the uncertainty that is life, the little moments of promise that peek out between duties and chores and the numbing work of daily life. "Crocker Dawes is an honorable man."

Mallika took a step back. "I don't like him coming to the house."

Deepa understood Mallika's determination to fend off the meddling of outsiders. Both had grown up with freedom, but in her short life Mallika had known a nation moving from strength to strength. At her daughter's age, Deepa had accepted her life of duty and pushed aside thoughts of anything else. But then two years ago she opened her mailbox one afternoon and pulled out the light blue airmail letter. The minute she touched it, before she knew what it was, her fingers tingled and she felt a frisson, as though her body knew before her mind. Perhaps she had not put aside the past; perhaps it only withdrew, biding its time, lingering safe if silent in her shroud of discipline to duty year after year, taking life's joys where she could find them. Perhaps even duty had its limits.

"Tonight I will tell you a story about this foreigner you dislike so much. Then perhaps you will know why I bring him to my house for a meal and call him an honorable man." Deepa turned back to the sink.

Twenty

Hotel Delite slipped into the humming and buzzing of midmorning, as tourists gathered up their things and headed out for the morning or, sometimes, the entire day. Between saying goodbye to the guests and checking schedules, Anita fielded phone calls from other hotels helping tourists find accommodation and even offered the telephone to one unattached woman from Germany trying to find a cheap room for the night. The hikers passed the desk just as the tourist expressed her frustration to Anita, and the two young men offered to help the fellow hiker. The trio went off for coffee with a list of hotels and cheap lodgings and great optimism.

The squeal of the desk chair in the office behind her alerted Anita to Auntie Meena's arrival. The sound of a sputtering motorbike announced Ravi, and the slap-slap of Moonu's feet warned Anita that the upstairs dining room was about to close for the morning.

"All have eaten?" Anita asked when Moonu reached the counter and leaned on it, punctuating his haggard look with a long sigh.

"All are eating but one."

"And which one?" Anita asked.

"Forche sir." Moonu turned to the staircase behind him, just in case he might appear, ready for breakfast.

"Well, if he hasn't come down by now you don't need to wait." Anita knew that was the reason for Moonu's doggy look and sent him back to the kitchen, with a lighter step as he planned the rest of his morning. She then turned her attention to a man coming down the steps from the parking lot to the front door. He was tall for an Indian, wearing belted dark slacks and a white shirt tucked in with black sandals scuffing the sand. His sunglasses were moderately expensive, and she considered his watch ordinary when he rested his hands on the counter. He asked to speak to Angela Deetcher, which he pronounced "Madam Disher."

"I am helping here." Auntie Meena materialized beside Anita and shifted her to the side, pushing her into the tall stool. "I am owner of Hotel Delite, hotel renowned on this fine beach for its excellent services to our guests, whom we regard as family. Family is having great importance. And we are extending all necessary considerations to our guests in making them know they are like family to us. Isn't this so, Anita?" She addressed this question to her niece without ever taking her eyes from the man in front of her.

"Perhaps you are telling Madam Disher I am come." He stepped back from the counter and gave a small bow. Anita found this charming if unexpected.

"I'll tell her." Anita reached for the telephone at the end of the counter but Auntie Meena put out her hand and rested it on Anita's, pushing the receiver into its cradle.

"You are having other duties, Anita." Meena continued to smile, but her attention remained fixed on the man at the counter, as though by keeping her eye on him she could impale him to the spot. She lifted her chin, strained to appear taller, and kept a rigid smile on her face. "Perhaps, sir, you are explaining your business?"

"Can you tell Madam Disher that Tengar Ram has come?" It was clear at least to Anita that the tall man standing there had no intention of being put off by Auntie Meena. But he remained polite and courteous, not slipping into the usual arrogant insistence that accompanied a second request. He was neither obsequious nor aggressive.

"Oh!" Auntie Meena leaned forward, her shoulders still locked in place. "Such an interesting name? What is your native place?"

Anita wondered if Tengar Ram was fooled by Meena's feigned interest but whether he was or not, he pressed his lips together, closed his eyes for a moment, and then answered.

"A small village outside Jaipur. You would not know it." He gave another tiny bow.

"Such a beautiful city, Jaipur, isn't it?"

"Yes, beautiful." He waited.

"And you are having family there? Do they work in the Pink City?" Meena leaned forward eagerly. "We are very backward here in Kerala. We have never had a palace so grand and so beautiful to earn such a name. The Pink City. It makes one think of the fabulous and the wondrous, and of course the gods who guide us. Your family works in the Pink City, yes?"

"I am coming from a small village. We are not working in the Pink City." He made a half-turn toward the telephone sitting on the counter and gave it a long look, but it didn't ring and Anita didn't pick up the handset.

Whatever he was going to say next was lost in the interest of listening to the voices coming down the hall. A look of panic spread over Auntie Meena, but that turned into great relief when Moonu and Sandra Stover came into view.

"You have slept well, Madam Stover?" Auntie Meena was at her most unctuous, and Anita thought she must have lost her mind. She'd already asked the guest this question at least four times since she arrived in a convent car earlier this morning.

"Yes, I was well cared for at the convent." Sandra offered everyone a lazy smile, and Anita thought she did look well rested and at peace.

"I am so very glad," Meena said.

Sandra turned to the man standing at the counter. "I saw you in Trivandrum, didn't I?"

"Yes, madam, I was there."

"I thought so. You were with Angela, weren't you?" Sandra seemed delighted to have made these connections and stood smiling up at him. "Such an interesting talk, wasn't it?"

"Most interesting, Madam. Dr. Rajkumar is well known throughout Asia for his breakthroughs and discoveries. We are all admiring him."

"He must be a wonderful teacher." Sandra tipped her head and smiled. "I did like his analogies between the human body and little machines running amok with disease." She stifled a laugh, pressing her lips together, as though fighting off hysteria.

"I have once studied with him," Tengar Ram said. "He is most humorous in classes as well. Most unusual for our sort of schooling. We are very serious." He looked pretty serious himself, Anita thought.

"I've noticed that, but I suppose there are reasons to take life seriously." Sandra paused to dwell on this thought for a moment. "Have you come to see Angela?"

"Yes, madam."

"Does she know you're here?"

"Not yet, Madam." He gave her a little bow. Again Anita found these expressions of courtesy charming but she imagined he might get quite tired of bowing and nodding, and she would get tired of watching it.

"I'm going upstairs now so I can let her know," Sandra said.

"Most pleased, Madam." Tengar bowed again.

"Not at all necessary, Madam Stover." Auntie Meena looked alarmed, but before she could stop her, Sandra waved away her concerns and headed for the stairs.

"It is so nice to be of use at least once in a while," Sandra said. "I don't know how people can stand going on vacation."

"Sandra!" Larry jumped up from a chair in the parlor and came hurrying toward her. "I've been waiting." Sandra stopped a few feet in front of him, and all three standing at the front desk turned to watch this disjointed meeting.

"Of course you have," Sandra said. "Of course you have." She took another step toward him and reached out to pat his arm.

"I thought we could—"

"Yes, of course. We can do whatever you want to do today." Sandra continued on to the stairs, turning at the bottom so that she was facing the front desk. "You deserve to have what you want too." And with that ambiguous statement she headed up the stairs, one slow step at a time and yet her step didn't sound, at least to Anita, heavy or burdened.

* * * * *

In the late morning quiet, after all the guests had scattered to their destinations—beaches, shopping, museums, late morning coffee or tea, Anita walked to the computer. Auntie Meena sat at the round table scowling at a stack of papers. Ravi managed to take over the registration desk without a single word to either woman, his radar telling him that Auntie Meena was in a dangerous mood. He moved in near silence, even managing to answer the telephone without letting anyone else hear the conversation.

"It cannot be." Auntie Meena muttered on the impossibility of something only she knew, pushing away the papers and staring at corners of the room as though looking for something hidden there.

Anita listened to the ping she'd been expecting and read the email on the screen. Then she read it again. She typed a quick answer, clicked on send, and leaned back in her chair. The more information she gathered about this very peculiar tour group, the more concerned she became, but the tropical sun of Kerala was burning off the mist of confusion, and she didn't like the landscape that was emerging. She pushed away from the computer desk, determined to get some answers before darkness fell again, obscuring all she had glimpsed of the truth.

"I do not believe it for a minute, not for a minute," Auntie Meena said.

Anita gave her aunt a careful look, and then headed for the locked boxes. Hotel Delite maintained a tall metal cabinet of separate locked drawers for guests of this as well as other hotels, where foreigners could stash their cash, tickets, and trinkets from shopping expeditions. The safe deposit boxes had held medications, antique bronze images, pebbles collected on the beach, travel documents, and love letters. Anita would not allow illegal drugs or anything for which there was no receipt, which had to be included with the purchased item. She felt a prude sometimes, but Hotel Delite was her livelihood as well as her home. She didn't want anything to happen to it, not after living through a harrowing experience when Auntie Meena had pledged the hotel for an outrageous sum of money. Anita slipped the key in the lock and turned.

"What are you doing?" Auntie Meena asked.

"When the tour checked into the hotel, Kenneth Maxinter deposited tickets and other travel documents here. We returned the passports but not the other items. Since he is dead, I have both keys, so I don't need to use the master key to enter." Anita pulled out the box.

"We should not have a master key," Meena said.

"And the world should not have thieves and liars," Anita said.

"I don't believe him either."

At that moment it occurred to Anita that her aunt had been carrying on a private conversation, and Anita had no idea what she was talking about. Meena chewed her lower lip as she stared at the table. "What're you talking about, Auntie? You sound upset." Anita rested the box on the table and sat down close to her aunt. "Tell me. Perhaps I can help."

"How can you help? How can anyone help?" Auntie Meena pressed her hands to her face and shook her head. "Am I not giving my poor pathetic heart to these guests?"

Anita settled in her chair, ready to listen to her aunt's lament. She knew almost the entire song by heart and nodded along with the expressions of grief, outrage, despair, and sorrowful disappointment. "And who has brought you to this misery?"

"How can you ask?" Meena sat up and rocked back and forth, like a tower in danger of overbalancing.

"I'm not clear on who has distressed you this time," Anita said. "I want to know."

Meena reached out and patted Anita's cheek. "Of course, you do. You are fairness personified." Meena closed her eyes, took a deep breath and exhaled. "It is that horrible man Tengar Ram." She gave a little shiver.

"He didn't seem horrible."

"He is deceitful."

"How is he deceitful?"

"He is stalking foreign women at intellectual events."

"Really?" Anita frowned, trying to catch up with her aunt. "Ah! You mean the professor who gave a talk in Trivandrum?"

"Exactly!"

"Did you follow her there?"

"Certainly not!" Meena did indignation well, in Anita's view. "I have seen the advertisement for this talk at Jubilee Hall, and Madam Deetcher is telling me she is attending this." Meena began to wring her hands.

"And you thought it sounded like just the kind of thing you'd enjoy."

"You mock me, Anita."

"Did you enjoy the talk?"

"He is a scoundrel preying on unhappy foreign women."

"So, you didn't enjoy the talk."

"How can I enjoy? I worry about my guests."

"So, is that where you first met Mr. Tengar Ram?"

Auntie Meena gasped. "I would not meet such a one."

"Of course not. Still, we must remember, Auntie, Madam Deetcher is an adult and a guest in our country, and even if we think she is acting foolishly by spending time with a young man who is nothing but a stranger, we can only warn her. We cannot stop her. And we cannot insult her by interfering."

"But she is a nice lady," Auntie Meena said.

"Yes, Auntie, she is a nice lady."

* * * * *

Moonu leaned around the corner of the office door and glanced from one woman to the other. When no one shouted at him, he stepped into the room and held out a tray. "Elevenses." He came further in and slid the tray across the table toward Auntie Meena. She reached for it, pulled it to her, and thanked him without looking up to see that he had already escaped the threatening atmosphere of the office.

"What are you doing, Anita?"

Auntie Meena leaned across the table to watch Anita pull papers and envelopes out of the box. She rifled through them and then spread them out on the table. "Interesting, isn't it, that no one has asked for their tickets or other papers. They don't seem to be worried about them at all."

"And why should they be worried?" Auntie Meena sat up just in case her honor had been impugned. She reached for the glass of milky coffee and sipped. "Very good. Moonu is reliable for this."

"Moonu is reliable for everything, Auntie." Anita sometimes thought her aunt avoided saying anything nice about the staff for fear she would be overwhelmed with affection for them. So, she grumbled.

"What have you found?"

"Tickets." Anita opened and glanced through a series of documents. "And travel insurance, it seems." She picked up each ticket a second time and read it through carefully, noting departure and arrival dates and locations.

"How many times are you going to read those tickets?" Meena said when she'd finished her coffee. "If you are not familiar with airport abbreviations, I am having a full listing just there." She nodded to the file sitting on the top of the desk, where she kept scattered bits of information that other people found on the computer but which eluded her whenever she logged on to search for them.

"I had an email this morning from the night manager at the hotel in Athens."

"Oh, very nice," Meena said. "You are establishing international friendships for Hotel Delite. Very nice indeed." She wriggled her shoulders.

"Perhaps, Auntie, but this time he sent interesting news." Anita collected the tickets, bundled them together again, and replaced them in the box. She slid the box back into its slot and locked it. She put away the key in her own locked box.

"Why are you doing that?" Meena asked.

"I think the information in the tickets needs to be managed carefully," Anita said. "Some may want to see it and others may not want it to be seen."

"Anita! I will not allow riddles. You know I am slow and easily confused." Meena was also one to put her foot down when she felt the ground beneath her slipping away, so now she stamped on it, as if holding the earth in place.

"Except when someone's trying to cheat you." Anita grinned and gave her a friendly poke in the arm.

"You mock me." Meena looked ready to cry but also smug at her own astute financial abilities.

"Teasing only." Anita sat down again.

"But you did not tell me why you are reading tickets?"

"The manager in the Athens hotel wanted me to know the authorities now think Georgio didn't die accidentally. They think he was murdered." She glanced at the computer sitting on the desk, and wondered what dark news it would deliver next.

Meena gasped. "Such a horrible thing for a hotel."

"According to the hotel clerk in Athens, another guest, someone not on the tour—a woman—told the police she heard Georgio arguing with someone the night before he was found dead."

"Oh, very sad for her. Very sad."

"But she reported it after the tour had left. He was found on the beach."

"Ah, so not our concern."

"Except that he might have been poisoned." Anita frowned. "Well, it seems he died from an overdose of his medication."

"Oh! Perhaps we should make a point of telling our guests to be most careful with their medications." Meena shifted in her chair, and Anita guessed she was trying to figure out how to do this without prying or meddling, or at least without anyone else thinking she was prying and meddling, which she most definitely was. "Perhaps we can offer to keep them here, in the office, and then we can deliver them as needed."

Anita stared at her aunt, who stopped speaking. Even she seemed to realize this was an absurd idea, impossible to suggest to the guests and even harder to carry out.

"Maybe not," Meena said after a moment.

"One of the guests here overheard an argument in Kenneth Maxinter's room the night before he was found dead," Anita said. "I wonder if there's a connection."

"A connection?" Auntie Meena said. "One is in Athens and the other is in Kerala. How is there a connection?" She placed the empty glasses on the tray and shoved it to the far edge of the table. "And why are you looking at tickets?"

"The police found Georgio's ticket in his room," Anita said.

"Ah! You informed the hotel about our locked boxes. This is a most appreciated service," Auntie Meena said.

"His ticket ended at Athens."

Auntie Meena looked startled, but, as Anita well knew, she would shift her thoughts to something else that made sense rather than puzzle out what such a discovery might mean. Anita waited.

"I think a buffet on Saturday evenings might be a nice addition," Auntie Meena said.

"You asked about the tickets."

Auntie Meena waved away the comment. "Not our concern. We are not to trouble ourselves over someone else's travel plans. Once guests depart, it is not our concern. And they are leaving soon, aren't they?" she asked hopefully.

"Crocker Dawes's ticket ends here, in Trivandrum." Anita brushed her hand across the smooth wood whose oiled sheen had long since been worn away beneath papers, suitcases, spilled coffee and tea, wooden trays, and other things. It was hardly worth thinking about refinishing it; no one had the time for it.

"I accept he is very fond of India." Auntie Meena pleated and unpleated the end of her sari. "It is very nice to have a foreigner know us so well and like us just as much, isn't it?"

Anita agreed, warmly. Despite her aunt's pride in the young nation, whose birth she had missed by a very few years, she harbored the pockets of inferiority that were one part of the legacy of living under the rule of foreigners. She wanted to be liked and approved of by Western tourists, who seemed to know how to do everything and to be undaunted by whatever came along.

"As does my father," Anita pointed out.

Auntie Meena winced. She had never forgiven Anita's father for marrying Meena's older sister and carrying her off to America, after his work in India was done. To this day Auntie Meena was not completely convinced her sister had not been kidnapped. "Yes, well, hmm. You shouldn't tease me, Anita. I am dutiful to your mother."

"And Sandra Stover's ticket ends in Saigon," Anita said.

"Saigon?" Auntie Meena stared at Anita. "Saigon? You are mistaken, yes?"

Anita shook her head. "Angela Deetcher's ticket ends in Sydney, Australia."

"I hear this is a fine place. Perhaps we shall visit one day."

"And Larry Forche's ticket ends in Tokyo." She repeated the name of the city.

"I, yes, I heard." Auntie Meena began reaching for ledgers, eager to bury herself in work.

"No, Auntie, you're not listening to me."

Auntie Meena tisked tisked a few times to dismiss her niece and then lifted the heavy cloth cover of the ledger and rested it on the table. She began turning pages until she came to the day's date.

"I've read the tickets carefully," Anita said.

"Of course you have." Meena peered at the column of figures.

"And no one has a return ticket that ends in the United States."

"Yes, we know this already."

"Except Kenneth Maxinter. He was the only one with a complete round-trip ticket."

Twenty-one

Anita removed the lens cap and slipped it into her pocket as she headed down the lane to her gallery. She'd been neglecting her photography over the last few days in favor of sussing out the secrets of the foreign tourists. So far she had almost nothing except the depressing news that all of them were planning on ending their days in foreign cities where they had once spent a memorable part of their lives.

For a brief few hours Anita had been willing to let the death of Kenneth Maxinter be ruled natural causes, perhaps a heart attack or a stroke. But the discovery of the otalam seeds in the spice mix changed her mind. As she stepped onto the Promenade she saw Larry Forche straight ahead, leaning over a pair of women sitting cross-legged on the ground and selling fruit.

The fruit vendors spread out their brightly colored cloths every morning in hopes of selling bowls of fresh, cut-up fruit to the tourists who wanted a snack but didn't want to leave the beach for a meal. The fruit, purchased that morning, or plucked from the vendor's yard on the way to the beach, was guaranteed fresh. The women kept two buckets of water nearby, to rinse out bowls. But they had turned from steel forks to plastic ones after it became clear that tourists were fastidious about utensils. Larry looked worried as the vendor held up one banana and then another.

"Do you need help?" Anita said as she drew near.

"I just want mango and pineapple," he said. "She keeps opening bananas and showing me." Anita could have covered for the woman by saying she thought he was dissatisfied with each banana, but this was only a ploy to sell more fruit. She jumped in and ordered the woman to make up the bowl of the two fruits Larry had pointed to. The vendor did so after scowling at Anita. With great relief, he reached for the bowl, handed over his rupees, and thanked Anita.

"Which way are you going?" she asked.

He spun around in a circle.

"The steps over here get shade from the guard's umbrella." Anita nodded to a spot a few feet further down the Promenade.

"I missed breakfast," he said as they walked together. He sat on the top step. Anita sat opposite, leaving a lane between them for others using the stairs.

"I think Sandra did also." Anita pulled the edge of her dupatta down over her forehead, and was glad she'd chosen a longer and wider scarf than usual to wear with her salwar set. The sun was rising and growing fierce, and her skin was already darker than her mother liked it to be. It was one of her mother's curiosities: whenever she and Anita spoke on the phone, she urged her daughter to stay out of the sun, even though Anita was light enough to pass for a Kashmiri. "It makes you dark," she said, dropping in the admonition among talk of family weddings, a new civic building, and political matters. Anita adjusted her dupatta.

"Yes," Larry said, not looking up as he worked his way through the chunks of fruit. Halfway through the bowl he stopped eating. "I guess I was hungrier than I realized."

"Understandable."

Larry's head jerked around. "Really?" His mouth twisted into a cynical smile. "I look like a fool, don't I?" He rested the fork in the bowl and watched the waves rushing ashore. The ocean was quiet today, with small breakers that made little noise on the smooth sand, like silk falling in folds across the floor. The water sped inland, leaving dark swales on the beach before slithering away.

Anita didn't know what to say to this insight because she hadn't given him much credit for self-awareness. "No," she said, shaking her head, "you look unhappy and concerned about your friend, Sandra."

He extended his legs down another step and rested the bowl on his now-level thighs. "Thank you for that." He kept his eyes on the bowl but he seemed to be thinking of other things. "Yes, she is a dear friend."

"Does she find this weather uncomfortable?" The question, she knew, could offend him, meant, as it was, to draw him toward the obvious feature of Sandra Stover, her wardrobe of wigs. Every time Anita saw her, she wondered how the woman could stand wearing one in this heat.

Larry picked up the plastic fork and began eating again. "She never complains." He ate more slowly now, savoring each bite. He had adjusted his wardrobe again this morning, wearing a light cotton shirt that looked like it had been made by one of the tailors in the resort, and light khaki shorts. He wore new sandals, perhaps purchased from one of the many vendors plying the beach with their wares.

"I hope the death of your tour guide won't upset your plans. We will of course do everything we can to help. It's a terrible thing to happen in our hotel and we'd like to make things right if we can."

Had she gone too far? He had to guess she was probing, seeking that one chink in the concrete wall that seemed to surround the tour guests.

"I won't miss him if that's what you mean." Larry finished the fruit and rested the fork in the bowl. In a nanosecond a young boy appeared behind him. Anita spoke to him and then looked over her shoulder. She told Larry it was all right to give him the bowl; he was here helping his grandmother. He handed it up with a skeptical look.

"That woman is his grandmother?"

Anita nodded.

"She doesn't look over forty."

"She probably isn't." Anita glanced back at the woman now taking the bowl and dumping it into a soapy bucket.

"The bowl was plastic. I thought I was supposed to just throw it away."

Anita laughed.

"The whole country is like that, isn't it?"

Bemused, Anita tried to grasp what he meant.

"I mean, someone watching you all the time, always knowing what you're doing."

"You make it sound like a police state, and we're nothing like that."

"I didn't mean it that way." He rubbed his hands over his thighs, down to his knees. "Sandra and I stopped for something to drink at one of those little cafes just behind the hotels on the other side our first afternoon. I think it was one of those family-owned places. There are just two tables in front of a one-story house, and the yard has a sapling fence."

"I think I know it," Anita said. "It faces a paved road that runs in front of a four-story hotel, and then climbs up a very steep hill."

"Yes, that's the one." Larry nodded. A curl broke loose and flopped over his forehead, almost covering one eye.

"That's Parvati's Cafe. How did you ever get back there?" Anita hadn't thought of Larry and Sandra as the adventurous types. Few tourists wandered that far away from the beach unless they were staying in the area.

"Sandra wanted to walk," he said, brushing away the curl. "We got thirsty so we went in and the owner chopped open two coconuts for us. Delicious."

"They're very fresh here."

"Sandra mentioned she'd had some little savory donuts at an Indian restaurant in the States and she loved them, so the owner called to his wife and she brought some out." He smiled at the memory. "We decided to go back the next day, and when we got there the table was already set with two coconuts and a plate of those donuts. We didn't even see him watching for us on the lane."

"We like to anticipate the needs of our guests." Anita knew that behavior was the norm in many hotels throughout India, but she had trained the staff not to meet the guests at the door with their favorite cold or hot drink. Such attention could be overwhelming for those used to doing everything for themselves. "Did you enjoy your second visit as much as your first?"

"I thought we did." Larry glanced at her and went back to staring at the beach. "But I must have been wrong. That's when Sandra decided she wanted to go to mass. We went back to the hotel and I'd wanted to change and go with her, but she left without me." Perspiration layered his face, like a thin sheen of gel. He lifted the hem of his shirt and wiped his face, making a circle twice with the fabric.

"You must have been worried when she didn't return. She doesn't seem very well sometimes."

"Sandra's dying." Larry's bald statement, delivered in an ordinary voice, should have shocked Anita, but it didn't. She'd already surmised as much. "I shouldn't tell you that, but she is. You can probably see it for yourself."

"Yes, but still I'm very sorry to hear that." She waited for him to continue but he seemed to feel he'd said enough. "Did Mr. Maxinter know?"

"Oh, he knew all right." Larry rested his head in his hands. "I never should have agreed to this. I just wanted to take care of her."

Her heart ached for him when she saw the pain in his eyes.

"I promised her I could make her final weeks good ones, the two of us together."

"And she wanted to travel?"

"She wanted not to be a burden to anyone. She could never have been a burden to me. Never. Can you imagine what it's like to find the love of your life, your soul mate, as hokey as that sounds, and then find you don't have any time left, either of you? I just wanted to take care of her but she insisted she would make her own end." He shut his eyes. "It was Ken got her into this. All of us. He talked us all into this."

"How do you mean?" Anita said, listening carefully for confirmation of her suspicions.

"Ken set up this trip for people in the support group, so we could go to where we'd been happiest. She signed up for this trip so I signed on too."

"You're all dying, aren't you?"

He blinked several times, then nodded. "Except Ken. The whole idea was to have joy at the end, to experience again the happiest moments of our lives. A stupid, stupid idea." He was venomous now, berating himself for making a decision that was unraveling his life. "Most of the people in the support group didn't go for the idea, or they interpreted it differently. But us, here, we're the ones who wanted to travel overseas."

"Whose idea was it originally, before Ken went to work on it?"

"It was always Ken's and only Ken's." He hunched over and glared at the tourists passing by on the beach below. A man carrying an umbrella came up the stairs, remarked on the awkwardness of the two of them sitting there, and to Anita's surprise Larry swore at him under his breath. The man halted for half a second, then continued on up the stairs.

"The police in Athens think Georgio, a member of your group, didn't die a natural death," Anita said. "Is that possible?"

Larry's shoulders tightened and after a moment he nodded. "Georgio began to change his mind. He had his meds, so his passing would be easy. Everyone has an extra supply to . . . Anyway, he told Angela he was having second thoughts."

"Did that surprise anyone?"

Larry shrugged. "Maybe. It bothered Angela that Ken didn't put Georgio on a plane back to the States, so he could be with what family he had left. I thought Ken was, well, too involved in Georgio's decision-making."

"Did you tell him that?"

Larry shook his head. "I didn't. But Angela did. She made it clear how she felt about Ken's behavior. Manipulative. That's what she called it. They had quite a row on the plane."

"But Georgio didn't get to change his mind. At least, that's what the police think. They're questioning how he died, whether it was accidental, suicide, or something more." She wondered how far she should go with this.

"Really? Ken said Georgio decided to go through with it, because he didn't want to die in pain. He felt so good that for a while he forgot how sick he was. And then he remembered and didn't want to go through what he'd been through before. That's what Ken told us."

"You're all supposed to die in the place where you were happiest," Anita said. "That's why no one has a ticket that returns to the States."

"So you've been checking our tickets." He was neither angry nor surprised.

"A healthy man died in our hotel, Mr. Forche, from taking poison in his food. I have to know who was responsible." Anita leaned forward. "Why would Kenneth Maxinter care if one of the tour members decided he wanted to live?" She felt Larry studying her, sizing her up, wondering if he could tell her everything or nothing.

"They were all afraid they might get sick in a different country instead of where they wanted to die." He opened his clasped hands, studying his palms. "Traveling overseas can be scary if you're not well. So Ken took out insurance policies to cover unexpected medical care before we got to our intended destinations." Larry's face twisted, and he clenched his fists.

"What else was in the policies?" Anita said, guessing the answer.

"A small life insurance payment."

"Made out to Kenneth Maxinter?"

Larry nodded. "Just to cover unexpected expenses, he said." He took a deep breath. "Angela said the whole thing was as good as murder. But we thought Georgio had changed his mind again and meant to go through with it. So we got on the plane in Athens."

"And here you are," Anita said, looking at his fists clenching and unclenching in anger. This man could kill someone with his bare hands. He wouldn't need poison or any other weapon.

* * * * *

Anita didn't try to detain Larry when he stood up, nodded and walked off, back toward the hotel. He marched down the Promenade and veered off along the canal. She waited a minute and then followed him. She caught sight of him as he passed the small shop sitting on the edge of the lane and turned up the hill. She supposed she shouldn't be surprised. After all, many tourists figured out that the intersecting lanes running away from the beach were an easier ascent than the steep paved road running from the beach up to Lighthouse Road. But the vacant lot is also where she found the otalam plant, and of all those in the resort area, this one was closest to Hotel Delite. Anita headed for the shop.

Rajan appeared behind the stacks of sweet biscuits, toothpaste, incense and other items. The boy waggled his head in greeting, his eyes alight with the prospect of a sale. "Did you see the foreigner who just passed here, the one who took the lane just there?"

"Seen." He sat up straighter behind the counter.

"Have you seen him here, on this lane, before?"

Rajan shut his eyes and clamped his lips shut, shaking his head. He was adamant he hadn't seen the man before. "He is not coming to shop. Once he is standing on the edge just there and telling his friend, no, not this way."

"She wanted to come this way?" Anita said.

"She said it's a nice walk, and he said, no, there is an odor."

"Did he point to the canal?"

"The canal stunk that day. She didn't think it was bad."

"What did she look like?"

"Very unusual hair."

"A wig?"

"Nice color but stiff."

How did Larry know the canal had an odor? When on earth had Sandra Stover and Larry Forche ever been apart long enough for either one of them to take a walk along the canal and perhaps even get into the vacant lot and find the otalam fruit?

Anita thanked Rajan, and headed back to the Promenade.

Twenty-two

Anita dropped a matted photo into the bin at the front of the gallery, and stood with her arms akimbo. After a few moments she looked down at Peeru, who seemed to be fussing around the bin on the far side, shifting the photos and trying not to knock the whole thing over.

"What are you doing?" She knew she sounded annoyed but she was so absorbed in her own thoughts that she didn't stop to correct herself.

"The photo, Amma. Upside down and backside to." He peered up at her with a worried look. Anita repeated his reply and then shifted her attention to the bin. When it dawned on her what he was talking about, she laughed and tapped her hand against her cheek.

"I wasn't thinking, Peeru. Of course, we must straighten it out. Thank you for noticing." She began to finger through the photos, found the offending item, and put it back in the correct position.

"Very worried, Amma."

"I have a lot to think about." Indeed, Anita now had much more to think about than she had expected. Her conversation with Larry Forche earlier in the morning had brought a few surprises, and her interview with young clerk Rajan brought more. "I think it's time for coffee." She pulled out a few rupees and handed them over to the boy. "Offer to bring Chinnappa and Kanjappa something as well."

Anita suppressed a smile as Peeru tucked the money into his pants and the accompanying growl from the tailor's shop arrived on cue. She waved off the boy and walked to the edge of the gallery platform and peered into the shop next door.

"You are spoiling him." Chinnappa spoke as he held up a silk blouse to examine a shoulder seam. "You will persuade him he is worthwhile."

"He is, Chinnappa."

"Bah!" He growled some more and spread the blouse on a table. He began to work his needle through the rose silk.

"He helps me gather information and manage the gallery." She didn't have to add that he had once, along with Chinnappa, saved her life right here in the resort. But that was a little while ago and the less said about it, the better.

Across the narrow lane, Kanjappa appeared in the doorway of his tiny bookstore. A young man thin and shy, he added each book to his collection as though it were a newborn relation. He smoothed the wrinkled cover, unfolded dog-eared pages, and fretted over water stains. He reglued pages sliding out, and shook every book to dislodge forgotten notes and currency. He didn't turn on the lights unless a customer was making a sincere effort to locate a book in the windowless interior. When he went off to his other job, the real job in his parents' eyes, he locked the door but left the tall bookshelves on the outside unattended. He counted on Peeru, among others, to keep an eye out for any obvious thieves. Tourists often picked up a book or two and returned later with payment or the book. It was an informal business.

"I heard about the guest dying," Kanjappa said to Anita. "Very sad. Such nice people. Will the tour continue?"

"I think so," Anita said. Peeru appeared at that moment, lifting glasses of mocha-colored coffee out of the wire basket and handing them around. The bookseller took his and sat on the bottom steps of the stairway leading to the shop above his. "You sound like you have met some of the people on the tour."

"One or two are coming," Kanjappa said.

"Did they buy anything?" Anita could imagine Chinnappa behind her rolling his eyes. He had strong opinions on tourists who visited and did not spend money.

"Only one is buying," the bookseller said. "The one with the limp."

Anita's interest was piqued. "Do you remember what she bought?"

"A science book." He had the delicate features of a young man who had yet to fill out the form he would have as an adult. Unlike many other men, he didn't have a mustache, and thus looked even more boyish.

"Do you remember the title? Was it anything to do with botanical matters?"

Again the bookseller shook his head. "No, it was about chemistry." He frowned and rubbed his hand over his chin. He always looked ready to engage in a story or joke or friendly banter. But at this moment he was thinking hard. "I know this book. *Climbing the Limitless Ladder*," he said. "It is an autobiography of our most famous chemist, Professor CNR Rao." He broke into a broad grin, like his usual self. "I have an old copy and madam bought it. A very good sale."

This intrigued Anita. Angela Deetcher found and purchased what was apparently an important title on science. Visitors left all sorts of books behind rather than lug them home or to the next stop on their journey. Perhaps this was a question for Pema; she might remember if she'd seen an unusual book during her cleanings. "Did she look at anything else?"

Kanjappa shook his head. "She said it is for gifting."

"Gifting? She's giving it to someone?" Anita took another sip of her coffee. Two couples in their fifties, probably, in bathing suits with towels and tote bags passed by on their way to the beach.

"Gifting," Kanjappa repeated. "She was walking with a young man and I heard them talking later, after making the purchase."

"That same day?"

"Same day."

"Do you know this man?"

Kanjappa shook his head. "He is not of this place. North, I think, perhaps Rajasthan."

Where Jaipur is located, Anita thought, where Tengar Ram is from. "What did they talk about?"

"He thanked her. He said she is a fine person who is most understanding." This statement pleased Kanjappa and he grinned. "A very nice compliment."

From across the lane came the expected harumph and Chinnappa's cynical mutterings.

* * * * *

Instead of closing for the lunch hour, Anita pulled her chair farther back in the gallery and settled herself in the cool interior. Kanjappa's report left her depressed, and she began to feel almost as gloomy and cynical as Chinnappa sounded. Auntie Meena had been fretting and worrying over Angela Deetcher's involvement with the Indian man Tengar Ram. Even though Anita had tried to downplay the relationship, she was beginning to think she had been wrong and her aunt had been right. Angela had bought him a gift.

Granted, a secondhand book from a small beach bookstore wasn't much of a gift, but it was a token of interest if purchased by a foreign woman and given to an Indian man, a much younger Indian man. Anita tried to push away other thoughts, including the changes in Angela's wardrobe and attitude. Anita's mood darkened without a cloud in the sky to blame it on.

Since the tour had arrived just a few days ago Anita had been consumed with the oddness of their trip, and then with Kenneth Maxinter's death. The whole thing had thrown her off balance, and she had neglected her other obligations. Once she had agreed to compose the photo essay, she had let that fall by the wayside also, and now it was nagging at her as the deadline approached. She had been taking photographs desultorily, thinking in the back of her mind that she had plenty to use in case she came up short on the list of intended ones. She picked up her camera and began to search through the recent shots she'd taken.

"See anything interesting?"

The question came from Crocker Dawes. He jumped up onto the platform, surprising Anita with his agility. She set aside her camera and welcomed him to the gallery.

"I saw the poster for your gallery near the counter in the hotel, so I thought I'd stop in. I've been out walking. It helps me think." He shoved his hands in his pockets, as though to prevent himself from doing any damage to the merchandise, and began a methodical stroll through the space, leaning in close to the photographs hanging on the back wall and placed on easels, and peering into the bins. "Nice work."

"Thank you." Anita waited for the questions to begin, but he kept on peering and walking. If he stopped a little longer to admire any photograph in particular, he winked at Peeru, who trotted behind him, before continuing his circuit.

"Choosing which ones to print next?" He nodded to her camera.

Anita explained the photo essay she was preparing and waited for what she regarded as the inevitable interrogation. She had faced numerous questions, as all artists did, and she longed for an original one. She waited, betting with herself as to which one Crocker would ask: Would it be how did she get into photography, or what were her goals (once someone had asked her that and she'd had no idea how to reply), or what was her inspiration, or what role did the deity play in her work (and it was all she could do not to mention the creation of the world)?

"I think the most beautiful scene I've experienced so far," Crocker said, "was looking up at the hotels late at night and seeing all that light and those palm trees."

Anita had to agree that this was indeed a beautiful scene wherever one stood, on the beach, on a lane, looking down from the top of a hill. The landscape was gorgeous. And, she thought, Crocker Dawes was a man who noticed. She liked that.

"I may be staying in the hotel longer than I originally planned," he said, turning to her. "I have some arrangements to make." He seemed more relaxed, his hands lifting from his pockets as he turned to the nearest photo bin. He flipped through but wasn't really looking at any one in particular.

"After the rest of the tour departs?"

"I hope that won't be a problem," he said.

"Not at all. Do you know where you're going?"

"Not far." He gave her a warm smile, as though she might know what he meant.

And she did.

* * * * *

By late evening, as the restaurants filled up and tourists strolled the Promenade to enjoy the white sheen laid down by the moon, Anita felt buoyant on her way back to Hotel Delite. There were moments when she knew how fortunate she was. Not just lucky, the way some people are, in being able to find the perfect sari at a good price at the last minute before a wedding, or in getting the last two tickets to a special dance performance and discovering the seats are located in the front row. Her good fortune was more than that. She felt it most often when those around her seemed the most troubled, pulled down by the darker feelings lying dormant, waiting for the right moment to spurt up and wreak havoc in the garden of a life.

Anita thought about the aunt who doted on her even if they often disagreed, the happiness in her mother's voice every time they spoke on the telephone, her father's encouragement when she wanted to try something new, all the members of the hotel staff who were more family than employees. And all the little things as well—the calm that embraced her at moments of terror or confusion, and the goat that seemed to find her amusing, its bright yellow eyes watching her, ready to charge.

At the top of the hill a guard pulled shut the large iron gates on the road leading up to the lighthouse. Tourists could visit during the day, following the paths and climbing the steps to the top, where they had a panoramic view of the resort and beyond. It occurred to Anita that such a photograph might be a good addition to the essay she was working on.

Crocker Dawes was enthusiastic about his favorite views, and Anita considered including one or two in the final collection. She had a number that might work, and if none met her demands, she could take more. She still had time. In her mind she began listing the shots she wanted to add to the three or four already selected. Crocker had a good eye, she'd concluded after listening to him describe scenes from his visit here. She made a note in her mobile, and tapped off.

Anita spotted Auntie Meena sitting at the reception desk as she came down the steps to the front door.

"You look tired, Auntie. You should retire and I'll take over."

Auntie Meena shifted on the stool and gazed around the hall. "Rest will not ease my soul."

"Oooh! Why so glum, Meenavelayamma." Anita stepped closer, offering her soothing words. Always traditional, Meena missed the older practices, including the traditional form of address for the mother's younger sister. But this evening it did nothing to lift her spirits.

"You are a good girl," Auntie Meena said. "A good girl."

"What's gone wrong?"

"What has gone right?"

"Ah, now you're toying."

"Toying? I offer perfect accommodations for single women and yet karma hounds me." Meena made a great effort to climb off the stool, as though the entire world was shifting on its axis.

"It's Madam Deetcher, isn't it?" Anita sighed, blowing out her lips. Her good mood vanished. "Let her have her fun, Auntie." She leaned forward to whisper in Malayalam, just in case a guest wandered near and understood. "It cannot last." Anita had to wonder, as she said this, if Auntie Meena understood what it meant to be on this tour, that Angela's time was limited, and she probably knew how long she had.

"You think she is dying?" Meena lifted her pallu, the end of her sari, to cover her mouth as she spoke. She glanced back, as though delivering a government secret. Anita felt like they were two women playing spies in a bad movie. "Not so, Anita, not so."

"No?"

Meena shook her head. "Today she went to the travel agent." She nodded to the open doorway, but Anita knew what she meant. "She booked a ticket for the States."

"Really?" Anita sat down on the stool with a thump. "But that's wonderful news, isn't it? It has to be good news." She tried to think through what this could mean—a change in her diagnosis, a new treatment possibility, a desire to live as long as she could at home with her companions and family. Anita was delighted at the possibility of Angela having new prospects.

"You are naive, Anita."

"Why can't you be happy for her, Auntie?"

"She is booking two tickets." Meena pulled her pallu tight around her, and her face paled. "Two. Think of it, Anita. Two tickets."

"Why a second ticket?"

"I asked the agent. Hamid Ali is just there." Meena liked Hamid. He was another young man making his way in the world who seemed to be in need of a mother, though he had a mother and aunts and sisters and nieces and was probably in need of having no relatives at all, at least once in a while.

"What did Hamid say?" Anita didn't think her aunt could look any worse but as the seconds passed her expression grew sadder and more miserable.

"He is politeness itself," Meena said. "He said Madam Deetcher and her friend, a young man, booked tickets and our guest is paying. The young man has a passport and Madam Deetcher is taking him to apply for a visa. They are flying to Chennai in four days time."

"Angela Deetcher is taking Tengar Ram to the States?" Anita could hardly believe this.

"What will become of her?" Meena began to sniffle and her lips trembled.

This was a good question, Anita thought, but perhaps not the right one. "I think we should be worrying about what will become of Tengar Ram. Angela Deetcher is American. She knows what to do if she has difficulties. But Tengar Ram is a poor boy from a poor village who will be lost in America if his patron abandons him. I'd be just as worried for him as for Madam Deetcher." Indeed, thought Anita, it was hard to decide which one to be more concerned about.

Twenty-three

Deepa refused to look at her daughter. In her view, Mallika had behaved badly, but the girl would never see it that way. She had sulked through the meal Deepa had prepared, clattered tin plates in the sink, and been short with Uma. When Crocker Dawes asked her in his quiet voice to explain her feelings, she spun around and glared at him. And so it began.

Again and again she repeated her insistence that her mother had greater obligations and no one in the family would let a foreigner take advantage of her. Deepa cringed when her daughter began sounding so hide-bound, a caricature of a young woman proud of her heritage.

His question to her signaled her opportunity to deliver a harangue she must have practiced for days. She sputtered and vented, inching her way forward until she was almost nose to nose with the foreigner, backing him up against the wall. He stared down at her, frowning and listening, but never answering. Uma rested her chin on the kitchen table, her eyes filling with tears of fear and confusion, her little fingers holding onto the edge. Deepa rested a hand on the little girl's head, smoothing out her hair, while the harangue went on, into the evening.

It was late. Mallika should have left for home an hour ago. But she wouldn't give in, wouldn't relent. Deepa called her name one more time, sharp.

“That's enough, Mallika.” Deepa stepped forward, forcing her daughter to return to her place by the table.

"I must go." Mallika swung around to face her mother. "We have a good man like Bhadar watching over our place here and you disregard him."

Deepa stopped her before she could get revved up again. "You must go now or you will have to stay all night." She hustled Uma off her chair and out to the yard. Mallika followed. She rested her bag on the scooter, and lifted her helmet. Deepa looked up at the tube light, already gone out. One more frustration. There were moments when the expected unreliability didn't make it any easier to tolerate, and she wished that once, just once, ordinary features of modern life would be reliable and safe and not disruptive. She glared at the dark lamp and turned to her daughter, but a shout called her back.

From the end of the lane she heard another shout, and then another. Both Crocker and Deepa hurried to the compound wall and looked over. In the dim evening light a man waved a stick at something on the ground.

"I knew it was you! I knew it! Troublemaker! Eater of snake entrails and excrement! Son of a sick goat!" The speaker rushed into the lane. Hunched over, his limbs flailing, he kicked at a figure crumpled at his feet. The man on the ground curled up tight, his hands protecting his head, as the angry man kicked him again and again, shoving him forward and thrashing him with the stick.

"That's Bhadar!" Deepa rose on her toes to see better.

"You think I am stupid? A fool? An imbecile? You eater of old food, food taken from the trash bin!" The man brought the stick down again on Bhadar's back as he tried to get to his feet and scramble away, a giant crab skittering across the lane, running this way and that, trying to escape the bamboo switch. The man lunged after him, bringing the stick down on his back, his head, his legs. "You think I don't know what you do with those lights? You think you can sneak around in the dark?"

Deepa hurried back to the veranda, flicked a switch, and flooded the compound with light. A man in the house opposite did the same, lighting up the area between them. The speaker chased Bhadar from side to side, giving him no rest as he rammed into compound walls. Men and women came out to see the commotion, flicking on the lights for their homes and illuminating Bhadar's stumbling, sprawling flight. When the two had reached the end of the lane where it intersected with another, the speaker raised the switch one last time, brought it down so hard everyone on the lane heard the crack. He followed this up with a curse on Bhadar and his entire family for the next ten generations. He spit on Bhadar. And then he pulled the sandal from his left foot and slapped the man on the head, back and forth, cursing and swearing and condemning him to eternal life as a rock, to be smashed to bits and ground into macadam and driven over for all his days by trucks and cows and elephants and smothered under dung. In his final words he barred the self-appointed guardian of the street from ever appearing on this lane again.

Bhadar disappeared around the corner. The neighbors watched the man march back to his home, slam shut the gate and then his front door. The neighbors glanced at each other, absorbing the many satisfying details of the humiliation of the self-appointed guard who had been a thorn under their feet for weeks, before returning to their homes and shutting off the lights.

"What was that?" Crocker asked Deepa, who was trying not to laugh.

"The homeowner has a young wife." Deepa cocked an eyebrow and looked down the lane again.

"He's not going to hurt her, is he?"

Deepa almost laughed. "No, I think not. She's foolish but I doubt Bhadar got more than a flirty smile. Her husband's anger is spent on Bhadar. But the husband has relatives in the hills. I think he'll send her to live there for a while." She grew serious, and sighed. "For a long time I have wondered why only our lane has so much trouble with the lights."

Deepa glanced at Mallika, but her daughter didn't look at her, and Deepa understood she was not yet ready to admit her shame at siding with one such as Bhadar.

"It's late," Crocker said. "I'm getting you a taxi, Mallika. The driver can put the scooter in the trunk." And with that, Crocker Dawes marched down the lane, his head back, his long legs stretching out and his arms swinging. Deepa stepped into the lane, ostensibly to watch for the taxi, but then she swung around to her daughter.

"That's how he walked into the village," Deepa said. "We came out of our houses to see him. He walked the miles from the bus station with a backpack. We thought he looked funny, the way he tipped his head back as though he had to peer over his nose. He's myopic, you know." She smiled at his retreating figure.

Twenty-four

The computer pinged and Anita slipped off the stool to check the hotel email. There were times when she felt like a dog on a leash, yanked here and yanked there and ordered about like a toy robot taking direction from a machine. Really, she thought, the things we humans do to ourselves. She glared at the computer and then sat down at the desk.

"Do not answer it, Anita." Auntie Meena sounded so tired that Anita lifted her hands from the keyboard and turned to her. "You know it is only bad news. What other news is there for us? Hotel Delite is cursed." She took her new favorite position, slouched in a chair staring at the table.

"We're not cursed, Auntie." Anita reached across to pat her arm. "We've survived worse." She did not mention the time her aunt had pledged the entire hotel to raise money for her reckless daughter, or the time a slew of guests decided to go on strike in favor of higher wages for hotel employees up and down the beach. The entire resort had been thrown into a tizzy with protesting tourists and staff until the guests couldn't get breakfast or a cold drink. Anita tried not to think about it.

"Am I not a good Hindu? Do I not make my ablutions faithfully?" Auntie Meena sank deeper in her chair.

"But Auntie, this tour group is a small matter and it will pass."

"Small matter?" Meena sat up and stared at her niece.

"Consider it a storm passing through. It's messy and loud and upsetting but it's not permanent." Anita returned to the computer and hoped she was right. She clicked on the email and read the few messages. "But it is a peculiar storm anyway."

Auntie Meena groaned. "More bad news, isn't it?"

"I'm not sure." Anita reread the email as Meena came to stand behind her.

"Who is this man who is writing to you?" Meena sniffed. "I do not approve, Anita. Your mother would not want you to have such correspondence with strange men. Not good, Anita, not good. You must promise me not to have this relationship."

Anita swung around to look at her aunt. "He's the hotel manager in Athens who's been helping us with information, Auntie. He's a professional friend, a colleague."

"Oh." Meena pinched her face to help her think harder about this. "Well, I suppose this is acceptable. But you are not to talk about other matters."

Anita smiled. "Promise, Auntie."

"What has he written?" Once she had overcome her scruples, Meena gave in to her curiosity. "Is it news?"

"It is indeed." Anita leaned back in her chair while Auntie Meena reread the email.

"Another ticket?"

"Another ticket. Larry Forche bought another ticket, from Tokyo to Los Angeles while he was in Greece," Anita said. And he kept that with him, she thought, instead of asking to put it with the others, in the safe deposit box. "So he at least plans to go home to America."

"But you have the tickets here," Meena said.

"Apparently I don't have all of them." Anita typed a quick reply to the manager and signed off. "But perhaps I can find out."

"Find out what?"

"Find out if I have all the travel information for our tour guests," Anita said.

"What does it matter?" Auntie Meena sat down again. "They are leaving soon and I am very glad. It is a bad thing to say, but I am glad. I am willing to love these guests because they are from the same country where your mother lives and I do not want anyone to think ill of her because I do not welcome them here to her native place. But I do not want them to stay. It is ungenerous of me but it is the truth." Auntie Meena continued in this vein, paying no attention to Anita watching her with a curious smile. Then, Anita turned around and began typing. "What are you doing, Anita? You are not telling my sister all of this, are you? I do not want her to know how much trouble I have here. She will think I am not capable and I am always assuring her I am most capable. Most capable."

"And indeed you are, Auntie. Indeed you are." Anita continued typing and hit send. "I'm asking Hamid something because he's the one who works with our guests most often." She turned around to Meena. "And he writes to people in the States late at night, so I can ask him questions at this hour and he'll answer if he can."

Anita continued to reassure her aunt until she was rewarded with a high ping. She spun around to her computer and read the email from Hamid. "Ah," she said. "As I suspected."

"What have you suspected? More trouble?" Auntie Meena shut her eyes and clapped her hands over her face. "It is too much for me."

"Another guest has changed a ticket," Anita said. "Hamid won't tell me who it is, but he says yes, another guest at Hotel Delite has changed a ticket." Anita read the email again, a second time. "He doesn't say and he doesn't hint, but I think I can guess which guest it is." She typed a quick thank you and logged off.

* * * * *

Anita sent her aunt to bed with the assurance that all would be well. She couldn't have said why she felt that way, but her aunt needed peace of mind in order to sleep, and right now Anita had little to offer in the way of optimistic predictions. A man lay dead, with evidence of murder and a slew of suspects, and little to point to any one of them. The police might be slow in responding to Dr. Premod's report but they would respond eventually, and Anita wanted to be ready. Nothing would be worse than having the hotel shut down for a murder investigation.

Anita checked the keys, noted that all the guests had returned, and locked up the office. She could hear Sanjay spreading out his mat in the parlor and the dog out in the compound chasing a cat or chipmunk or some other creature doomed to be his preoccupation for the night. He had once harassed a crow until it turned on him, and since then had left the birds mostly alone.

"This." Sanjay plunked a small plastic phone case on the counter and returned to his mat. Anita reached for it, turned it over, but found no name or label on it. She opened the case and punched on the cell phone. Immediately, without requiring a password, a number of photos floated up in rows across the screen.

After a moment she recognized the setting. This was the island in the lagoon just to the north, connected by a footbridge to the mainland. Tour guides led tourists down narrow paths between houses. Here tourists could watch coir fiber from coconuts being woven into rope, and exchange a few words with the children playing in yards or helping their mothers preparing a meal. Feeling only a little guilty, Anita scrolled through the pictures. She'd spent time there herself, taking photos and enjoying the quiet. Even though an expanded road brought traffic within sight of the footbridge at one end of the island, it was quiet as soon as one moved out of sight of the highway.

"Someone will miss this." Anita tried to guess who most likely owned the phone and settled on Larry Forche. She would begin with his room. He had spoken about a visit he and Sandra Stover had made to a small village near the water on their first day.

At the top of the stairs, on the second floor, Anita took a last look at the photos. She paused to enlarge one near the end. She studied it for so long that she failed to hear a door open and footsteps approach.

"I'm glad you find that so interesting." Larry reached out and snatched the phone.

"I'm so sorry." Anita waited for some response. "I thought it might have identifying information but those very nice photographs came up."

"I got the phone at the last minute, sort of as a backup." He turned off the phone and slipped it into his pocket.

"I was just getting ready to go from room to room, to ask who might have left it downstairs." She was used to the reaction of foreign tourists who recovered a lost object, the relief at regaining possession or the surprise at being proved right—that the object was nearby. But Larry's response wasn't quite like that. "Sanjay found it in the parlor and brought it to the desk. The photos are lovely."

Larry's expression softened as he pulled out the phone and held it in his palm. "Thanks. It was the nicest visit."

"That was your first day, wasn't it?"

"The day we got in," he said. "Sandra didn't want to rest. She wanted to get out and see everything she could. I thought she'd be tired after the flight."

"How did you pick that part of the area?" Anita had not been surprised at first that guests from Hotel Delite found themselves touring the little island. After all, Hotel Delite was a budget hotel, and its guests rarely opted for the expensive elephant rides or private car tours of the city. But it usually took a few days before someone managed to persuade them to enjoy a boat ride on the lagoon and a stop on the island. Yet Sandra and Larry found this modest tour on the first day.

"Sandra wanted to see the countryside so she could—" He stopped. "She thought all the time about what her students would like."

"That's right; she's a schoolteacher, isn't she?" Anita recalled the documents each guest had to fill out on arrival. Many of the guests were writers, journalists, poets, and the police gave them little notice. But the constable who had arrived and viewed the passports and applications for this tour group had remarked on the occupations. Perhaps, he said to Anita, the schoolteacher will find good things to say about us to her students and they will learn about India as a free country.

"That's not how she started out," he said. "She wanted to be a scientist." He sounded bitter, as though her disappointments were his as well.

Anita glanced at the phone still resting in his palm.

"Thanks for finding this." Larry again slipped the phone into his pocket. "Good night."

* * * * *

Anita left the hotel in Sanjay's capable hands for the night and returned to her suite over the garage. Whenever she shut the door behind her, she felt she'd entered another world, one of her own making, offering solitude, comfort, and sanity.

The brightly printed curtains billowed into the room, tossed about by the light evening breeze and beckoning her to the balcony. Far out on the horizon the fishing boats lined up, their kerosene lanterns enticing fish to the surface, and the fishermen's nets. She leaned on the parapet and gazed down at the black guard dog sniffing along the picket fence, pawing the ground, and then trotting farther down the terrace. The animal entertained himself for most of the night in the guise of protecting the property. Rarely did she hear him bark.

Anita pulled out the chair and settled at her desk. She had meant to crawl into bed and let sleep lull her into calm, anything so she didn't have to think about the body of Kenneth Maxinter curled up in a final anguish on the bed, the members of the tour scattering themselves across the globe in answer to their terminal diagnoses, and the otalam seeds that could have killed Ravi and herself. Sometimes the extent to which luck, or fate, played a role frightened her. It seemed to remove any chance for good intentions or hard work to affect ordinary events.

She popped the photo card out of her camera and began the process of transferring the images to her computer. She had expected to be finished with the photo essay days ago but the death of the hotel guest couldn't be ignored and now she was so far behind that she wondered if she should reschedule. She named the file folder and opened the first image.

Crocker Dawes had mentioned the experiences and moments that struck him, and Anita thought that would be a good start. If something captured the attention of one tourist, the image was worth considering. She recalled his list and clicked through the images in her file, looking for some that might fit his description. But even as she did so, she heard that little voice in her head telling her she was veering off track. When did she let other people tell her what photos to highlight? After all, Crocker Dawes wasn't a gallery director or another artist known for his brilliant eye, someone who could have an impact on her career.

Anita put her feelings down to being tired and continued searching.

The first image captured a procession of devotees carrying a murti of Balabhadra Kali, and Anita stopped for a wistful moment before clicking to the next one. This picture caught the light from numerous hotels sparkling on the water, and she remembered where she was standing when she took it. Unfortunately, it wasn't nearly as captivating as the lived experience, and she closed it down.

The next series of photos were taken from a spot on the beach late in the evening, when the waves lapping on the sand sounded like a secret being shared. It was that moment between late evening and night, between the rough and tumble daytime waves calling the adventuresome into the sea, and the quiet, stealthy waves that slithered forward in the night that made her think of the ocean as a creature that well hid its true, mercurial nature. She clicked on the first in the series and was surprised to see Sanjay in the doorway to the kitchen. He was holding out his hand to the dog. It had to be after eleven o'clock, she estimated, and Sanjay was sharing a treat with the animal.

The next one in the series captured light spilling out from open doorways onto balconies. From her position on the beach the windows seemed to billow outward with light. She felt a glow low in her midriff, a sign she had come upon something to pay attention to. She enlarged the shot. This one was special. She could feel it.

In the hope of finding another one with a different angle that balanced the two upper windows, Anita opened the next picture, taken at the same time at the same place but from a slightly different angle. Here again, the light billowed outward, carving out space in the darkness, and the distance between windows was perfect. Perfect. Except for one problem. It looked like a shadow had fallen on the curtain, one that hadn't been there in the previous image. Anita enlarged the shot.

The scene grew grainier as it increased in size, but her first guess had been correct. A shadow from someone in the room had fallen into the light, a slight imperfection that ruined it for her. She clicked out of this one and tried two more shots. The shadow grew clearer in the next two but disappeared in the last one. She went back to the first one and clicked through the five pictures of the night scene. But by the last one Anita was no longer interested in erasing the shadow.

She slipped the photo card back into her camera and brought up the images, checking the dates. She had taken this series of the hotel rooms on the night after the tour group's arrival from Greece. This was the night Kenneth Maxinter had eaten the otalam seeds and died.

Anita walked out onto the balcony and looked across the parking lot to the hotel. From this angle she could see the edge of one balcony and the light falling onto the terrace from the rooms beyond, but she could not see anyone standing on a balcony. She had asked the guests if anyone had argued with the dead man in his room, but each one insisted that he or she had not. Even though Larry heard voices that sounded like an argument, no one had admitted to being in the room. Anita had wondered at the time if the victim was listening to a radio program or playing a CD. But she had her answer now. She returned to the computer.

With the help of her software, Anita enhanced the image again and again until she could make out details. She moved in closer until her nose was almost touching the screen. She could make out the hair and a profile and a tilt of the head as though the person were looking up at someone who was taller. It seemed to be clear to her who this was, and yet she found it hard to believe. Why this one?

There was no obvious answer to that question, and she knew it. But she also knew she had almost all she needed to confront a murderer. Almost. And she'd get the rest tomorrow.

Twenty-five

Anita slept fitfully through the night, waking and sleeping, sore from alternately sprawling and curling up on the settee. Exhausted from staring at the computer screen late into the night and too tired to undress and crawl into bed, she'd collapsed on the settee and promised herself she'd nap just for a moment. She left photographs strewn on the floor, the computer dark and humming, the door to the balcony ajar. But if she hadn't worked at the computer until forced to give in to weariness, she might not have heard the soft rustling just outside. Anita sat up, listened and padded to the door, pulling it open.

The reflected light from a streetlamp caught the look of surprise on Deepa Nayar's face as she jumped back against the stair railing, embarrassed. Anita took a step onto the landing and stubbed her toe on a basket.

"What's this?"

Deepa managed an embarrassed smile. "A gift for you."

Anita stepped back to get a better look at the flat-bottomed basket covered with a folded-over kitchen towel and a stick placed across the top, to keep off crows. She picked up the basket and lifted a corner of the towel and gave a little gasp of delight. "Modakams. These are modakams." She looked at Deepa in wonder. "You just made these?"

"Prasadam, for you, Anita Missi."

In the world of Indian families, Deepa was old enough to be Anita's mother, but their positions in the world were very different, not only as employee and employer but also less and more educated, family caste, and more. Hence, Deepa could address Anita as Missi, as if she were a young girl of status, and

Anita could use the familiar form of address, but Anita was careful how she spoke to people. She wasn't comfortable addressing those considered her inferiors with such terms, but now, in surprise, she used the familiar address with Deepa, more as a marker of friendship than status.

"What have I done to deserve this?" Anita held the basket closer to her face and inhaled the fragrance of the freshly steamed sweets. In this part of India people made the steamed dumplings with sweet fillings on Vinayaka Chaturthi, Ganapati's special day, in the month of Chingam. But that was months ago, in August-September.

"This last evening was Sankasthti Chaturthi Puja," Deepa said.

"Oh, so it was." Anita tried to think why that mattered. Her face cleared as she worked it out. "The tour group arrived five days ago now, on the first day after the full moon day, and yesterday was the fourth day. And you made these for the puja after moonrise, in the evening." Anita's face lit up with warmth and understanding. "You fasted all day?"

"And I made the offerings to Ganesha, and I offered thanks to those who have been his servant in aiding me."

Anita shifted her gaze from the modakams to Deepa and back again. Deepa relaxed against the railing long in need of a coat of paint and a plaster patch here and there. She was a woman without sentimentality or a remnant of girlishness, a woman who'd faced how hard life could be and loved it anyway, a woman who never expected anything but hardship and saw no reason to complain.

"You've made a decision, haven't you?" Anita said.

"Yes, my decision is made. I've spoken with my daughter, and she has spoken with her husband in the Gulf. There is no need for more discussion."

Anita could just imagine the conversations. Deepa was embarking on a path untrod in her experience and in the experience of everyone else she knew. She could be leaving behind her entire world, or expanding it to something better than she ever expected. Neither she nor her family would know until it was too late to turn back. "I'm very happy for you."

"It will be a happiness shorter than one would want, but longer than I expected." Deepa let her hand fall to her sari, which was the sari of the Nayar lady, white with a red border and a matching blouse, or choli. She wasn't wearing her usual work sari. She arranged the pleats falling over her leg, her left foot resting on a lower step. "But hope is there." She stood up, like a soldier called to arms, lifted her chin and peered at Anita. "Hope is there and many fine medical people are there also." She pressed her lips together, firm in her convictions. "Time is also there. Happiness in the time."

"Things have moved swiftly," Anita said, lowering the basket.

"But properly." Deepa adjusted the cloth on the basket. "The first letter from my old friend brought great confusion but also forgotten warmth. The letter was full of questions, but I answered them and agreed to meet, and Ganesha has aided me. And now, for the last step we take, again I seek the aid of Ganesha, and I am grateful." The two women gazed at each other, and then Deepa nodded and hurried down the steps. Anita held the basket of modakams, the sweet dumplings known to be Ganesha's favorites, tight against her waist.

Twenty-six

Once awakened by Deepa, Anita resigned herself to an early morning in the hotel and a long day managing guests. She began with the two hikers, who were ready to check out. She handed over the sheaf of bills, meal and laundry chits stapled to the room chits, and left the two Australians to review each one. They moved to the corner of the counter and began thumbing through each piece of paper, muttering while Anita turned her attention elsewhere. She had been so focused on the curious behavior of the American tour group that she had given almost no thought to the other guests. Fortunately, the other guests didn't seem to want any attention. The young Dutch couple with their child, in room three, had checked out and two Spanish women had checked in.

Mr. and Mrs. Allbret strolled past on their way to the dining room for breakfast, nodding and smiling to Anita. Anita could hear her aunt greeting them in the doorway and ushering them to their favorite table.

"It is so much higher than we expected," Gene said, the taller of the two.

"It's the taxes." Anita pulled the stack of bills toward her and began reviewing them.

"But there are taxes on taxes," Ron said.

Anita shrugged, as if to say, I don't write the laws, I just live with them.

"Is there perhaps a student reduction?" Ron squinted at her, and the distress in his eyes seemed painfully real to Anita. She felt sorry for them. Hotel Delite was hardly the most expensive hotel on the beach, and the two young men had not indulged in any additional expenses. They'd been careful with their money, taking the bus or walking, buying food for a picnic rather than eating in restaurants, and tipping modestly whenever they received a service. She glanced over her shoulder, as though Auntie Meena might be there watching her.

"Let me take another look." She withdrew into the office and began toying with a calculator. The hotel had lost money with the empty rooms reserved for the tour group, but Gene had stopped her from making a fatal mistake. He was the one who had noticed the seeds in the spices that she had collected from Kenneth Maxinter's room, and would have eaten if he hadn't come along and stopped her. That should count for something, shouldn't it? Anita made a few changes in the master billing and returned to the front desk.

"Perhaps this is better," she said, handing over the bill.

Gene and Ron read the cover sheet and both blinked. They stumbled over each other in their eagerness to pull out their wallets and pay before Anita could change her mind. She took their money, stamped their bills paid in full, and dated them.

"I hope you'll continue your botanical studies," Anita said.

"I didn't expect to get so much encouragement here," Gene said. "Meeting Sandra was great."

Anita counted out the change. "I didn't realize you'd had a chance to talk with her. When was this?"

"When she came out of the church, the other night," Ron said. "We walked with her to the convent. It was already getting dark and she was worried about walking alone."

"She'd heard all the warnings about women going out alone even before eight o'clock," Gene added. "We offered to walk her down. None of us realized how far it was."

"But it seemed to really matter to her," Ron said. "I thought she could visit the convent another time, but she insisted. She wanted to see someone there, but it was a good thing as it turned out."

"I didn't realize," Anita said. "And she told you something about Indian plants?"

"Gene was showing off," Ron said, "talking about the plants hanging over the wall of the Ganapati Temple. That's how we found out she had started life as a botanist. But then she started teaching grade school to support herself while she finished her graduate degree and after that, well, I guess in the States it's hard to make the switch from one school system to another." Ron shrugged.

"So she'd studied Indian plants," Anita said. "That's very rare here, to have a tourist who knows so much."

"She knew a little about poisonous plants because, she said, people grow them as garden plants. You know, flowers for the table, and all that." Ron leaned on his elbow, enjoying the conversation. "She said most people in the States have enough poisonous plants in their gardens to kill off the entire town they live in." He hooted at the thought.

"Otalam is related to oleander," Gene said, still happy to show off a little of what he'd learned. "She said it's dangerous for foreigners because it looks like the mangos you see hanging on trees in people's gardens. Except it's a lot smaller."

"Yes, it is smaller and deadly," Anita said.

"She gave me some good ideas for what to work on," Gene said. "A lucky encounter."

"Yes," Anita said. "A lucky encounter."

"It's been an awesome trip," Ron said.

She finished making change and slid the bills across the counter. "I hope you'll return to Hotel Delite someday," she said, and meant it.

* * * * *

The main office of Hotel Delite grew quieter as Anita pushed the door until it almost closed. She could hear voices passing by but the speakers sounded distant enough that she could avoid being drawn into conversation. Ravi had taken his place at the desk and begun his daily duties of charming everyone, sometimes even Auntie Meena. Not for the first time Anita thanked her lucky stars for Ravi's arrival some years ago, a neatly typed resume in his black plastic brief case and his lips trembling with a nervous smile.

Anita checked the convent's telephone number and punched it in. A quiet but firm voice answered, with that tone of suspicion and warning to anyone whose call might be a waste of her time. Anita asked to speak to an assistant in the main office.

In the background she could hear the occasional whoop of students in a nearby classroom as they settled in for the morning.

"Oh, Anita Chechi!" The cheerful voice greeted her. "Very busy now, but ready to be of assistance." Sophia Jacobs was a few years younger than Anita but far more settled in her life. She had grown up in the Vanchiyoor neighborhood of Trivandrum, attended Holy Angels Convent School and the University of Kerala, and married into a family that also lived in the area. She and Anita often chatted about goings-on in the city.

Just last year a crisis at the resort had driven away a number of guests late in the season, and rather than cancel reservations outright, Anita had tried to find them alternative accommodations. To her relief, the convent offered to take in two of her guests, two young Danish women traveling through Asia. The women accepted the offer, and everyone was happy. This was something of a thank-you for the rescue of a visiting cleric who'd been locked out of his hotel when the roof began to leak in the northwest monsoon. Hotel Delite offered him a room at reduced rates, and he was profuse in his thanks.

"You had an overnight guest just this past week," Anita said.

"Oh, yes," Sophia said. "I arranged a car for her in the morning. Such a surprise to come into the office and there she is." Sophia's laugh tinkled through the phone.

"Did she rest well?" Anita asked.

"I think so." Sophia paused to speak to someone else in the room. "She told me she is leaving well rested and restored in body and soul."

"I'm glad to hear it."

"Father Paul Mar blessed her as she was leaving."

"A blessing? Of course." Anita paused to consider this. "Is he there every day now?"

"No, no," Sophia said. "Only on the Wednesday he gives mass and then in the morning next day he stops for a brief consultation with this office. And then he is gone." Papers began to rustle on the desk and Sophia's voice grew cooler, reminding Anita that the day's business was under way and Sophia had things to do. Anita thanked her and punched off.

Out at the registration desk someone laughed, a newspaper slapped down onto the counter, and feet scuffed out the door. The day's activities had begun. Anita pushed back her chair and stood up. By now Dr. Premod was sure to have passed on her report to the police, and the report had been sent through channels. It wouldn't be long before someone showed an interest in the guests of Hotel Delite. It was time for Anita to take the next and last step.

* * * * *

Anita emerged from the office planning what she would say to the tour members only to find the hall blocked by Auntie Meena pacing back and forth. She looked both frantic and determined, her lips pressed together, clasping and unclasping her hands.

"Auntie," Anita said stepping in front of her. She raised her hands to halt the other woman's pacing and held her in place with a hand on each arm. "You're distressed."

"And why wouldn't I be distressed?" Several strands of Auntie Meena's hair had already fought their way out of the bun tied at the nape of her neck, and were beginning to flare outward, as though sending electrical charges into the air. "I am greeting and welcoming to the breakfast. Very good public relations, isn't it?"

"You're always gracious." Anita began to nudge her aunt farther down the hall, away from the dining room. Ravi glanced in their direction and then blanched. He knew a crisis simmering on the front burner when he saw it, and turned to study the hieroglyphics of the registration book.

"But I am thwarted, Anita. Thwarted!"

Anita maneuvered the older woman toward a chair in the office and Meena fell into it, almost tipping it over. "How are you thwarted, Auntie?" Meena shoved a handwritten note at Anita, a simple request from Angela Deetcher to have her bill drawn up.

"Am I not offering fullest protection?"

"Of course." From what, Anita wondered.

"Am I not guiding and advising?"

"Of course, always." But for what?

At the desk Anita heard the now familiar voice of Tengar Ram. Auntie Meena covered her face with her hands and wept.

"Ah!" Anita sat down on a nearby chair and pulled it closer to her aunt. "Perhaps it is nothing. Perhaps you see more danger than is there."

"Is she not a woman traveling alone? Without husband? Without brothers? Without family? Do not our men—oh, the shame of it—prey on foreign women?"

"Not all of them, Auntie." Anita started at her aunt's expression. "But they are only going on a short trip. It's a simple meeting in Chennai. It may come to nothing."

"It is not nothing, Anita. He is leading her to ruin." Meena gasped for breath between sobs. "I must stop it."

"Perhaps it cannot be stopped, Auntie."

"Of course it can be stopped. Will not the police assist?"

"No," Anita said, shaking her head so that her hair also threatened to rebel.

"No police?"

"No," Anita said, more gently. "But let me inquire, Auntie. Perhaps I have some influence."

"Will you? You will do this? You will save our reputation and you will save this woman, this good foreign woman, from ruin?"

Anita opened her mouth to speak, swallowed, and said, "I will offer the very best guidance, knowing how you feel about all this."

Auntie Meena grabbed Anita's hands and kissed them, pressing her mouth onto her niece's knuckles again and again. With effort Anita extracted her hands. She called to Ravi for a coffee tray for her aunt, and left her with strict instructions to remain in the office, so that she, Anita, could carry out her plan.

"You have a plan?" Auntie Meena asked, gazing up at her. "Oh, child, you are the finest of daughters and the finest of nieces. Forgive my many foolish complaints. You will save this woman from ruin." She grabbed Anita's hands again before she could flee the office, gave one final strong squeeze, and shoved her niece's hands away from her. "Go! Go! Save her!"

Twenty-seven

"You're looking pretty grim, Moonu." Anita walked up behind the waiter as he placed cutlery and teacups on a tray in the kitchen. He gave her a sideways glance without moving his head and punctuated the movement with a little grunt.

"He is offended." Pohty, the cook, spoke over his shoulder as he prepared eggs for one of the guests.

Anita closed her eyes and took a deep breath. Sometimes she wondered if it would be easier to fire all the staff and let the guests fend for themselves. It would certainly be simpler. "And what is it this time?"

Moonu's head jerked up and he glared at her over his long nose. "You are not seeing?" With gestures that belonged in a Bollywood movie, the waiter closed his eyes, tipped his head back, and sniffed three times. "That man from North is sitting at table with Madam."

Anita turned in the doorway just as Tengar Ram walked into the hall from the dining room. He stopped and bobbed his head in greeting.

"I'm just leaving," Tengar Ram said with a shy smile. "Getting a taxi."

Anita offered a few words and then headed into the dining room. If she moved fast enough she might be able to have the dreaded conversation with Angela Deetcher before she slipped out of the hotel and out of the protective environment of the resort for good.

Angela welcomed Anita with a graceful wave of her hand toward the chair opposite her at the small table. From her seat Angela could see the first tourists spreading out their beach towels and setting up umbrellas. The morning yoga practitioners had come and gone, the villagers using the far end as a latrine had ceased their steady arrival and departures, and the washerman had already begun laying out sheets to dry on the rocks. The morning was advancing.

"I noticed that you left a message with Ravi to prepare your bill," Anita said.

"Yes, I'm leaving today. I'd like to see a little more of South India before we fly out from Chennai," Angela said. She had placed her knife and fork at 4:20 on her plate, and Anita knew Moonu would swoop down and remove it as soon as he noticed. She spotted the waiter advancing across the dining room. Anita ordered a cup of coffee.

"Do you know what you want to see?" Anita asked.

"The three temple cities. They're quite old, I'm told."

"Madurai, Tanjore, and Kanchipuram are three of the finest temple cities anywhere in the world," Anita said. "Shall I arrange a guide for you?" The question brought her very close to the dangerous topic she wanted to discuss, and she all but held her breath waiting for a reply that would allow her to delve into the issue pushing Auntie Meena over the edge. Angela smiled, and in that glimmer of acknowledgment, Anita realized they understood each other. "I would be glad to book rooms for you," Anita continued, "in hotels we know to be comfortable and accommodating."

Angela nodded and poured herself another cup of coffee when Anita received hers. "I remember the look on your aunt's face when she saw Tengar Ram the first time. I think he was holding a door open for me and your aunt looked like she was about to faint. For a moment I thought she was ill, but then I saw she was looking at Tengar Ram, not me." She began to stir her coffee though she hadn't added milk or sugar, and continued stirring as she leaned back in her chair. "I saw him at the lecture held in Jubilee Hall but we didn't speak until we ran into each other at the bookstore." She gave the spoon another twirl and put it down, rested her arms on the table and glanced out the window. "I should have brought a bathing suit. It would have been fun."

"Suits are available here," Anita said. It was the expected comment, and neither woman meant it to go any further.

"I'm sure by now you've figured out most of what's going on with us," Angela said. "But I appreciate whatever it is you are trying to do."

Anita gave a halfhearted laugh. "I'm not trying to do anything except keep my aunt from collapsing and—"

"And a guest from making a terrible mistake." Angela nodded. "I can see it in their eyes, the taxi drivers and the waiters and even the guides in the museum and art gallery. They welcome me with the usual effusive greeting reserved for foreign tourists and then scowl when they see Tengar Ram come up behind me."

"We mean well. That's the most I can offer." Anita tipped her head to one side and turned to listen to snatches of conversation from the other guests. No one else from the tour had come in for breakfast, but the other guests had filed in with happy chatter about their plans for the day. "Will you still be going to Australia, as you planned?"

"No." As if to punctuate the statement, Angela pushed the coffee cup away and pulled her hands into her lap. "No, I've changed my plane reservations and both Tengar Ram and I will fly back to the States, directly, with no stopovers."

"I see." It was now or never, Anita decided. "If I may, is this fair to Tengar Ram?"

Angela's mouth fell open and she squinted at Anita, then leaned forward. "I beg your pardon?"

"I said, is it fair to Tengar Ram. After all, he is a young Indian man with no connections in the States, and you, well—" Anita paused and took another plunge. "Whatever choice you make about your life is your business, but I am wondering if Tengar Ram will find himself stranded and broke, overstaying his tourist visa, and in more trouble than he can handle."

Angela closed her mouth but she continued to stare at Anita. Soon the chemist's eyes began to sparkle with incipient tears blinked back, and though she tried to contain a smile, her lips twitched and her cheeks crinkled with the lines that framed humor. "You are perhaps the only one who would see it that way."

"Not really."

"Yes, really, because you have been there and you understand the challenges a foreigner faces. I can hear it in your speech—you learned English from Americans." Angela let her smile free and her eyes filled with warmth. "My oh my." She shook her head and looked ready to laugh. "Do you remember my telling you that I had spent the happiest year of my life in Sydney, Australia? All of us on the tour were traveling to the places on earth where we'd been the happiest. We have been trying to go back in time. But of course, we can't. You can have the best experience only once in your life. You can't go back and relive the best year of your life."

"No," Anita agreed. "But you can be happy there."

"Yes, that's possible, I suppose, Anita. May I?" Anita nodded and Angela continued. "But I'm a scientist. I've had a successful career in my field, and I have a reputation to be proud of. I was happy. At least I thought I was. And then . . ."

"And then?"

"And then I thought about how I was ending my career and my life," Angela said. "And I was disappointed in myself." She waited while Moonu cleared away the remaining dishes. The noise of the other diners blended into a comforting background. "It unsettled me. I began to think I had avoided other things in life, focusing so much on my work."

Anita wasn't surprised she was unsettled. A terminal diagnosis for a woman only in her fifties would unsettle anyone. But she didn't see how Tengar Ram played into this.

"Perhaps it's the climate here, or the natural beauty, or the color or the food." Angela laughed. "Probably the food."

"People do loosen up when they come here," Anita said.

"And then I met Tengar Ram. I recognized him when I was browsing in a bookstore after the lecture." Angela's hand went to the pendant she was wearing, and Anita wondered if he had given it to her. "We were in the same section way in the back. Do you know Modern Book Centre?"

Anita nodded. It was her favorite bookstore, after Kanjappa's secondhand books in the resort. "What section were you in?"

"Science."

"Oh." Anita couldn't help wondering if Tengar Ram had somehow manipulated the meeting.

"He's a student in chemistry." Angela leaned forward. "I can see you're skeptical but it's true. He had a scholarship to a prestigious university in Delhi but he lost it in the political changeover." For a moment she flashed a look of challenge and impatience, and Anita imagined her in a lab pressing her assistants to explain what they were doing. "I quizzed him. His training is sound. You look surprised."

"I admit it, I am. I had no idea."

"No, of course not. He says nothing about it. He's here because he's hoping to make some money and perhaps find a sponsor. He heard rich North Indians come here, and he was hoping to meet someone in the science field. He came to meet people in the IT world, but that went nowhere."

"He told you all this?"

"He told me some of it and I did some digging on my own," Angela said, leaning back again. "The world of science is its own country, a nation underlying all others. I got in touch with some of my colleagues and asked them to check into his story, and they did. It checked out."

"I'm sorry he's had so much trouble." Anita felt chastened and not a little ashamed for the assumptions she and her aunt had made.

"That's why I'm taking him to the States." Angela tipped her chin up and shifted her shoulders. "I'm a scientist and I know what my end will be like. Ken talked me into doing what he said I was entitled to, a year living where I'd been happiest. He got me when I was vulnerable, and I went along with it. And now, even though I think he was wrong, it's a stroke of luck that I was talked into it."

"I don't understand," Anita said. And indeed she didn't. She was about as confused now as she could be. "You think Ken was wrong when he brought you halfway around the world."

"He was a swindler. I can see that now. But because he almost got away with swindling me, he introduced me to what I really want, to what I can do at the end of my life."

"Tengar Ram?" Anita said. This didn't make sense.

"Tengar Ram. I'm dying and I have no family, but I'm a scientist. I don't have to leave an end. I can leave a beginning. I'm putting Tengar Ram into school in the States, with a sponsor and money to pay for his tuition and the rest of it. I won't live long enough to see him graduate but I will see him enrolled in a good program. He's the beginning I'm leaving behind."

* * * * *

Anita followed Angela Deetcher into the parlor. Tengar Ram jumped up from his chair when she appeared, but his smile didn't fade or alter when he saw Anita.

"Could I ask one more question?" Anita had little time left before Angela checked out and was gone for good. The other woman turned to her and lifted an eyebrow.

"Please," Angela said with a nod.

"I found three envelopes in Kenneth Maxinter's room, one tucked into a journal." At first she thought she had figured out the purpose of the pre-addressed envelopes but when she couldn't find the fourth one, she started to rethink her conclusions.

"Whose was missing?" Angela asked with the whisper of a smile.

"You know, don't you?" Anita took a little step back. Every time she felt she had figured out the foreign tourists in this group, one or another of them surprised her. She took note of the phrasing: "whose," not "which one."

Angela turned just enough to give Tengar Ram a reassuring smile. He walked over to the table, picked up a magazine and began flipping through the pages. "The names to which the envelopes are addressed are perhaps unfamiliar to you. Ken asked each one of us to provide contact information of a close relative or figure who could act for us, so that he had someone to write to at our deaths. He wanted to make sure the information was conveyed to our families and friends and colleagues."

"He was very organized."

"Oh, yes." Angela's head began to turn just a bit, toward Tengar Ram, and Anita appreciated that the stranger from North India had given her a reason to go on living. But there was more. He had also given her a way to access her feelings, to let her deeper self emerge. She could be excited about her future even while acknowledging her time was limited. Once again she could belong to something larger than herself and feel herself growing into it. "Ken dotted his i-s and crossed his t-s."

"Whose envelope is missing?" Anita asked.

"Mine was addressed to my married sister, whom I haven't seen in almost a dozen years." She recited the name. Anita reached into a large white envelope and extracted a small one.

"You'll want to keep this," Anita said, handing over the small envelope. She glanced inside the large one again. "Only one left."

Angela nodded. "What happened to the others?"

"I asked Crocker Dawes about one, and he explained it was addressed to his ex-wife, and took it back. You have yours. And the one I have left has a name and address on it that doesn't match any of the passport information I have on the tour members."

"And you want me to tell you whose it is?"

Anita could see Tengar Ram behind Angela listening intently; he'd let the magazine rest on his lap, his fingers holding up the pages.

"I've guessed a few things, but I'd like to be certain," Anita said.

"Yes, of course," Angela said. India has changed her, Anita thought. She's no longer the stiff, cautious scientist who arrived here five days ago. "In London Larry asked for his back. He said he wanted a different person to be notified. But I knew he wouldn't replace it. The envelope you have isn't for Larry."

"Because Larry shouldn't have been included in the group," Anita said.

"Exactly." Angela nodded with an almost conspiratorial smile. "You figured that out, did you?"

"Yes. But I think it's best to have confirmation before taking any action."

Angela laughed. “Well, I leave that to you. I have a few things to attend to before our departure.” She turned to Tengar Ram, then turned back and touched Anita on the arm. “I would not have allowed this to happen to me in the States,” she said. “But everything is different now.”

The women parted, and Anita felt she'd met a woman of courage and resourcefulness whom she would always admire. She wished Angela Deetcher had chosen to stay a little longer, if only for Anita to have the chance to learn more about her, and from her.

* * * * *

Anita found Auntie Meena where she'd left her, in the office, her hands clasped in her lap tearing apart an embroidered handkerchief. Anita glanced at Ravi, who shrank on the stool, pretending to be absorbed in the registration book.

“Really, Ravi,” Anita said, leaning on the counter. “I'm not going to feed you to the dogs.”

Ravi gasped. “You are not even to be joking, Anita Chechi.”

“That bad?”

Ravi glanced into the office and then slid a piece of paper across the counter toward Anita. “A new request. I made the call just now. The nurse is coming.”

Anita read the note. “Who gave this to you?”

“Madam Stover. She called to order breakfast in her room and asked if there is a service for a nurse to come to her. If not, she asked about nearby hospitals.” Ravi waited for Anita to say something.

Anita slipped the paper into her pocket. “Tell me at once if Madam Stover leaves the hotel. Don't delay. Come find me.” Both stopped to listen to the clatter of heavy-soled sandals on the stairs, and waited for Crocker Dawes to come into view. Anita sensed Ravi stiffen and when he greeted the guest politely there was an unmistakable formality in his tone.

Anita greeted Crocker also. “You have plans for the day?” He seemed a little tired this morning but since she had seen so little of him, she didn't know if this was how he normally looked. She hoped it wasn't anything else.

“I'll be sorry to leave,” Crocker said.

"Ah, you are leaving?" Ravi sat up straighter. "Am I to prepare your bill?"

Crocker nodded. "I am leaving, but not right away. I'll be here for a while longer." He seemed unbothered by Ravi's apparent eagerness for his departure. "But at least I'm not going far."

"Not going far?" Ravi paled. He was the polite young man who would never admit to disapproving of anything a guest did, but he couldn't conceal his feelings from Anita this morning. He did disapprove. "Will you require a taxi?"

Crocker shook his head. "Just going up the hill a bit."

"Ah." Ravi waggled his head.

Crocker turned to Anita. "I may ask your advice in a few months, in case, well, in case I want to extend my visa and I run into trouble."

"Foreigners aren't allowed to remain in the country for longer than six months at a time," Anita said. "And you have to make a special application for that."

"That is correct. Only six months." Ravi offered a firm look, pulling his mouth into a grimace. "You are required to leave the country. Hardly worth staying now, isn't it?"

Crocker listened to this in silence. "Anyway, Miss Anita, if I'm still around in six months, I may ask for your help."

"I'd be glad to help, in any way I can." He began to thank her but she raised her hand. "No mention." Anita was very fond of Deepa and the prospect of this new future made the morning shimmer. "We have a lot of contacts and I think we'll be able to work something out."

"Thank you." With a beaming and somewhat foolish smile, he nodded to both and hurried out the door.

"You don't like him, do you?" Anita said to Ravi.

Ravi shrugged. "My opinion is of no matter." He sank down on his stool, rested an elbow on the counter, and propped his head in his hand. "Such immoral behaviors we are having here."

Anita began to laugh. "You are definitely not a romantic. But it's all right, Ravi. He's an old friend of Deepa's and he means to follow good behavior."

Ravi shifted enough to look at her. “You say this only because your father is Amrikan.”

“Really, Ravi, not you, too!”

Challenged, Ravi sat up. “Are we not seeing this shocking behavior? Madam Deetcher and—” he lowered his voice to a whisper—” and that man from North, and and and—”

“And what?” Anita asked. “They're not doing anything wrong and she's generous.”

“Ah yes. This is true.” Ravi pursed his lips and gave this serious consideration. “These Amrikans very generous. Even the poor ones.”

Anita suppressed a laugh. “Even the poor ones,” she repeated. “Just keep an eye out for Sandra Stover.”

“And not the other one?”

“Oh, yes, of course. Larry Forche.” Anita paused. “Yes, let me know if he leaves the hotel. But I'm thinking if Sandra stays here, he will too. If she leaves, he'll follow. Has he ever gone out alone?” Anita knew he had, now that she thought about it, but not often. And so had Sandra Stover.

“Yes, going.” Ravi waggled his head. “Few times. Madam Stover is taking a nap and Mr. Forche is going for a little walk.”

“Yes, Ravi, keep an eye on them both.”

With a purpose for his morning, Ravi sat up straighter and scrutinized his domain.

“And now, for Auntie Meena,” Anita said. This, she knew, was the bigger challenge: convincing her aunt that Angela Deetcher wasn't catapulting herself straight to her doom.

Twenty-eight

Auntie Meena wiped the end of the sari over her face one more time before sighing in resignation. She stared across the office, not seeing what was in front of her, but only the dire straits she imagined she had fallen into, dragging along her hotel, family, and guests. From outside the office came the sounds of hotel staffers at work—soft voices, the occasional laugh, feet hurrying up or down stairs, the call of a taxi driver hoping to corral a customer, the bleat of a goat wandering the lane.

Anita loved the sounds of life along the ocean, the easy flow of work and pleasure, even when things were difficult. She was used to the songs of lament that issued from every woman who worked in the area, and most she had heard a dozen times at least. The personal songs were refined and reworked and polished until they could have been published as poetry, but they were stories of the women's lives told as long tales of misery that carried on a tradition in the literature of Kerala.

Auntie Meena lived and thrived in that tradition, and Anita wondered if she too would find a place there. It hadn't happened yet, but then she hadn't fallen in love. Anand, dear sweet Anand, had found another to love before she had grown serious. His turn away from her had hurt, but she hadn't yet felt it as a betrayal and probably never would. She'd found his careful distance a mark of safety, though she understood that only after she realized he was in love with a man, not another woman. Anita let her mind ramble through these thoughts while Auntie Meena composed herself.

"We do not understand how different these tour guests are," Meena said. "Even at their arrival they are different. And now we understand why."

"Ah," Anita said, sitting up. "So you're grieving for them knowing their fate is coming soon."

"They are dying, isn't it?" Auntie Meena's eyes were red from crying and rubbing.

The fate visited upon her guests would capture Meena's sympathy regardless of what misery they might have brought down on Hotel Delite. Auntie Meena could be guaranteed to open her heart in compassion even if she harbored resentment or disapproval for a guest's folly. Right now, Anita guessed, her aunt was probably trying to identify a good doctor for the two guests remaining, Larry Forche and Sandra Stover.

Crocker Dawes would soon leave to live with Deepa Nayar, to Auntie Meena's shock, but even here she was torn between disapproval at this behavior and fey delight at Deepa's good fortune in having the love of a decent man in her later years even if it wasn't going to last long. Meena put Angela Deetcher's decision to return to the States with her protege Tengar Ram from her thoughts. That one confused her.

"And do the police not want to keep them here?" Auntie Meena asked.

Anita shook her head. "Not yet, anyway. They might be stopped at the airport, but so far I've heard nothing. Neither has Dr. Premod, and she turned in the report."

"Hmm." Meena leaned back in her chair, oblivious to her disheveled look. "Are we doing anything more?"

"No, Auntie. I will speak to Mr. Forche and Miss Stover, but that's all." Anita brushed creases from the dupatta draped over her shoulder and sat up. "Why are you giving me such a suspicious look?"

"They are leaving us, Anita." Meena's face flushed and she sat up straighter in her chair. "Going. Onward to other destinations."

"Well, yes, I do think they're all leaving the hotel if not today then very soon," Anita said, ready to make her escape. "Before you wanted them to go, and now you get your wish."

Meena's face twisted in anguish as she grabbed her pallu and pulled her fists to her chest.

"We must let them go, Auntie. It is not my doing, but theirs." She went out to the registration desk. "Ravi, ask Moonu to bring elevenses for Auntie." Anita stepped into the hall. "And why are you looking so miserable yourself?"

Ravi glanced through the doorway and then leaned toward Anita. "Sometimes, Chechi, perhaps your aunt is right. Perhaps we are letting authorities take these matters forward, yes?"

Anita couldn't avoid feeling hurt at Ravi's betrayal. "I had no idea you were so timid, Ravi."

"I am not being timid," he said in a hoarse whisper. "I want your auntie to be at peace. That is all."

"Ravi, do you see authorities taking charge of this man's death? Kenneth Maxinter died in this hotel, in our care." Anita tugged on her dupatta for emphasis.

"But not under our care, really." Ravi struggled to find another argument. "Perhaps, you can step aside and the authorities can take over?"

"No." Anita took a step back and glared at him, but then an idea came to her. "Ravi," she said with a smile, which brought suspicion and dread flooding his face, "I haven't noticed this before but you are a true ally of Auntie Meena. She will be pleased to know this about you. It will give her great comfort."

Ravi's face grew pale. "Do not say this, Anita Chechi. She will notice me."

"Yes, Ravi, she will notice you." Anita cocked her head to one side and waited.

"I say no more, Anita Chechi." Ravi resettled himself on the stool. "You are cruel to me, Anita Chechi."

"Now that, Ravi, is exactly what Auntie Meena would say." Anita winked at him and headed for the staircase.

* * * * *

Anita climbed to the second floor and turned left at the landing. Larry Forche had been given room four, which had a balcony whose outer southern parapet did not extend beyond the wall of the hotel. No one standing on Larry's balcony could see more than the corner of the balcony of room five, and beyond that was room six, which had been Kenneth Maxinter's room. Larry's door might look out on the hallway and the doors for the other guest rooms, but from his balcony his view was limited to the ocean and the terrace below, and, Anita reminded herself, her own balcony above the parking garage. She knocked on the door.

Anita listened to the sound of objects scraping against other objects, perhaps a chair dragged across a floor, or a suitcase, or drawers being closed. She waited, then knocked again. When the sounds diminished but still no one came to the door, Anita pulled the bundle of keys from her waist and rattled them. She had learned that the sound of a jumble of keys rattling in front of the door often captured the attention of those within. She held the keys up and jiggled them again. She heard a bolt drawn back and a handle turn. Larry peered at her through the crack in the door.

"You asked to have your bill prepared," Anita said.

"Is there a problem?"

"No problem."

Larry tried to push the door closed but Anita's foot was in it. He glanced down, then up at her. "What do you want?"

"I would like to enter." The jumble of keys rested in her upturned palm. He stepped back, pulling the door open. She thanked him and walked in, noting the packed suitcase sitting on the floor by the bed, the desk drawers standing open, and the closet doors ajar. "Is your flight today?"

"As long as I pay my bill, what do you care?"

The last few days had been a parade of the ways India can change people, frightening them with its richness in food and color, its closeness to nature—a world without the safe boundaries between humans and the untamed world that foreigners are used to—enticing them to open themselves up to life, startling them with its variety. She had watched Angela Deetcher change in unexpected ways, and Crocker Dawes discover more about himself than he was ready for. She had seen the change in Sandra Stover and in Larry Forche, but it had taken her longer to figure it out.

Anita looked around for a chair, walked to the desk, and sat down. "Why did you come on this tour?"

"Excuse me?" Larry started, his shoulders jerking back. "That's none of your business."

"It has become so," she said. "The authorities know how Kenneth Maxinter died, and they will arrive soon and start asking questions. You will be expected to answer these questions, so perhaps you can tell me first." Anita watched the shifting expressions on Larry's face, his knees begin to bend as he leaned toward the twin bed. The bright red cheeks he had arrived with at last grew pale, and his forehead, always pale, now pinkened. His wispy gray hair stuck to his head in the heat despite the overhead fan. He was once again wearing the khaki slacks and white shirt of his arrival. "You're not one who is dying, are you? Don't bother lying. The police can easily establish the truth—our doctors here are very good, as good as yours at home."

Larry eased himself onto the bed, staring at the off-white counterpane still crumpled from a night of restless sleep. He had sunk into himself as well, farther down than he had dared to go for some time. His struggle was obvious, and she waited for his breath to grow short. When he gasped for breath, he drew a small red inhaler from his pants pocket and put it to his mouth. He closed his eyes, inhaled, and exhaled, letting his breath ease.

"No, I went into remission." He stared at the floor, sadness filling his jowls, weighing him down.

"And you didn't tell anyone?"

He shook his head. "When I understood what the trip was really for, I stayed on with the support group to be with Sandra. I thought I could talk her out of her plans." He studied Anita sitting in the chair, expressions flickering and then fading in his eyes. "I promised to take care of her all the way to the end, if she'd just come home with me. At first she wouldn't even listen, and then, something changed her, and she kept saying she couldn't leave. She had to see it through. I didn't realize what she was talking about."

Anita leaned toward him, the wooden chair creaking. "She chose Saigon as her last stop. Why?"

"That doesn't matter. It had to do with her stepfather. She adored him. He was Vietnamese, one of the refugees from the war, and he married her mother. They visited his country, and those were very happy times. It all fell apart when her mother got sick, he died, and some other stuff." Larry took a deep breath. "She figured out what was going on with Ken and the group."

"She knew Kenneth Maxinter was taking advantage of all of you?"

"She figured it out. The support group back in the States was for patients with terminal diagnoses, but Ken started to sort it out into two or three groups, and one of them was for people with no close family. He implied it was because we needed to lean on each other and not feel bad about being alone. In the other groups people talked a lot about their families and how much help they were, and Ken said that would just make us dissatisfied and unhappy, and remind us how isolated we were."

"You were very vulnerable," Anita said.

"Sandra started to feel there was something wrong after we got to Athens. She'd been hinting at a few things—the way Ken kept all our documents, the travel insurance, the way he always spent the last night with the patient. Georgio told her he had changed his mind, that seeing Greece again he was happy to be alive and he wanted to stay that way as long as possible."

"Did Sandra think Ken killed him?"

"He died, didn't he?"

"So she was afraid that Ken would make sure the patients died as planned so he could collect on the insurance," Anita said. Larry had once again taken to staring at the counterpane, pulling it to create tall ridges, separating it from the sheet beneath. "Why didn't she just tell him you had changed your minds?"

"Look, Miss Anita. He was a louse, okay? A real shit. He preyed on people who were dying, getting them when they were at their worst, with no one to help them. He promised them a beautiful happy ending, and we jumped at it because we were pathetic losers and cowards and we were desperate for something, anything to give us an escape." His face reddened and his lips twisted together. "It's done. There's nothing anyone can do about it. Okay?"

"It's a sad end to what was supposed to be an uplifting journey."

"Yeah." He pushed himself off the bed.

"You'll be going back alone to the States then?"

"Yeah," he said, his hands on his hips.

"That's too bad. You were very good to Sandra. Anyone could see how much you cared."

"Yeah, well, that's over." He began to move as though his whole body were stiff or sore. "You done?"

"You said you have no family. And Sandra has no family. What will she do without you?"

He stared at her, growing still. "She'll cope. She'll find some guy who needs to be of use and she'll latch onto him."

"That sounds unfair and bitter, Mr. Forche."

"She liked me better when I was dying. Look, I have a plane to catch if you don't mind."

* * * * *

Anita crossed the wide hallway to Sandra Stover's room and knocked. Auntie Meena gave rooms four, five, and six to the three men in the group, ensuring that no woman would find herself opening and closing her door with men on either side of her. The non-arriving Georgio had been assigned room nine, opposite rooms five and six, ensuring that the two female members of the tour, Sandra and Angela, were separated from the men as much as possible in rooms seven and eight, at the opposite end of the small hotel. Auntie Meena was nothing if not proper. On any other occasion the assignment of rooms for the guests would have amused Anita. She knocked on the door.

"I thought I heard voices," Sandra said, as she opened the door. She ushered Anita inside and motioned her to a chair, as though this were an ordinary visit in her home.

Where to begin? Anita thought. She walked to the balcony, which faced the compound and the beach to the south. This was one of her favorite rooms, with the palm trees waving just overhead, the view down the coast, and the spots of color from drying sheets and saris. She turned around and clasped her hands in front of her. She felt like a schoolgirl confronting a teacher ready to scold her for some infraction.

"You have something on your mind," Sandra said, sitting on the edge of the bed.

Since first noticing the wigs Sandra wore, Anita considered Sandra Stover's graceful demeanor and movements part of her coping with a terminal illness, but now, as she stood across from the hotel guest, Anita decided this was her normal manner. Sandra Stover was a gracious woman, always poised and receptive. Perhaps it was the teacher in her, or perhaps it was her true nature. Whatever it was, she seemed an especially lovely person who didn't deserve what was coming.

"I understand you intend to stay in India," Anita began. She recognized the infinitesimal changes in the other woman as she steeled herself for the conversation to come.

"You know all about us now, don't you?" Sandra turned just enough to see the suitcase sitting on a low table near the armoire. The top was unzipped, letting it sit askew on the body. The doors to the armoire were open, revealing an assortment of blouses and dresses and slacks. A second suitcase sat inside the armoire, on the floor, and Anita guessed that this one held Sandra's many wigs. "Of course, I can't leave now, can I?"

Anita glanced down at Sandra's hands resting in her lap, palms upward. When foreign women stayed any length of time, Anita wondered if she'd lived longer in the States would she have better fingernails or a larger wardrobe or a different hairstyle. She noticed how American women walked, with an ease and swing she never expected to see in Indian women. Sandra was among the more self-contained foreign women she'd met, but she guessed that was partly because of her role as a teacher and partly a result of her disease.

"How did you find the service at Christ Church?" Anita asked as she sat down.

Sandra leaned forward as though she had trouble hearing, then smiled. "Mostly recognizable. The two hikers told you they ran into me there?"

Anita nodded. "And they walked with you to Holy Angels Convent, where you spent the night."

"Yes, the sisters took me in for the night." Sandra flexed her fingers, trying to relax. "I'm a Catholic, you know."

"I didn't know," Anita said. "Did you find the priest you were looking for?"

Sandra offered the perfect smile to ease the correction. “I wasn't looking for a particular priest.”

“But you wanted to talk to one.” Anita raised a hand as Sandra began to speak. “I called the convent office and talked with a friend. You went there, on the advice of someone at Christ Church, because you felt the need for confession sooner rather than later. You got to Holy Angels, and they accommodated you by calling in a priest who was there on other business. You made your confession.”

“You're very well informed.” Sandra pressed her lips together, to hold back whatever it was she didn't want to say. “That's right.” She stood and began fussing with open doors and misaligned chairs.

“You had something to confess,” Anita said. “And I'm supposed to know what it is.”

Sandra laughed. She rested her hands on a chair back and looked around the room. “There's been only one thing consuming everyone here.”

“Consuming? It seemed to me no one cared about Kenneth Maxinter, or his death. All of you who were traveling with him went about your days as though he was nothing to you.”

“That's a little harsh.”

“In your case, I agree. I think you were troubled by what happened to Ken. I think that's why you went to see the priest. You had something to confess.”

“Yes, I did.” Sandra offered a smile, her chin lifted.

“But not his murder.” Anita crossed her legs and leaned back in the chair, as though she were settling in for a long, comfy chat. “Larry is a very bitter man.”

Sandra lowered herself into a chair, her face a mask of disdain. “I went to confession because I needed to. I've changed my travel plans, so I can remain here in India, where I think the police will want to interview me. They will want to interview me, and I shall remain here for them to do so.”

“They won't arrest you for Ken's murder.”

Sandra stiffened and swiveled forward in her chair.

"The trouble with this tacit arrangement you've made with Larry, to let him go home while you stay here and die before you can come to trial, is that the evidence is against you."

"Exactly," Sandra said, breaking into a nervous smile.

"Exactly against you being the killer." Anita waved her hand when Sandra began to argue. "I was just talking to Larry and I was so surprised that he was willing to let me think you were guilty. You knew he picked the otalam fruit during your walk on the first day, and you knew he put those seeds into the spice mixture in Ken's room."

"I don't know what Larry has told you," Sandra said.

"You knew I was suspicious and you knew I'd taken the spice mixture to the doctor, and she would have to report her findings to the police."

"You're making accusations that are insulting to Larry and to me."

"You can take the accusation of murder without admitting to it, and you will not be violating your principles," Anita said. "Larry can return home to a longer life while you remain here and die. You haven't long, I know." Anita winced as she said this, angry that she had to bring both Sandra's fate and Larry's treachery into one. "Why is Larry leaving early?"

"I've told him it's pointless for him to stay. He's been so helpful and attentive, but I'm not going to spend my last few weeks with him. I told him after Ken died."

"That must have been a shock for him."

"He said some terrible things."

"He thought once Ken was dead, you would see your commitment to suicide was foolish and you would let him take you home. But he was wrong."

"You shouldn't be thinking Larry is responsible," Sandra said. "You don't know that he is."

"But I do know." Anita rubbed together the thumb and fingers of her left hand, as she had when she'd begun to count the reasons to look at Larry Forche. "He had a terrible bout of diarrhea on the first night after your first full day here, even though you and he had eaten the same foods throughout the day. I didn't think anything of it until later. Otalam is deadly if ingested, but even handling it can be dangerous. Some folk remedies call for otalam seeds to be taken as a purgative but it's rarely used because it's so risky. Larry made himself sick just by handling the raw fruit and seeds.

"I didn't think anything of it at first, but the next day Pema, our maidservant, brought down Larry's shoes to clean because they were so dirty, and I wondered how he'd done that. Then one of our staff found the remains of the squashed fruit out in the yard, carelessly thrown into a plastic bag and then on the trash heap." She paused, to contain her anger. "He could have killed one of our animals."

Sandra started to speak, but Anita held up a hand.

"I'm not through," she said. "The problem for me was, I couldn't figure out why Larry would kill someone like Ken. He was annoying, I suppose, but the whole tour seemed odd and I couldn't figure out if the death had been an accident or intentional."

"It could have been an accident." Sandra had the sudden eagerness of someone who has discovered an out, an escape, and rushed to take it. "That's the most logical explanation, isn't it?"

"No, it isn't." Anita looked at her hands. Some years ago even she had once felt a slight tingling after handling a few pieces of flesh from the otalam fruit. She had picked it up, then dropped it at once and washed her hands, glad that she hadn't rubbed her forehead or her eyes while trying to think, a bad habit she was thereafter determined to break.

"You're worried about the reputation of your hotel. Is that it?" Sandra said.

"Did you have an argument with Ken the night he died?"

Sandra looked confused, then shook her head.

"Do you remember Larry saying he thought he heard Ken arguing with someone? He was the only one who heard it, but then after Larry kept talking about it, Crocker and Angela said they might have heard something. Larry made good use of the power of suggestion. By the time he was through talking I almost believed him too." Anita wanted to get through this, force Sandra to admit that it had not been an accident, but there was no easy path here.

"What's your point?" Sandra said.

"Larry convinced everyone they heard Ken arguing with someone, so if we could figure out who that someone was, we'd have the murderer. We could jump to the obvious conclusions and that would be that. It was supposed to be a wild-goose chase. But Larry didn't know that Ken did have a visitor that night, someone who spent a minute or two admiring the view from his balcony. You."

"You're guessing," Sandra said.

"I was on the beach taking photographs, and I took one of you on the balcony. I didn't notice you when I was shooting—I was looking for something else, but when I put the shot on the screen at home, there you were, on Ken's balcony on your first full night, and quite late too."

Sandra grew pale and groaned. "Damn." Barely a whisper.

"Larry didn't know because he can't see the other two balconies from his. His room is too far back. And he had no idea you'd gone in to see Ken. No idea whatsoever. Why did you?"

"Oh, Larry, Larry, Larry!" Sandra got up and walked to the balcony doorway and crossed her arms. After a moment she turned to Anita, and leaned one shoulder against the doorjamb, steadying herself. "I went to Ken's room to tell him I felt things were changing with us, all of us. We were uneasy that Georgio had been left in Athens, and we weren't sure he wanted to die. Ken tried to convince me that he had but I started to think something was wrong. Maybe Georgio felt as we did, unsure as we got closer and closer to our destinations. Ken didn't know about Crocker Dawes." Sandra smiled, a warm smile of delight and a little impishness.

"What didn't Ken know?"

"He didn't know Crocker was planning on getting married to his old sweetheart here and live as long as he could. At least that was his dream." Sandra returned to her chair. "He had no intention of committing suicide. He never told Ken about the Indian woman. On the plane he was so excited he could barely contain himself. I asked him if seeing India again was that important to him, and he said, It's not India. It's the people he knows there. Then he told me about Deepa. Is that right?"

Anita nodded.

"That's a pretty name," Sandra said.

"Deepa. It means light, a lamp, shining."

"Well, that sure is the right name for her. It was like his life had started all over again. He was beyond happy." Sandra tipped her head back and gazed up at the ceiling before returning her attention to Anita. "I had to talk to Ken after that. We had to make a change. This was all wrong."

Twenty-nine

When Anita made her way downstairs again the entryway of Hotel Delite was in its usual state in late morning when guests were checking out and new ones were checking in. Those who arrived on the early morning flights often went straight to their rooms if available and completed the registration process hours later, after a good morning's sleep. Others left their luggage and wandered off until later in the afternoon.

Anita found a twisty path among the suitcases and backpacks and cloth bags stuffed to bursting with gifts and souvenirs. Ravi handled these periods of transition with little difficulty, and even Auntie Meena coped well if the process didn't take more than an hour to get everyone sorted out. But it was hard to tell if this morning things were going well because Auntie Meena began the day in a glum mood and it wasn't getting any better. After it was all over, things had to get better. Anita glanced at her watch, wondering how much longer all this sorting-out would take.

Ravi handed a key over the counter and Sanjay picked up a suitcase, balanced it on his head, and knelt down to pick up another. He trotted off with two suitcases on his head and a young couple trailing along behind. Fortunately, he didn't have far to go, only to room two, on the same floor. The suitcases thinned out, fewer people milled around the counter, and the chatter subsided. Auntie Meena wiped the sweat from her brow, and turned into the office, her shoulders hunched over.

"This one," Ravi said, pointing to a suitcase. A taxi driver picked it up and headed up the stairs. "Only one remaining."

"Hmm?" Anita barely heard him. She feared she'd never get Sandra Stover's resolute expression out of her mind.

"Madam Stover. Only one," Ravi said. "Madam Deetcher is standing just there with her car. Tengar Ram has very detailed directions. Crocker Dawes has gone out for the day. And Mr. Forche is just there, departing."

"What? Larry Forche is leaving?" Anita bolted around the counter. "He can't."

"Yes, he can," Ravi said. "Bill is paid. All is in order."

"But I told you—" Anita spotted Larry Forche pointing to the boot of a taxi, where the driver deposited the suitcase, rearranging a small carry-on bag according to Larry's directions. Before Anita could call out, however, a small gray jeep came down the lane and parked by the compound wall. A man climbed out of the passenger side and gave orders to the driver. Anita saw the officer's hat, and so did Larry. She didn't know why the CID officer had driven down the lane, but she could guess. It looked like Larry must have made a similar guess because he urged the driver to get moving, but the driver pointed to the other car blocking his path. Larry slipped around the side of the car and quick-marched up the hill.

"Wait!" Anita ran up the short stairs to the parking lot. No one paid any attention to her. Except one man. Tengar Ram looked at her, looked at Larry, looked at the CID man, and bolted for the lane. Larry must have sensed something was happening because he glanced over his shoulder and took off running. The crowds were thicker at this time of day as tourists moved between hotel rooms and the beaches and shops. Larry dodged among them, but Tengar Ram was quicker and began to close the distance between them. He yelled into the crowd and in an instant two men jumped off a low stone wall where they'd been smoking cigarettes and gossiping and lunged into Larry's path. Tengar Ram threw himself onto Larry and the two men landed hard on the paved roadway. And in the magic that is India, about ten men materialized in a circle around the men on the ground, lifted up Larry and pinned him to a compound wall with nothing more than their patient, steady stares.

By the time Anita reached Larry and Tengar Ram, a crowd had grown, and true to the nature of crowds in India, the men and women stood somber faced as they watched the incident play out. No one spoke. Instead they stood shoulder to shoulder, perhaps crowded a little closer, and watched those involved in the capture of Larry Forche as though it were the most ordinary of television shows. They barely moved as others pushed their way through the crowd. The CID officer's driver shouldered his way through first, and behind him at a stately pace came the CID officer.

"Is this the man?" the CID man asked.

Anita nodded. "But I suppose that depends on which man you're talking about."

"The man—or woman—who might get away." The officer stared at Larry backed against the wall. "The person Dr. Premod warned us about."

"Yes, that's the one." Anita rested her hands on her hips, able to smile at last.

"And this one?" The CID officer indicated Tengar Ram.

"A friend," Anita said. "A friend of Hotel Delite."

The CID man looked the North Indian up and down and then at Anita and then at the man against the wall. He made this triangle again and then grunted. "You are fortunate in your friends." The officer stepped away and waved his driver over. A constable from the guard post on the Promenade threaded his way to the center of the group. He shackled Larry's wrists. Larry began to swear and struggle, twisting against the two men holding his arms. He managed to swing his face close to Anita's. She recoiled from the rage in his eyes and winced at his labored breathing. She was surprised he'd even been able to run as he had.

"Why on earth did you run, Larry?" Anita asked, suddenly feeling sorry for him. "What did you think was going to happen?"

"I thought—" He looked at the CID officer and his driver, at their neat uniforms and belts.

"You thought what?" Anita followed his look, confused.

"I'd rather be dead than spend the rest of my life in prison in this country with—" He stopped and looked around him.

"He thought the cop was going to shoot him," came a foreigner's voice from the crowd.

"Is that true, Larry? Did you? Did you think someone was going to shoot you?" Anita took a quick step back. She glanced at the CID officer, who responded with a lift of his eyebrow and a shrug. The constable and police driver half-walked and half-carried Larry away.

The crowd parted for the three men, then flowed along behind them, like a stream that has found a new channel.

"What has he done?" Tengar Ram said, brushing the sand and dirt from his shirt and slacks.

Anita had forgotten he was still there. Of course he didn't know. Angela Deetcher wouldn't have known about Anita's suspicions, or the evidence she'd put together against Larry.

"One of our guests died suddenly," Anita said, "and we think Larry Forche is responsible. Poison." She began to follow the crowd but turned around to look at him when she heard a gasp.

Tengar Ram's eyebrows rose and his eyes widened. And then his expression changed, from surprise to wonder to disdain. "He has done this?"

"That's what the evidence suggests," Anita said.

He stared at the crowd moving up the hill, at the three men at the head of it. "The man is a fool." There was no doubting Tengar Ram's attitude now.

"I suppose anyone who commits murder and tries to get away with it could be called a fool."

He shook his head so hard and so fast it was like watching a tuning fork vibrate. "Not so, not so. A desperate man in this country may have no hope, but an American always has hope." How quickly he has caught the disease of faith, Anita thought. He clapped his hands to rid them of sand. "You know I am leaving with Professor Deetcher."

"Yes, I know. We're very happy for you at Hotel Delite," Anita said, surprised at this sudden switch in the conversation.

He glanced at her and she wondered if Auntie Meena had made her displeasure known to either him or the professor. "I hope it is the opportunity you dream of."

"It is a great opportunity, greater than I had dreamed of. But no matter what happens," he said, "it can only be better than the prospects I face here." He forced a smile and, remembering his manners, he bowed before following the crowd up the hill.

* * * * *

It didn't take long for the lane to return to its usual quiet. Anita hoped to relax in the hotel office, but she knew it wasn't to be when she saw Pema standing in the doorway. Anita thought of the maidservant, Pema, as a quiet figure, not quite docile, but amenable to most of the requests the hotel made of her. But Anita was now revising that opinion. The maidservant stood just inside the office door, her light blue-flowered print sari somewhat worn but still clean, her hands clasped in front of her.

"Very reasonable, Amma." Auntie Meena gave Pema the saddest look Anita had seen in quite some time, and that was saying something, considering what the hotel had just been through with the American tour group. "Husband is saying, dangerousness pay is reasonable."

Anita sat down at the table, rested her head on her hand, and tried not to laugh. "And what is the danger, Pema?"

"This man. Murderer." Pema managed to look indignant and serious, but she would probably have to become angry if she wanted to keep from breaking down and laughing. "And the otalam inside the hotel."

Anita leaned toward her aunt. "Dangerousness pay." She wondered how long she'd have to wait but she knew it would come—Auntie Meena's reaction. Would it be the cousin of Vesuvius, or the hiss of a snake? Would Pema quake and regret her request, or would she shrug and accept the decision? Just how angry was Auntie Meena now?

"And assisting pay." Pema seemed to think she now had the advantage and pressed harder. "Am I not finding evidence on sahib's shoes? Am I not to be paid for ferreting out information of dangerous man, a killer in our midst?" She was about to go on in this vein, working herself into a high pitch of self-importance when Anita sat up and waved at her.

"Enough, Pema, enough." Anita nodded to the computer, which was now pinging to announce incoming email.

"You are expecting?" Auntie Meena said. "CID is contacting?"

"Not the CID. States." She glanced at Pema and then leaned toward her aunt and spoke softly. "A small rise in pay. Not so much. But she is a good worker and we like her."

This evaluation seemed to annoy Pema and she clapped her hands on her hips, no longer the modest maidservant, and glared at Anita. "Very good worker, Chechi. Liking is not enough. I deserve a rise in pay."

Anita suppressed a laugh and smiled at the maidservant instead. "You will get, Pema. You will get."

Delighted with this, Pema waggled her head and wiggled her way out of the office. Anita could hear her muttering to herself as she disappeared down the hallway, "Getting a rise, Pema, getting a rise."

"How can you have done this?" Auntie Meena said. "Hotel Delite is as good as empty. I hope this pinging brings more tourists seeking reservations." She watched Anita slide into the desk chair and click onto her email. She leaned forward and read through three short emails before sending one reply.

"All our rooms will be booked by this afternoon," Anita said. "The tourist office has a few lost travelers. Sandra Stover is still in room seven, the rooms on this floor are filled, and a family is enquiring about family room, room nine. And next week is even better."

"Oooh!" Auntie Meena started to get up and then fell back into her chair. "I am forgetting Madam Stover. Where is she to go? She has no one now that Mr. Forche is taken away."

"I wouldn't mourn for him, Auntie. He was willing to abandon her to a charge of murder." Anita scowled at the computer and began to type, the sound of the keys filling the room with soft rhythmic plunks.

"But he loved her," Auntie Meena said.

"You are such a romantic, Auntie."

"Surely it is a misunderstanding."

"Yes, of course, and that's why he ran down the road and Tengar Ram chased him." Anita finished typing and clicked on send. “And caught him, Auntie. He performed a great service.” She spun around in her chair to see how her aunt took this accolade of the North Indian's conduct.

“Hmm. I see he is doing this.” She frowned, reluctant to admit she could have been wrong. “Yes, virtue is there.”

Anita leaned over and patted her aunt's hand.

“But I am telling Madam Deetcher she is to be calling me from States if behavior untoward is arising.” Auntie Meena tried to look fierce.

“And I'm sure she will do just that, Auntie.” Anita stood up.

“Where are you going now?”

“I am going to tell Sandra Stover that I have contacted her stepsister, her only close relative, to tell her about the circumstances here.”

“Oh, yes, very good, Anita, very good.”

“And Madam Stover will remain here until her stepsister can arrive or persuade Sandra Stover to return to the States and the care of her family.” Anita headed for the hallway, and braced herself to face the other woman.

Thirty

Eighteen days after the last member of the American tour left, with the exception of Larry Forche, who was in prison, and Crocker Dawes, who had remained at Hotel Delite, Anita and Auntie Meena turned a corner in the last blackness of night onto a lane bright with oil lamps lining the tops of compound walls and overhead streamers creating a tunnel of flowers. Yellow blossoms dangled from tall banana stalks marking the entrance to Deepa Nayar's house. The compound was also decorated, and in the center of the yard stood a small covered platform, the marriage mandapa. Small bowl lamps shimmered in the pre-dawn darkness. It was nearing four o'clock in the morning.

Anita and Auntie Meena found themselves part of a small crowd of family and friends inside the compound gate. Anita tugged at her silk sari, which tended to slide, and wished she'd used a safety pin to hold the top in place.

"Why are marriages always scheduled for this time of night?" Anita said, looking around for a place to sit.

"Shh. It is auspicious time." Auntie Meena became effusive when she saw the mandapa decorated with plantain stalks, a large bowl of paddy, and offerings of fruit. "Very nice." She began to coo, always a good sign. "And the brass lamps! And the flowers!" She continued in this vein, listing all the accoutrements of a proper wedding.

When Crocker Dawes first informed the people of the hotel that he intended to marry Deepa Nayar in a traditional Hindu wedding, Auntie Meena was at first shocked, then saddened, convinced this was the beginning of the end for

Deepa. She almost refused to attend, but an hour ago she appeared at Anita's door urging her to hurry up.

"There!" Meena pointed to a spot on the ground and dragged Anita over. "Good view from here." She sat cross-legged on the ground and nodded to those she knew. "Where is the chair? Is he carrying it in?"

"No chairs, Auntie." Anita rearranged her sari. "I really don't like silk."

"Not liking silk?" Auntie Meena stared at her with wide-open eyes. Anita might have said she was becoming a streetwalker.

"No chairs, Auntie, because Crocker has been practicing sitting cross-legged for months, ever since he knew he was coming to India." Anita did wonder, however, how long he'd be able to stand it if his muscles and skeleton weren't used to this posture. She waved to Ravi sitting among the men on the opposite side of the yard.

"Who are those foreigners with Ravi?" Meena asked.

"One is the husband of Crocker's cousin. Crocker has asked Ravi to look after him," Anita said.

"Oh, no," Meena said. "Is he ill also?"

Anita shook her head. "Crocker was afraid he wouldn't understand how to behave and sit down in the women's section or kiss his wife or something like that." Meena winced.

"Very wise." Meena looked around. "And that girl there?" She nodded to a teenage girl sitting near Deepa's granddaughter, Uma. "Surely she is too old to be here?"

Anita found the girl indicated. She was wearing a long silk skirt and an overblouse, but they didn't look like they'd been made in India. She was clearly an older teenager. "I think that's the cousin's daughter, and the cousin wouldn't come without her."

"Oh, very attentive mother." Auntie Meena murmured about this a minute longer.

Just then Malllika appeared and sat down beside Uma.

"And where is the teenager's mother?" Meena asked

"She's getting ready in the house," Anita said. "Crocker's cousin will take the place of an elder sister and tie the necklace around Deepa's neck." Anita had been amused but also impressed when Crocker went over the details with Anita at the time of booking rooms for the various relatives and friends coming for the wedding. Though it was short notice, his generous offer to pay for everyone's airfare had persuaded his guests and family to accept the invitation, and they began arriving over the last few days, at three in the morning after twenty-hour flights, looking dazed and exhausted.

"And who will serve as Deepa's father and mother?" Meena scanned the crowd as though she could spot the likely candidate.

"Her uncle and aunts are coming from their village," Anita said. She leaned closer. "They remember Crocker when he was a young man. The uncle worked with him. It's exciting, isn't it?"

"There is nothing romantic about building latrines, Anita." Auntie Meena settled back into her conviction that the marriage would be a disaster and she looked forward to telling her friends about the catastrophe for the rest of her life.

Whatever the future, the present was beautiful and sweet. Rustling and activity near the house drew everyone's attention. Deepa's uncle knelt near the mandapa and an assistant priest deposited a large brass tray in front of him. On the tray were piled several silk saris with wide gold borders, three envelopes, and a small box of gold jewelry. Auntie Meena was speechless. She elbowed Anita in the side and managed to squeeze out a squeak.

"Yes, I can see," Anita said as she lifted and sighted her camera.

Auntie Meena put her hand over the camera and whispered her niece to stop that. Photographing was rude. Anita tipped her head to the side, Meena looked behind her, and there a dozen or more women held up their cell phones to get a good shot of the dowry. Meena sighed and shrugged.

The uncle ran his hands over the saris, poked among the jewelry, and scanned the contents of the envelopes. He nodded to the assistant priest, who returned to the house, his duty of delivering Crocker Dawes's required marital gifts completed. And very satisfactory they were, too. The entire group of guests murmured approval on that score.

"So much?" Auntie Meena had recovered her voice. She looked upon the wedding with new interest.

More noise drew everyone's attention back to the house. The groom followed his cousin through the crowd. The American woman, in a long linen skirt and silk blouse, carried the obligatory tray of offerings, the eight auspicious items. She looked more worried about stepping on people's hands and feet than on her other duties, but she managed to make it safely to the mandapa. She, as the important sister, was given a chair. Deepa followed in the same manner. After her came two cousins carrying the brass trays, and her uncle behind them. The priest directed them where to sit on the mandapa, with the bride and groom. With some effort and help from Ravi, Crocker managed to sit down cross-legged.

"These adjustments in the requirements," Meena said, "mean nothing. They have a very fine priest, you know. Every puja he performs is most auspicious for the patron." She continued to watch every movement of the priest, every response by the bride or groom, the graceful gestures of Crocker's cousin to tie the tali necklace, the exchange of garlands, and the placement of the kumkum powder on the bride's forehead. When it came time for Crocker to lead Deepa in walking around the fire seven times, Ravi and the priest had to help him stand up. Undaunted, he and his bride circumambulated the fire the required number of times.

After the wedding feast, when large vats of rice and bowls of curries disappeared almost instantly and children ate their parents' small bananas when left untouched on the banana leaf, Auntie Meena and Anita made their way back to the hotel.

"Very nice," Auntie Meena said. "I always believe such a wedding portends a fine future."

"Really?" Anita managed not to laugh and point out the obvious incongruity between this and her aunt's earlier predictions.

"Really, Anita. So I offered my assistance. A small gift."

"Assistance? Oh Sweet Auntie, how lovely of you. What did you do?"

"I arranged for Deepa and Mr. Crocker to have a week on their own, with full service and all attentions." Meena gave Anita a smug smile.

"You gave them a room for a week? That's very generous of you, Auntie."

"No, no, Anita, not me. You. I am giving them your suite for a week. Even now Pema is getting everything ready." Meena gave a tight smile. "And you are staying in my suite with me."

"What?" Anita stopped in the road and stared at her aunt. A week living knee to knee with her aunt? At that moment Anita didn't know if she was furious with her aunt or prouder of her than she'd ever been before. But she would know in a week.

-End-

About the Author

Susan Oleksiw writes the Anita Ray series featuring an Indian American photographer living at her aunt's tourist hotel in South India. *In Sita's Shadow* is the fifth in the series (the first is *Under the Eye of Kali*, 2010). She also writes the Mellingham series featuring Chief of Police Joe Silva, beginning with *Murder in Mellingham* (1993), and most recently *Come About for Murder* (2016). In 2018 the first in a new series was published: *Below the Tree Line: A Pioneer Valley Mystery*, featuring Felicity O'Brien, farmer and healer.

Susan is well known for her articles on crime fiction; her first publication in this area was *A Reader's Guide to the Classic British Mystery* (1988). She co-edited *The Oxford Companion to Crime and Mystery Writing* (1999), as well as contributing several articles. Her short stories have appeared in *Alfred Hitchcock Mystery Magazine* and numerous anthologies.

A co-founder of Level Best Books, Susan has recently joined with two other writers to found another publishing venture. Crime Spell Books will continue to publish the series of anthologies known as Best New England Crime Stories. The 2022 volume is entitled *Deadly Nightshade*.

Susan lives and writes outside Boston.

www.susanoleksiw.com

Made in the USA
Las Vegas, NV
04 October 2022

56547781R00142